Make My World Complete
by
Michael Khatkar

Published by
Filament Publishing Ltd
16, Croydon Road, Waddon, Croydon,
Surrey, CR0 4PA, United Kingdom
Telephone +44 (0)20 8688 2598
Fax +44 (0)20 7183 7186
info@filamentpublishing.com
www.filamentpublishing.com

ISBN 987-1-912256-75-4
Printed by IngramSpark

Contents

Dedication

L ife is excruciatingly short.

If you have people that make your world complete, hold onto them, for they are priceless!

Thank you to those in my life that make every day worthwhile; you give purpose to my world and complete it.

Introduction

A mysterious book weaved deep into the lives of three people entwined by tragedy, regret, pain and romance.

There is no escape from the circumstances of choice, as physical and psychological retribution haunts the individuals, plummeting their maladjusted lives to inhuman levels of degradation and adversity.

Catastrophe blights their days with despair and misfortune, pushing them to extreme depths of carnal and mental deterioration, catalysed by their unpredictable and insecure tryst.

Three dysfunctional lives directed and deviated by a book titled 'Make my World Complete' malignantly bonding them together, questioning their individual interpretations of love & life itself.

Disconcerting and volatile, 'Make my World Complete' will drag you through an identical whirlwind of extreme emotions as experienced by the characters, compelling you to examine the essence of your own purpose and the life you live.

Chapter 1
Jolene

The beautiful passion of beginnings. Outcomes, the possibility of endings. The ripple of waves contorting and flexing life all deemed irrelevant, this enchanted delight, a basal fluttering in time clasping untold certainty, collapsing the universe into a solitary touch. Messages of ecstasy galloping ferociously through the corpuscles of life, electrifying their path with tracks of boundless joy, spreading the word swifter than a multiplying disease intent on reproducing malignancy. Cells bursting in a symphony of animalistic fervour as the delicate pressure of her moist lips on his neck twitched his concealed manliness into eager anticipation.

'Do you like that?'

Her words were delicately woven silk, rich raven in colour brushing his awakened skin with intimacy and promise, simply reciprocated with an involuntary nod, barely moving but silently responsive. Heaven winked in apprehension and poetically mumbled its approval as her hand caressed his dauntless red-blooded firmness as it happily responded with the breakneck gush of blood that flowed into it.

'I miss you, I miss you so much, I do, I miss you and it's killing me.'

The salacious desire of beginnings screeched to a grinding halt, feverous boiling blood dried to a fine red powder, athletic cells became sluggish and expelled their catalytic oxygen. The dampness of sexual warmth transformed to a deadly barren landscape of deficiency and nothingness. The seventeen dispirited words showered down on Ash as he turned to face the woman that was promising such blissful adventure.

Her eyes were uncontrollably weeping, painfully crimson with deep-seated sorrow, his reflection in her dilated pupils emblazoned her agony, there was only him in her vision, he was all she wanted, he was the dawning and termination of life itself.

'I miss you, I miss you so much, I do, I miss you and it's killing me.'

The words he desperately wanted to say formed in his mind and floated as images into her psyche, each one synchronised with the hurtful anguish overpowering her emotions.

'You make my world complete, you do, you make my world complete.'

She acknowledged his silent sincerity, as the sentence washed her agony and her melancholy stare intensified.

'I miss you. I miss you so much, Ash.'

'I know you do. I want you to stay forever. Don't ever leave me. Stay by my side. I will love you until the end of time. Please don't cry, I am here for you.'

An unceremonious darkness shadowed the room, whitening her already pallid complexion, her cheek bones edged from her skin, protruding and severely angled as an intimidating grimace distorted her face. There was an all-consuming pain as she swung her head back, stretching the skin over her throat, pouring out an unexpected blood curdling scream. Ash was stunned into stillness and completely helpless as the love of his life howled in distress and fell to the floor cracking the back of her head upon the solidness of her landing.

'Save me, save me, save me, Ash. Don't let me die. I don't want to die. I want to make your world complete. Please don't let me die.'

Ash squeezed his eyes shut, he knew this was a nightmare, he knew he could wake and leave this destressing scene, he knew he could wake and return to the comfort of his bed and gaze upon his beautiful Jolene, who assuredly would be lying next to him. His nightmare had him imprisoned, upon opening his eyes he was still present in the unfolding calamity, still witnessing the grotesque malady the love of his life was being dispensed.

A mouthful of cloudy mist was forced from Jolene's lungs as she lay bleeding on the floor, accompanied by a scrunching crack, as the fragile bones in her neck twisted into submission and splintered with a sickening grind, signifying the abrupt end of her life.

Ash wakes. Sobbing and sweating in equal quantities but at least he escaped his torturous nightmare and came back to the tranquillity of his perfect and content life, in bed with the one person that made his life complete, his wife Jolene.

He turned to ogle the sleeping beauty lying beside him. Every waking day, this was his ritual, to offer a silent 'thank you' to the universe that somehow engineered their paths to meet. Ash was eternally grateful for his life and for the beautiful woman that he had vowed to cherish through every living day, every solitary moment until life turned to death. Ash was hopelessly in love, entwined in the poetry of togetherness, existing in a unique, blissful world, an impenetrable union that created strength, power and a hopefulness for the future that only deep renderings of the heart can accomplish. He lived life with one almighty wish, simply that Jolene would outlive him because he could no longer visualise a life without her.

There was a volcanic rumble in Ash's chest, his protective ribcage couldn't ebb the flow of bleakness that pounded from his bursting heart as it erupted a fierce and untenable gloominess. He was incapable of a logical explanation to calm the demoralised discharge of morose grief burning through his shaking body. There was no explanation, there was no reasoning and no justification for his surroundings or the intensity of the pain burrowing through every pore of his body, a pain only comforted by the lava of adrenalin spouting from his frenzied emotions. A billion microorganisms that gelled together, constructing blood, bones and the essence of Ash's life stood back and wailed in hysteria and disbelief.

His beautiful wife was not where she should be, next to him. This was not his bed, this was not his home. This was not his life.

Chapter 2
Nine Seconds

'Slow down, slow down, I'm sorry, I didn't mean to say that, please, Ash. Please slow down!'

Ash's vision was distorted as angry tears welled in his eyes and his only answer to Jolene was a berserk scream. He couldn't muster the calmer sentence his brain had pieced together, so there was no logic in his outpouring.

'It's all your fault! You made this happen, you have destroyed my world, I knew you would, I knew you would do it. I hope you're happy now, I hope you're really happy now. He is dead and I blame you, it's all you. I wish I had never met you. It's all your fault!'

'I'm sorry! I'm sorry! I'm sorry! All I said was there was no need to drive so fast, I wanted us to get there in one piece.'

'You liar! You lying little cow! You said don't drive so fast, it's not like you've seen him for years. That's what you said, you ungrateful bitch! How could you, how could you say that! My dad just died! Do you understand that?! Do you even care?! My dad has just died and all you can say is, it's not like you've seen him for years! You selfish, selfish, ungrateful little bitch! How dare you say that to me! How dare you, Jolene! How dare you!'

'Ash! Watch that car!'

One, two, three, four, five, six, seven, eight, nine seconds later the world has been deconstructed, rearranged and designed into a new version. Nine seconds for the architect of the universe to call upon its greatest artists, surveyors and builders to plan, draw and reconstruct an original masterpiece and change the meandering existences of untold numbers of people. Ash didn't see the car that was directly in his path. Had he noticed it his brief journey through life would have been travelled on a different road and he would have reached a completely different destination.

The frantic swerve to the left to avoid the oncoming car, coupled with the excessive enraged speed Ash was driving at, diverted the trajectory of the vehicle into the steel fence which encompassed the winding ring-road they were travelling on. The spiralling, winding system of roads that brought the teeming hoards of impatient traffic into the city and circumnavigated it straight back out avoiding the residential areas via exit slip roads, was a feat of modern day engineering, however it wasn't built to withstand a direct pummelling from a speeding car travelling at eighty miles an hour. The sturdy fence of steel poles and criss-crossed mesh, snapped with the resistance of a toothpick being playfully handled after dinner and gracefully let the uncontrollable car dominate its presence, barely damaging the pristine metallic blue bodywork. The fence respectfully left the ultimate car crushing crescendo for the waiting road, which was forty feet below, silently looking up and watching the drama unfold, patiently awaiting the majestic pleasure of pulverising one of the man-made monstrosities that callously drove over its tarmac for decades.

It was already the third second of the lethal nine seconds of annihilation, the link between the fence and the crumbling tragedy that was abiding its time beneath, equalled three and a half airborne seconds.

The words 'Ash! Watch that car!' were echoing in the flying vehicle, Ash's brain was assembling a reply whilst simultaneously assessing the grave danger that was visually apparent but still too breakneck for any kind of defensive reaction, except the habitual response Ash's arm always involuntarily managed, anytime he had jolted the car with his zesty braking. Amidst the frantic screaming, on cue, his right arm lashed out to protect Jolene from the threatening jolt. The impending carnage of a car travelling at eighty miles an hour and dropping forty feet through the air would require an arm of celestial intervention to have even the slightest effect on the outcome, however in those three and a half seconds, Jolene's mind threw in the towel, it was pointless conjuring up a plan when bloodshed and gore was so menacingly unavoidable and instead the physical sight and ungracious punch of Ash's arm placated the catastrophic riot in her head and transformed it into a quiet stroll on a warm summer evening. All was quiet, there was a closing warmth as the beauty of the sunset cast its shadow and said 'au revoir' to the intrepid day that had so heroically conquered night and in that ephemeral twinkling in time, love demanded the stage and energetically bounded in for the farewell performance 'I love you, Ash'.

The curtains instantaneously closed as Jolene's swan-song became the crowning glory and saturated the car with an abundance of devotion. There was no desperate torment, not even a tingle of pain as the gruesome impingement of the concrete road below became a nine second show stopper and splattered Jolene's love-gorged head clean from her delicate shoulders, apathetically erasing thirty years of breathing into an unrecognisable abstract of blood and bones. Ash was not discharged from life, albeit he achieved the finest line between living and dying, as any organ or bone that made up his human form both inside and out that could be punctured, broken burst or mangled was affected by the immense explosive impact. His heart had punctually stopped seconds after Jolene muttered the immortal words, 'I love you, Ash', but his brain stayed gravely active, monitoring, deciphering and subconsciously remembering every detail of the breath-taking melodrama. There was more death flowing through Ash's veins than life but loving words betrothed to him from the adoring wife he was willing to die for animated his mind and soul to survive, sparkling his blood with stamina and vitality against all the odds of the crushing accident and relentless wreckage.

The macabre combination of entangled metal, bodily parts and blood formed a mass weave of twisted melancholy and told the broken tale of lost love, an incomplete world and a journey that began in despondency with the news of bereavement and unexpectedly ended in catastrophe. Nine seconds that crucified love and yet painfully monumentalised it beyond comprehension, stealing one breath and leaving another breathless. The emergency services began the arduous task of dismantling the destroyed car with the grisly remains of two obliterated humans welded into its mangled frame. Almost every bone in Ash's body was shattered but his crippled arm was miraculously still comforting Jolene's headless corpse.

Chapter 3
Shattered

An overwhelming abundance of deliciousness
The crowning glory, brimming with ambrosia
Without the worldly angst, anger and fuss
A blessed life, a path so clear.
Wake up! Wake up! Mr Death is always so near,
Keep him as your foe and let his lesson be learnt
For this life, albeit so colourful and dear,
In time will diminish and darken as it's burnt
Celebrate today and drink the beauty up
Everything you see is in your beautiful cup.
Leave no hallowed moment to squander
Leave no divine day to carelessly wander.
Embrace every sacred breath as your last
For some that revered beauty has already past.
Exclusively enthroned, bustling with power
But the ultimate darkness approaches fast
So lift up your goblet and cherish the light
Scare the dark clouds and gloat with a fight
Wake every day with a will to shout loudly
And stand resurrected and announce proudly,
This life is mine and I will worship all time
And when my days are done I will fight some more
And when death takes me to my final door
I will not cower and gaze upon the floor.
I will scandalously cartwheel into the dark
Knowing all my days were fabulously stark
Not a granted moment was ever cheated
This world where I have left my precious mark.
Come to me darkness for my world is completed.

'Shut up! Shut up! Shut up! I don't want to hear any more. I want to go now. I need to see Jolene. Where is my wife? What have you done with her? I want to see my wife! I need to go, I need to go now!'

The ward nurse jumped in surprise, Ash's sedation had clearly worn off as he woke to the gentle reading she was doing. The book on his bedside, spattered in blood, was one of the very few intact belongings recovered from the nine seconds of carnage. Over the two weeks, throughout Ash's semi-comatose state, she would often read excerpts from the book, partly borne of her compassion as a nurse and partly as a cognitive therapy for the broken patient, in the hope the familiar words were penetrating his dormant brain and soul, carefully regenerating his mind.

'I'm sorry, I didn't mean to wake you. You need rest, you need more time to recover. I will go and fetch the doctor who will explain more to you.'

'I don't need a doctor! I want to go. I want to go now. I need to leave. Where's Jolene? I want Jolene, and put that book down! How dare you touch my dad's book! Put it down! Put it down! Put down my dad's book now!'

A blistering shockwave shuddered through Ash's demolished body as his brain awakened by the mention of his dad and sent him a chilling flashback.

'Hi, Ash, I'm sorry. I'm sorry. You need to come home. It's your dad. He's dead.'

The bleak phone call from Jolene that immediately forced Ash's world into chaos and perspective, coupled with the insensibility of a second reminder, having forgotten the tragic news that his dad was dead, stunned Ash's anger into stillness. There was a mammoth collision. His little existence was hit by an invading meteorite from outer space, with a merciless impact, a conquering fury that dumbfounded his senses, even his tears were thrown into confusion, too insignificant within themselves to demonstrate the sorrow of a life without dad. Ash was still. Completely frozen of any movement. He attempted to visualise his dismembered life, his brain was transmitting signals of emotional disorder, demanding sadness and encouraging him to pounce from his bed and attempt to glue together the cracks forced upon him.

'The funeral. I need to go to the funeral. My dad's funeral. I need to get there, when is the funeral? Let me go! I need to speak to my father before his funeral!' The agitation rippled through Ash's voice as his disconcerted thoughts honed in on the funeral, with the idea he may not be able to apologise for his indiscretions towards his dad.

'I'm sorry, Ash. Your father's funeral was eight days ago, you've been very unwell and mostly in a coma, so the funeral had to ahead; my name is Dr Kemp and I've been looking after you.'

The dam burst. The tears were set free, as the true horror and disbelief of missing his own father's funeral started to filter through to Ash's consciousness.

'No! No! No! No! No! No! No!' Ash's mind was awash with a tidal wave of troublesome images surrounding the picture of his dear father, each landscape appearing in his eyes was further accompanied with a wailed 'No!', as Ash attempted to lift himself from the hospital bed.

'I want to go. Let me go. Where is Jolene? I want Jolene! Please, please, please let me go!'

Dr Kemp placed his hand on Ash's shoulder as the nurse lay a small amount of pressure on his thigh. Ash jiggled even harder, rattling the cold steel hospital bed, as startled onlookers walking past the bedroom, peered in to see what the rowdy calamity was all about.

'Get your hands off me! I need to go! You cannot keep me here! I want to go now! Let me go!'

Ash's face was contorted with hatred and outrage, froth bubbled from the edges of his mouth, foaming and spluttering as it met the overflow of tears streaming from his red eyes.

'I'm sorry, Ash. I'm sorry, you can't move. You have major internal complications, a broken spine, multiple bone fractures and I'm afraid both of your legs are paralysed.' Dr Kemp reluctantly blurted out Ash's pitiful physical incapacity, as each word fell upon Ash's skull, hammered home like a leaden blacksmith's hammer, flattening the entirety of his resolve to lift himself from the bed and leave the hospital. The noise in his head was deafening, the pummel of the hammer shattered his brain and squeezed the fragmented grey matter into one singular consoling word. The only word that quenched the burning convulsions tearing his battered mind apart. The only word that was capable of rescuing his rapidly drowning life, as the tidal wave continued to apathetically wipe out his essence.

'Jolene! Jolene! Jolene! Jolene! Jolene! Jolene! Jolene! Where is my Jolene? I want my Jolene! I want my Jolene!'

The nurse looked at the doctor as tears filled her blue eyes and rolled down her cheek. Through his own gushing eyes Ash noticed the nurse's expression.

'Jolene! What's wrong with Jolene? Oh God, please no God! Please God, not my Jolene as well. No God! Not Jolene! What's happened to my wife?! What's happened to my Jolene?'

The nurse looked away as her resolve avalanched downhill and her flow of tears deluged her otherwise unaffected composure. Dr Kemp sighed, slightly increased the touch on Ash's shoulder and with his own hardened tears welling in his eyes, preparing for the battle ahead, he proceeded to shatter every single reason Ash clung onto to live another moment.

'I'm sorry, Ash. Jolene died in the car crash.'

Chapter 4
Time

Bruised, violated and severely crushed
You left me to die
Where were you time, when I needed you to progress?
Uncertainty and melancholy, you became so shy
And yet for others you wantonly fly.
Why for this destroyed soul should you be less?
Leaving me in this carnage and mess
Every day you force me to cry
As you stand back, laugh and lie.
Time, you are no friend to me,
While you refuse to let me be
You will forever be my enemy, until these tears run dry.
You may stand silent and shun your responsibility
Raising a glass to your only decree,
While you ignore me and watch me die.
You hold onto the past and never set me free.
Time, you are a villain and a brazen crook
You promised so much but everything you took.
I have no fight left in me, so take a look
I have no choice, I have no life
And wait for you to remove the bleeding knife.
Time, you erase my pages and close my book
Goodbye for now, I will close my eyes
And live in hope that you will hear my sighs.

Time was not prepared to heal Ash's wounds. Physically and mentally he was in a state of timeless placidity. The past was a gargantuan roadblock, through which there was no diversion, no advance and no passage. His father's book, still stained from the nine seconds of bloodshed, both pacified and tortured his soul and was his immutable companion as it captured what was left of his life. He read the poem titled 'Time' again, as each word soaked into his skin, it recognised his plight and wrapped him in the warmth of a listening, comforting friend.

The blanket of timeless memory covered Ash's head. Fate had simply approached him and with a hefty heave-ho had launched the blanket over him, shrouding the continuum of seconds, minutes, hours, days, weeks and months. It was irremovable, his vision was darkness and gloom as the world continued to spin in the glories of spring and summer. The two beautiful seasons of rebirth and illumination whizzed past him, as the slumber and death of nature subsided into a crispy brown autumn. It had been seven months since the fatal twist in Ash's life had bluntly robbed his perception of a crowning future. A calamitous nine seconds that threatened to remain the only timepiece by which Ash's earth was going to be measured by. Humanity was flourishing as the globe endured the programme of the cosmos, spinning around the glowing sun, in its invincible three hundred and sixty five day cycle. Ash's days crumbled into nights, which disintegrated into daytime, the appearance of the sun and moon was irrelevant, fate's indefinite blanket only projected a single hue into Ash's eyesight, an exhaustive eclipse of blackness.

'You all left me, you left me. Where are you? Dad! Jolene! C'mon, you can come back now. Come and wake me up. Please wake me up. Please wake me up. Please wake me up! I want you to come back to me! Where are you? I know you are there! I know you can hear me. I know you can see me! Come back, it's easy! We can all start again, we can all be happy again, we can all be happy. Please, please, please, please! Dad! Jolene! Please come back to me!'

Ash's reflection glared back at him, as his solicitude and disquiet poured from his strained vocal chords and his dejected words happily bounced back from the window pane he was staring into.

This window was Ash's maladjusted companion, the Samaritan that harboured Ash's outpourings of emotion and the uncompassionate fiend that displayed the fanfare of the world that had been pitilessly snatched from him. A window that offered magnificent glory, a window that listened day after day, after day and a window that then crushed Ash with reflections of the broken man he was, wheelchair bound and pathetic, incapable of basic human functioning and ablutions, he detested the world displayed on the other side of the schizophrenic window. Ash didn't want an existence without what he had lost, there was no life for him. The baneful nine seconds had terminated the passing of time. There was no future for Ash.

'You're not coming back are you?! You're never coming back. Dad! Jolene! You're not coming back. I know you're not coming back. You don't care do you?! Look at me, look at me. I can't even walk. I'm helpless without you, I'm nothing alone. I have nothing, I am nothing and I don't want anything. I only want to die. If you won't come back to my world then take me into yours. I want to die, I want to die. I want to come to you. Then we can be together again. I don't want to live anymore. I only want to die!'

'You don't mean that, Ash. C'mon, let's get you sorted and into bed. I'm sure you'll feel better in the morning.'

The allaying words from Ash's care nurse sprayed further fuel to Ash's explosive and despairing rage, as she turned his wheelchair around and rolled him from the lounge into the bedroom for his evening ritual of basic activity, to aid his feeble handicapped body into bed.

'No! Please, just let me die. I'm tired of living. I'm tired of life. I'm tired of everything. It's time to say goodbye. I don't want to live another second.'

Chapter 5
Isolation

A thousand, miniscule pieces,
Indelible emotions and chest creases.
All that remains of a heart once so strong,
Forever isolated, with so much wrong.
All around me there is loss and no gain,
Even time has taught me to feel the pain.
Alone, lost, my soul is weeping loud,
Once there were people, no more crowd.
No one to see, no one to observe,
All these tears and no facial curve.
Deep inside me there is a scream,
Out it pours but it could be a dream
Because no one to care, no one to share.
This is my living nightmare.

'It's the only thing he does. Day after day he reads this book and for the last six days he has read that poem over and over again. It's almost as if it has become an obsession. It was written by his late father. It appears to reflect his heartfelt emotions. It's almost as if some of it was written as a bizarre biography of Ash's current inner feelings. I'm really not sure if it is helping him, or pushing him further into his own isolated world.'

Nurse Grace handed the book over to John Sommers, the Director of Rehabilitation, at the Teers House Hospital, the emotional disorder institution that Ash had been administered to since the heinous accident.

'I'm assuming you took this whilst he was asleep? You need to return it before he awakes. If he gets solace from the words within this book, it will help him recover. Rehabilitation from extreme trauma requires a central focus and as long as this book isn't detrimental to his recovery, it's a valuable tool, that might just help make Ash's world complete again. Monitor his relationship with the book closely

21

and see if you can buy your own copy to try and understand what's going on in his head.'

Teresa gingerly returned the book to Ash's bedside table, where it had remained for the seven months since he arrived and since she had been assigned as his carer nurse.

'What are you doing? Why did you touch my book? No one is allowed to touch my book. It's all I have in the world, it's my only belonging.'

Ash hadn't realised Teresa had taken the book away but had stirred just as she was putting it back in its customary position, next to Ash's emergency call button.

'Sorry, Ash, I was just checking to see if your call button was on. I do that every night. I didn't mean to touch your book. I know how precious it is to you. I really am sorry.'

Ash turned to pick the book up, knocking the emergency call button to the floor.

'Ok, I just worry sometimes that I will lose it. It's all I have. This book is my world.'

Ash placed the book upon his chest, clasping it with both hands as if his heart had pushed past his ribcage and skin and was now resting on his body and the only way of resuscitating it, was to squeeze it tight to maintain its vital beating. His dad's book was his heart, it was his life. It was the beginning and ending to all his morbid days. The bleakness that had drenched all that Ash lived for had pushed him into a corner of despair and isolation with the passing of time blanketed out, an extinguished candle flame that once shone so bright but had now flickered into oblivion with no means of relighting it back to its blazing eminence. Words from the book were the only glimmer of hope from the abandoned world Ash reluctantly inhabited. The backwoods of his mind shrivelled all reality, he was detached and deserted and the only consolation from his solitary confinement was his dad's book, 'Make my World Complete'.

Chapter 6
'Make My World Complete'

The unequivocal moment, two worlds collide,
Commingle and contrive.
A gigantic force unknown to humans,
So uniquely vast in size
So immense in sentimental declaration,
The sublime celebration
So Herculean with innuendo
So unexpected with shocking exaltation
In that sudden provocation, now so torrid,
Teeming and free
Fire-powered resolution, there is no solution.
Boldness and purpose twinkle fiery in the soul
Melted together, commanding as one
Dominant and dynamic, gutsy and energetic
Amalgamated hearts, imprisoned in emotional glory.
Ultimate transcendent love, the incomparable
And majestic story.

Teresa's copy of 'Make my World Complete' by Sitara Kai Khusa, Ash's late father, arrived. The intriguing poem of the same title on the back cover, spoke of intense romance and deep passionate love. She stared, engrossed at the haunting words as each letter of every word perforated her skin and inscribed itself within the sullen segment of her mind and sprinkled a sensation of first love upon it. Romance was dormant in Teresa's life. She had dedicated herself to a life of caring and rehabilitation of patients suffering from mental health conditions. On too many occasions her blood had been poisoned by enthusiastic love affairs that promised an abundance of intimate companionship and fairy-tale romance but delivered the shackles of battered emotions, a bruised ego and a disfigured confirmation of love. Her most recent mutilation of passion, hammered a deep nail into her already wooden heart. Every romantic affirmation was present. Her amorous liaison was raw chiselled handsomeness, with equal measures of charm and wit, a strong athletic body with energetic love making to match. Simon was heaven-sent perfection, a seductive vision of dreaminess. He ploughed down her walls with bulldozer ease, she had melted into his eyes and wore his words with pride and wanton desire. She had succumbed, against all the odds of her damaged romantic past of poets who transformed into psychopaths and devoted husbands who surrendered to the lure of younger, sexier women.

Simon was a king among the shattered ruins of past lovers, Teresa's walls of resolve took a deep breath, sighed in ecstasy and tumbled, as did her uncontrollable body, submissive to his persuasion, seduced by his masculine allure. Simon's downfall from the lofty summit of sexual and emotional success was a lurking evil, hibernating deep within his charismatic mind. A slumbering monster of commanding magnitude, once wakened, unconditionally caustic and shamelessly cut-throat. It was his Achilles heel, his atrocious weakness. It was jealousy. Controlling his wisdom, detrimental to his words and a persistent, dictatorial authority over his anger. The resentment that jealousy brewed resulted in physical dominance and pain and a full frontal attack on the very emotion that Simon was able to cement and solidify within Teresa, when they first met, her self-esteem.

Teresa was broken. Simon, in the nine months they were romantically involved, shredded her confidence into unrecognisable ribbons of regret, injected her mind with belittling contamination, that left her vulnerable and gorged with loathing about herself. The poison was ensconced in every pore of her body, it shouted obscenities about her weight, her face, her career, even her future prospects. Every aspect of her life was brittle if not already disintegrated into a pulverised mishap. Her skin, below her visible neckline, was a rugged road-map of bites and bruises, as jealousy had no limits and no conscience along her hellish journey of defiled love. Simon's radical change from the mysterious charmer, to a bullying lowlife, as spite became his unrelenting catalyst, destroyed every Shakespearean sonnet Teresa had adored, every ballad she had heard and every notion that love and romance were not fantasies but really did exist in this grey, cynical world. Teresa's dreams of holding hands, whispering poetry, delivering hand-held flowers, asking the bride-to-be's father permission to marry his daughter were ambushed, abused and left bleeding to an untimely death. There was no romance, only mediocrity and second-best relationships. Teresa was done. Her life was destined to be void of the wholesome goodness she had fantasised about since she had little pigtails and believed one day her prince would come.

One simple poem on the back cover of a book she had never heard of, spewed a torrent of passionate words. A tsunami had been created and every morsel of anguish, every crumb of agony, every fragment of adversity contrived by feeble, despicable lovers was annihilated as the omnipotence of magical words cleansed her tainted soul and left the wonder of the 'unequivocal moment' floating in her conscience, distinguishing itself from the remnants of her past and preparing itself to be recognised one day. Love had been resurrected from the smouldering pyre and within its smoke Shakespeare's 'Shall I compare thee to a summer's day?' bowed a welcome return bringing with it Teresa's perennial hope.

Chapter 7
Waiting

I was conceived at birth
And until your final breath I will be waiting
I have no rules, I have no agenda
But I am forever creating.
I'm not in your heart, I'm in your senses, in every pore
I will thrive on your sadness, I will lurch in your tears
I will be waiting and I will wait for years.
One day, I will pounce, I will bound through your door
I will fill you with commotion to your deepest core
There is a struggle in this invasion but I will not resign
I will ambush you with desire, make you mine.
This is my promise, this is my only law
Nothing in your world can give you more.
Lay down your life for unrelenting love is your fate
Don't forsake my absence, it will be worth the wait.

'I will wait for you, love. Take all the time you need. I'm never going to stop, I'm never going to give up, I'm going to keep you in my life and I will wait for my unequivocal moment. I know you will happen and I know it will be worth the wait.'

Teresa's warm breath created a circle of mist on the mirror, as she whispered to love and applied her ruby red lipstick, with an additional exhale the misty patch grew larger, giving her a foggy canvas to squeakily draw a heart shape using her finger. It made her smile as she left her apartment for work, musing about love and romance and the anticipation of feeling its entire delight deluge her existence. As the chapters of 'Make my World Complete' immersed themselves into Teresa's psyche, her doubts and insecurities waded further out to sea; after only a few days of reading she felt transformed. From the distance there were haunting echoes and mumblings that she was ugly and undesirable but the oceans were vast and the drifting was constant, as each word became a powerful oar, brushing against the waves and building a chasm between what she was and what she was made to believe. Whereas every waking day her reflection had been overshadowed by the insults and attacks that Simon had happily inflicted upon her mental and physical being, that same bulge in her stomach, the wrinkled lines of laughter on her face and the natural drooping of her naked breasts were no longer objects of laughter and scorn but bewitching attributes that someone, somewhere would cherish and applaud.

In the capacious world there is a person, potentially multitudes of people, that are in search of everything that Teresa has to offer. A person that will undeniably accept Teresa exactly how she stands and instead of squeezing and poking her stomach and calling her fat, her delicate womanly excess will be kissed and caressed. Someone that will look at her wrinkles and instead of mocking her age, tell her he wants to see more laughter lines, ones he can help her create with the merriment they are going to share. Someone who's only regret is not the sight of southward bound breasts falling foul to the magnetism of age and gravity but that he wished they could have met sooner and grown older together. Teresa's unequivocal moment was out there in the vastness of the world and someone was prepared and longing to make her world complete and live in the magic of symbiosis as she equally completed his world.

Teresa's journey to work floated by on a cloud of blissful foresight as her meandering imagination fluttered through scenarios of romantic liaisons. Lazy Sunday afternoons together reading the papers and conversing about the stories and articles within them, mutually wanting to hold hands whilst strolling aimlessly through parks, the whisper of passionate language being exchanged prior to making love and enraptured sleep wrapped together in the sticky warmth of post sexual delirium. A beautifully drawn strategy of romance, the blueprint of love, a parchment written by experienced lovers, Teresa was ogling it with cheerful glee, until the disturbing racket from her ward, stone-heartedly scrunched her perfect manifesto into a screwed up ball of paper and flung it into the waste paper basket. Teresa scuttled into the room, rapidly tying her uniform hat as she made her way to the source of the noise.

'Wait! Wait for what you fucker?! I'm done waiting! I have nothing to wait for! Nothing to live for. Everything is to die for! Keep away from me! I have to do this, I have to find my way. I don't belong here! This world is not for me!'

Surrounding Ash's bed was a group of medical staff, a swathe of white coats wafting back and forth. Teresa pushed two of them apart to view the commotion from the ringside. The vision was a spectacular explosion of crimson and white. Ash was sat upright in his bed, with an abstract splattering of his own blood in dappled formation over the crisp white bed linen and crumpled duvet.

'I don't want to be here anymore. I don't want to be alive, when all I know is death! Stay away from me! Stay away and let me go! Let me go! I need to go!'

Ash's voice was a bold mixture of aggression and fear. The aggressive nature of his angered exchange was accompanied by a waving of the oak handled knife he had in his right hand, it was violently directed at the medics attempting to disarm him.

Then there was an underlying vibration of fear as his voice momentarily softened, 'Please tell them to back off. Teresa, please tell them. They don't know my pain. Tell them to go away! Leave me alone. Let me be!'

'Ok, Ash, I will but you need to put that knife down. Please put the knife down.'

The sharpness of the knife edge blunted into submission with the glare that Ash pierced Teresa's eyes with, he plunged into her sight and gouged her eyeballs as his distressed sneer spoke of pain she wouldn't even dare to quantify or understand and yet she was transiently immersed into his damned world of loss, her heart plummeted from a cliff edge and fell into the darkness of his defeated emotions. One stare and moments became hours and hours became days. Teresa's thoughts were catapulted into a downcast world of bereavement, albeit she had escaped the reality of death in her thirty six years of life, everyone she knew and cared for was still breathing. Suddenly a deep melancholy had overwhelmed her and Ash's injured life crushed her entity.

'You will understand more than anyone, Teresa. I just know you will understand.'

With the swiftness of an orchestra conductor brandishing his baton, Ash swung the knife through the laceration he had already caused on his left wrist. Blood vessels squelched out liquid as they were gashed open. The whiteness of the sheets was decorated in soaking warm redness as Teresa lunged forward and grabbed Ash's hand, crunching his knuckle as he held onto the knife handle. He yanked hard pulling her medium frame forward onto his immobile legs, Teresa's face was mottled with Ash's blood, matching the lipstick she had adoringly applied to her lips, as Ash attempted to control her with his freshly disfigured wrist. She tasted his blood as spraying droplets entered her mouth, bizarrely adding to the melodrama his stare had already kindled in her brain. The other medics took their cue from Teresa's actions and pounced on Ash, loosening his grip on the knife and restraining his movement.

'I need to die. Just let me be. This world is not for me. I need my dad, I need my Jolene!'

Ash's tears washed a clear track through the blood that was spattered across his face. Teresa straightened herself, realising she had fallen upon Ash's book, it was on the same chapter she had been reading, entitled 'Waiting, a conversation with love.'

One set of words that had incited two exceptionally alternative responses, two opposing sides of the spectrum, from complete affirmation to total negation. From simply accepting that love will ultimately deliver all his promises, to the pitying remembrance of love that is lost and never to be reacquainted in the living world. Love's slumbering poem crowned Teresa with the assurance that true romance will track her down and kidnap her and abiding her time for that unequivocal moment, the artistry of that sublime happening is worth a lifetime of waiting, its expectancy being as dexterous as the enchantment itself. The same poem embraced Ash's resolve and fortified his belief that such an unparalleled moment of true love couldn't possibly occur a second time in his lifetime, therefore his wait was over and it was time to enter the grave battlefield of death to be reunited with his incomparable love, for undoubtedly such a bottomless, yearning love would have crossed the barriers between life and death and would be waiting in anticipation of his homecoming.

Chapter 8
Penance

'I can't stop it! I can't control it! He is never going to leave me! He will take me, he will take me! He will make me suffer! He won't stop until I've been punished! He won't stop until I've paid for what I did! He will never let go, until he has his revenge. He wants his revenge! I have to pay! I have to suffer for what I did! I have no choice!'

Every word echoed through the featherweight walls, cracking the silence of dawn. The petrified shrill in mother's voice was pickaxe sharp and the customary wake-up call on most mornings, followed by the creak of Ash's bedroom door as Dad crept in to comfort him from the screaming, and repeat the same words he used every time Mum's tirade replaced the electronic alarm, 'Mum's just had another dream. Good timing, my son, it's time to wake anyway.'

The cold black structure assuredly peered over the rooftops. It was always there, it never let Ash down. The stalwart backbone of Paris, simply winking its hulking, tenacious residence with its consolatory whisper through the morning mist, 'Les gens du matin, je suis la Tour Eiffel et je vais vous garde en securite'.

'There it is, my son. Watching over Paris. Like an iron robot, always keeping us safe from harm, always watching over the people of Paris, always there whenever you're feeling insecure. Always ready to uphold the power of life.'

From an early age, Ash's dad had complimented the focal point of audacious strength in the city and utilised its firmness as a metaphor for emotional courage, conviction of character and the realisation of ambitions and dreams.

'Stand tall and brave, Ash. The world can be a scary place but if you stand tall and brave it will bow down to you and support your dreams and keep you strong. Be strong today, Ash. Be like the Eiffel Tower. Tall, strong and always happy.'

At the delicate age of twelve, the Eiffel Tower was an omnipresent grandfather for Ash, in a life that was seemingly appeasing and carefree; excluding inexplicable alarm calls courtesy of Mum, days were abundant with joy and encouragement.

'Dad, why does Mum keep shouting in her dreams? It scares me.'

'Well, Ash, firstly don't let it scare you. Mum is fine and happy. She just has dreams that wake her up, just like the dreams you sometimes have. Secondly, all adults have things that have happened in the past and sometimes those things are bad memories that keep haunting us, trying to stay alive. We all have them, just like mum does. The main thing is, you shouldn't worry because it's nothing to worry about. Remember, you need to be like Mr Eiffel. Nothing matters to him, not the weather, not what people say, not even bad memories. Mr Eiffel stays strong no matter what is going on. Don't forget that Ash, you too have to be like Mr Eiffel. Now be extra strong and quickly get ready for school, while I take a shower and then we can have breakfast.'

'Ok, Dad, je suis Monsieur Eiffel!'

The Eiffel Tower appreciated the admiration, impenetrably standing firm in the chaos of the Paris traffic, saluting anyone idolising his grandiose personification for valour, stability and perseverance, but today his dependability was about to be immeasurably tested.

'Rebecca! Rebecca! Rebecca!'

Three shouts of his mother's name and Ash's world froze as the Eiffel Tower could do no more than shed a tear and crumble into a heap of isolated, dysfunctional frigid metal. It was time to simply abdicate the authority that had been granted to him by Ash's dad, he was defeated, renounced by a glimpse of Mum's feet dangling above his parents' bed, with Dad's arms wrapped around her naked calves. Mr Eiffel wasn't prepared for this vision, his steely arms were unable to stretch and stop Ash from entering the room where dad was shouting Mum's name.

'Adieu, Ash! Je suis desole!'

The buckled remains of a once undaunted, impregnable edifice evaporated into a desolate crater as Ash witnessed the full horror unfolding in his parents' bedroom.

'Help me, Ash! Help me hold your mother while I untie her. Help me, Ash, or she will die!'

Ash, still in his pyjama suit, did as he was told. Without registering the complete shock of the surreal situation, he replaced his dad's embrace around his mum's legs.

'Push her up, Ash! Push her up! You need to push her up! Push! Push! Push!'

Ash simply didn't have the strength in his twelve-year-old arms to push upwards a fully grown woman that was being pulled by fate and gravity.

'Be strong! You can do it! Ash, be strong!'

Together they cried, spluttered and screamed but the tourniquet around Mum's neck sternly carried out the instructions it had been given, crunching her windpipe and brashly severing the entry of oxygen to her brain long enough to bid farewell to life.

The heap of a broken, sobbing family, in the decadent suburb of Paris, caked in vomit from the dead woman was an unrecognisable batter of naked flesh, a young lad and a father who had been unable to save a wife and mother from her own destruction.

'Why, Rebecca?! Why have you done this to us?! We love you so much, we need you! Where have you gone? Where have you gone? Where have you gone?! Where? Why? Why? Why?'

At the pubescent age of twelve, terror, torture and anguish had paraded with the distasteful loss of Ash's mother, even the lofty command of the Eiffel Tower had been swiftly incapacitated as the mysteries of living and dying had played their merciless game, shrouding a father and son with a cloak of darkness and misery.

'And that's the last memory I have of my mum, holding her dead body, while it crushed me into the soft bed, I couldn't move. I was hoping it was all a horrible dream, that I was about to wake from. I didn't wake. She never came back and life changed forever. I never understood why she had to leave us, I never understood what was troubling her. I never understood what dad meant by bad memories. We never spoke of that day again, I never got to ask dad what was haunting her. Mum took with her a piece of our lives that wasn't replaceable, we both died a little that day. Why did you ask about my mother?'

The tragedy of Ash's story creased a furrow of disturbance into Teresa's forehead. Why wouldn't the story of Ash's mother be harrowing? She should have known it would not have had a joyous ending, that somehow it was simply going to fall in line with the other broken pieces that glued this shattered man together, creating a mosaic of misery, utterly distinguishable from the regular lives of normal people, where naturally death and grief are unavoidable but not necessarily plunging to abstract remoteness and fathomless suffering.

'Oh, Ash. It was simply hope that talking about your mother might have made you smile and think of good things, think of things that make you happy. I'm so, so sorry. I had no idea about your mum. I had no idea something so horrible had happened. I don't know what to say, except I'm sorry for asking and I'm sorry about what happened to her.'

'Not a day passes when I don't remember my mum taking her life. Not a day goes by when I don't wonder why she did that to us, why she broke our happy family. Why she killed my dad on that day, my dad who loved her so much. It still makes me angry. If only I could speak with her for five minutes, just to ask her why, why, why. She was all my dad lived for. I remember him reading to her, lovey romantic poems that he had penned especially for her. On the day she died, his writing died too. He never wrote a single word after writing her eulogy. It was almost as if all his inspiration disappeared to the place where she had gone. I hope they have found each other and I hope they are happy again. I know they will be watching over Jolene because dad understood love and he knew how much I loved Jolene. I just wish my life would end so I can be with them again. I don't have a place in this world anymore.'

Ash's head drooped as the final words left his dejected heart, via his mouth and he meandered into the closest world he knew to actual death, deep sleep. His days and nights all rolled into edgy debilitation as he remained under heavy sedation since his attempts to cut his own life short had been thwarted. There was no alternative other than to dampen his belief that euthanasia was the only solution to a life he could no longer bear, begrudging every day he was still breathing.

'I'm pushing, I'm pushing. Mum, where are you?'

Teresa rolled Ash's wheelchair away from the window as he sleep-whispered remnants of the conversation she had sparked within his scarred memory. The terrifying image of what she imagined he was dreaming about drew some of his sorrow into her own world.

33

As the Eiffel Tower stood subdued and incompetent, staring oafishly upon the suicide scene of despair, her vision was lucid.

'It's time to say goodbye, you want this. You have waited for this moment. Well, be happy now, your time has come.'

There was no colour in Rebecca's face, she already looked bereft of life, pallid and withdrawn. Her tears had retreated back into her resolute eyes, they were reluctantly repressed as her fiery emotions were determined to challenge the miraculous sparks of vitality she was naturally born with. The noose, silken and red glided around her neck, in the unfamiliar circumstances of her being scantily clad and sat on her bed, rather than dolled up and adding a final touch before leaving home. This departure was unique, it had no return ticket in mind. It was a one way journey, away from Paris and away from the reality of living. Cushioned with intricate salmon and gold brocade, the majestic wooden boudoir stool was invited upon the bed, always one suppressed by the derrières of those it was made to please and support, it didn't hesitate with the curious instruction as it sturdily balanced on the springiness of the mattress. Rebecca's baby pink negligee swooped past her curves as she confidently stood up on the stool, denouncing the modesty it provided, balancing herself by gripping the wooden beam in the ceiling, once the impressive selling feature of the bedroom, representing timeless baroque charm, now innocently party to a conspiracy to kill, an accessory to murder, willingly allowing Rebecca to tighten the cloth around its girth.

'My love, there's only you in my life...'

Rebecca hesitated and listened to the quirky racket coming from the bathroom, as her husband attempted to tunefully sing their signature tune, 'Endless Love'; her heart fluttered as she remembered the Paris café she was sat in, dreaming of love and romance when Mr Sitara Kai Khusa miraculously appeared from nowhere and fired a love-bullet through her heart, capturing and imprisoning it with a life sentence of poetic beauty in a magical relationship that was heaven-sent and dream-worthy. It had been the most illustrious occurrence of her life. Her very own unequivocal moment, under the gaze of the French icon of love, the Eiffel Tower.

'...My endless love.'

Rebecca joined in with the last verse, holding the final climactic note as she kicked away the stool. Tears flooded her eyes as her crowning memory was washed away, grotesquely satisfying her penance with her own life. Her consciousness carelessly fluttered away with a deep remorseful sigh, there was no need to wait for a last minute reprieve, Rebecca's resolve was impenetrable and beyond speculation, even with the faint echo as her husband found her dangling body and shouted her name there was no need to look back. Life was now futile and death inevitable.

Teresa walked away from Ash's ward. The corridor was isolated and cold, with the clank of evening therapies in the background as nurses scuttled around the patients. Ash's story circled her mind in the formation of confused and angry bees buzzing around their disturbed nest, looking for answers and vengeance and yet in their bravery, scared and fragile in the huge unknown world around them and the uncovered perils within it.

Chapter 9
Eulogy

'My dear sweet Rebecca. Snatched away from your loving family. Incomplete and battered, how will we ever be the same again without your smile and charm to light up our darkest days? You epitomised gratefulness and made us appreciate the fullness of life with your presence.

The day before you came, life for me was meaningless and adrift. Stranded on an empty shipwrecked vessel, aimlessly detached and looking for dry land, I was hopeless and lost, with nothing on the horizon, except more anguish and heartache. Then the vision of faultless bloom. That unequivocal moment when I saw you under the watchful scrutiny of the Eiffel Tower, you made my world complete. Thousands of fractured and disjointed segments of my life simply magnetised together and made me whole again. I realised all my agony, all my shattered days, all my shredded emotions were destined to happen in order to bring me to your café in Paris, to meet you, the true love of my life.

For over a decade, my waking ritual remained the same; every morning I thanked God for the magic spell you cast upon me, for our wonderful son, Ash and the sunshine you shone into our lives. We were ordained to meet, it was binding fate that joined our fragmented worlds together. Now, there is nothing. The world without you is bleak and intimidating. You've said goodbye and with your flight I'm eternally grounded, trapped in this human shell of sorrow. I have no escape without you. I don't expect people to understand how I feel because I know most people never witness true love, therefore they cannot comprehend my internal dying, so I will humbly attempt to describe you, so at least people will grasp the enchantment that was you.

Rebecca, my love, your faultless skin, the sensuality of your curves, the allurement of your deep eyes, to the hypnotic vision of your entirety, you were lovable and loved. I have the greatest of sympathy for those that don't meet a complete partner such as you.

One that amplifies all that is captivating and causes an earthquake in the soul, making the meekest of characters enraptured with strength they never knew existed, within themselves. An ounce of you was worth a tonne of listless people that don't appreciate the power of living. Without you, I am a part of that entourage. No reason. No plan. No future and no vision. Thank you, Rebecca, for once completing my shrivelled life, I will forever be grateful that I was able to witness such gigantic bewitchery in your eyes. Only you would understand my incomplete life now. You've taken the quill from my hand, ended my chapters and closed my book. My story began and ceased with you. Goodbye, darling. This is my last poem, my final words and I dedicate them to you.

Rebecca

My senses moonstruck and possessed
My manly details charmed and obsessed
Your lingering eyes looked and caressed.
Your spellbound rapture opened my book
Captivated my physique, tempted and shook.
In my dreams you were an elusive fascination
An unreachable, entranced creation.
And in my truth a magical reality that set me free.
You, Rebecca lit my fire and rooted my tree.
Birds tweeted your song and appeared with glee.
My days were dark, with your candle I could see.
Now I am blind and misery has become me
You've caged the birds, you've killed me reluctantly.
Rebecca, I am confined to death without you
You were my lungs, my heart and my soul
I have no breath, I have no beat. I have no goal.
I count these burdensome days until my eyes will shut
Only then will I be released from this relentless rut
And I will search for you for an eternity
Without you there is no life, I cannot be.
Rebecca, I will find you. Please darling wait for me.

Sitara Kai Khusa

Teresa was defenceless, abandoned and powerless as the cracks in her mental damn were breached with the pressure of the eulogy Ash's father had penned for his deceased mother. Her internet search for his words had been effortless and now her face was a contorted mess of tangled emotions, deluged with tears of grieving and desperate bafflement. Why did Rebecca take her own life? It appeared to be exemplary in every imaginable way, from the accomplishment of heart rendering passion to the wonderful sense of family togetherness and belonging that was the nucleus of their life.

Chapter 10
Obsession

Creased and torn is my brooding face
Sleep is a mystery, darkness I chase.
There were days and nights so clear
They have rolled into oneness with this fear
It burns, it rasps, it burdens my every thought
I am captivated, I am prisoner. I am truly caught.
I see no release from this deadly plague
I once lived a life so easy and vague.
My fields are on fire, the smoke fills my brain
It poisons my blood and pours it down the drain.
It's not a conundrum, I know my feeling
I understand the futility of attempted healing.
Nothing, nothing, nothing is an anecdote!
It's my obsession that has the winning vote.
I'm crumbling inside, it's my unyielding neurosis
Buzzing loudly, contorting with craze
My unwanted delusion, it's not just a phase
Don't leave me now, my infatuation. My crush,
The monkey on my shoulder, my sweet tooth rush
I have no independence, I have no liberty
You have become my shackles, you are my decree.
I'm blind to the world in this escalating insanity.
I'm in a wicked trance, lost in unknown witchery
A lure so deep, only death could set me free.

There was no escape from the captivation of 'Make my World Complete'. Ash's dad had cast an inescapable net upon Teresa's life with his twisting words of unconditional love, passion and melancholy. 'Obsession' was a neurotic poem relating to the binding enraptures of swimming in the fixation of another person, caught in that deadly rapid flow, a torrent of meandering power, rendering one forlorn and handcuffed. Unable to resist the merciless energy and magnetism of another human being, a body and mind transformed to the finest powder of iron filings, polarised and incapacitated, intent on only one singular direction. Pulled and pummelled, weakened into submission. The pondering words of 'Obsession' penetrated Teresa's pores and drowned her with the disturbing reality, that she was obsessed too.

Her days and nights rolled into a single expression of passing time, her once dry wafting fields delicately moving with the wind of her lazy thoughts, now ravaged with disorderly fire. The smoke blocked all other priorities; she was bewitched. Her liberty had become her restrained insanity. Teresa was bordering on the realms of craziness. It was witchery. Ash's dissected life, his dad's book and the direful and inexplicable demise of his mother, were the only subjects that occupied her thinking and her wilted brain. The heady compulsion to unearth the truth behind Rebecca's suicide churned a steaming cauldron of speculation, conspiracies and unrefuted questions. What was she hiding? Why? Why? Why? Did she intentionally take her own life, knowing it would destroy her adoring family, especially the life of her loyal and passionate husband? She had everything. Even the Eiffel Tower was in her back garden, winking his appreciation of their lives. What was Rebecca hiding? What was so strong that she had to give her life up for it?

Teresa desperately needed answers.

The grief-stricken puzzle was a road block in her life that she simply could not manoeuvre around. Her driving obsession was fuelled by Ash's miserable existence, somehow Teresa knew the answers to the mystery of his mother, might unleash his life into the living world again, but she was also very aware that was not the conclusive reason for her budding compulsion. There was a grey area in her psyche, exacerbated further as she turned each page of his father's book, as every word lured her deeper into their cryptic past.

Daily, Teresa poured over the doleful eulogy penned by Ash's father looking for clues; there had to be a reason. Her infatuation was spiralling downwards into the depths of delusion. Between the passion, desire and romance of 'Make my World Complete' and the utter depression of Sitara Kai Khusa's parting words to his dear wife, Teresa's engrossment was planted, nourished by the book and emotionally decapitated and starved by the eulogy. A silent tiger, without a blink staring at its prey, waiting for an appropriate moment to pounce and satisfy the insatiable and burgeoning hunger, it was another evening at home and Teresa was fixated on Sitara's words of despair, piercing her glassy stare through the pages of the newspaper she had printed from the internet. She blinked in astonishment. Her eyes widened and an excited pang cavorted through her head, the shrill of elation discharged adrenalin into her bloodstream and the drum of her heartbeat pounded from her chest as her temperature rose by three degrees and heightened her senses as the optimum second for the tiger to jump arrived. How could she have missed the words underneath the main obituary?

Completely absorbed by Rebecca's poem, she simply hadn't cast her eyes to either side of Sitara's declaration of love and sorrow.

My dear, dear Rebecca. I have no words to express my grief that you are no longer of this world, all I can say is without you, my world would have died before it had even started. You were my only angel, my only saviour and simply the only person alive that I would have gladly given my life for. You will forever be my heroine and I will die a happy woman, knowing that I once had the greatest person alive in my life. You allowed me to breathe. You gave me hope. All my love forever.

Goodbye, Rebecca.

Dawn.

One hundred elementary words, combined in this setting and context, were a landslide distorting the terrain and prickling yet another dimension into the already multi-layered drama.

Who was Dawn? What on earth did Rebecca do to receive such a heart-warming accolade?

Teresa had unwittingly entered a maze and now she was lost with a burning obsession to escape and once again see the light. Her tears were confused as they followed the heavy tracks of their predecessors, pushed out by a jumble of mashed emotions, from the exhilaration of discovering Dawn's eulogy, to the escalating mournfulness of tragic lost lives.

For every word of 'Make my World Complete' that Teresa absorbed, there was a molecule of her make-up altered for infinity, instantly metamorphosing her thoughts and cunningly manipulating her moods. At the very precise moment she had gathered an ounce of willpower to stop thinking about the Khusa family, the words of 'The Spiral', Sitara's expression of human mentality spiralling out of control but then achieving the confidence to go forth, hammered another nail of gusto into her, obliterating her obstinacy.

The Spiral

Winding downwards into the wilderness of loneliness
The wind is sharp against the skin you did caress
The mountains are steep as they stand in my way
Underneath there is darkness and black.
I know my shaken emotions will crack
C'mon solidarity, join my thoughts and let me be
Help me fight this spiral until I taste victory
I crave transformation into upwards shooting rockets
Until my eyes are wide and bulging from their sockets
I have my confidence, I have my resolve
And the beguiling mysteries I will solve.
The time has come to capture my passion. I will evolve.
The stony mountains will crumble into dust with fear
I will guide myself through a path so clear.
Whatever I'm in, I will be all in
Until my unfinished symphonies bellow a din.
This is my calling, no more sprawling
Bye, bye spiral you tried but no more falling.
My bags are packed and it's onwards to my journey
I won't look back, for that's way, way behind me.
I will relentlessly trek, until I am content and free.

Teresa's sleep pattern was restored, her slumber was intense as the logger-heads of her mind joined forces and prepared for an identical battle. There was no more bemusement, her path had been cleared of the debris of over-thinking and procrastination. A lucid goal had been set and upon that bed her brain could finally rest. Teresa accepted the only way forward was to feed her harrowing obsession and discover the truth behind the lamentable and fractured Khusas.

Chapter 11
The Black Dog

Patience, discipline
And humour were my helpful bedfellows
Cherishing my life, cavorting with nature,
With birdsong in my heart.
A lengthy, colourful season
Wrapped in the glowing sun.
You were a distant echo, bereft of any substance.
A muted burden upon others, their gripe not mine.
The clouds gathered, days darkened, no longer fine.
You have bounded into my beautiful green park.
The rain has poured, the sun is bleached
And in my ears you carelessly bark.
You are my shadow black dog,
You have lapped my light
For every day that was bright,
You have squinted my sight
Silently you stare and sit at my feet,
Not a whimper, it's me you greet
Invisible to the world, other people matter not,
In my little cup you are the poison shot.
You are man's best friend, you are entirely loyal
And you will put me deep under the soil.
Black dog, you are here to stay and stronger you grow
In these dark days I know you will keep me low.
This is your true and rightful place,
the only lines and frowns on my face.

'Thank you, Ash. Your writing is lovely but the words are so sad, of course you won't be depressed forever, of course you will get better, of course there is light at the end of the tunnel. Your black dog will bound off as quick as it arrived and once again your sun will shine.'

'I'm so glad you like it, Teresa, but I think we all know I'm never going to recover. There is no way to recover. There is no sun because there is no solution. I doubt I will ever leave this place. I doubt I will ever be allowed into society again. Which is fine because I never want to be part of a society that doesn't have a place for me. I would rather spend my last days here, hopelessly waiting until the black dog finally puts me out of my misery. Death or absolute insanity are the only bedfellows that are welcome in my life.'

The dark clouds painted a drab, lumbering scene as Teresa peered out of the window in Ash's ward and caught her appearance. What happened to the morning sunshine that greeted her as she skipped to work with her renewed drive? Why were the dispiriting words of another dejected patient eradicating her resolve? Ash was one of the many hopeless entities at Teers House Hospital, none of the other patients had this affect upon her, however Ash's inherited bleakness clouded Teresa's glow. His eclipse was in her world and when he outpoured his suffering, the moon swallowed her sun, obscuring her rays of optimism.

'Find me death! Find me death! Find me death! Take me home death!' Ash's sedation was avidly circulating his bloodstream, his beleaguered body attempted to fight the onslaught but was rugby tackled to the floor yet still had the last word by sending tears marching to his eyes and begging words of death to his lips. With a snuffled snore Ash returned to his delicate slice of death, his silent world where memories were muted and the drugs overpowered his dreams and stole his subconscious. There was no window to consciously dream for Ash, as his dreams were a cruel reminder of his lost life and only existed in two genres, life or death. His face scrunched into a painful grimace. Dreamworld was following through with its very specific job description:

Dreamworld Job Description – Your role is to simply conjure all the images and feelings from the past and create one of two stories, both of which will make the waking dreamer feel lost and forlorn.

Story 1 – The LIFE Scenario. A vivid picture of how life once was. Remind the dreamer of all the beautiful feelings that existed, particularly precise moments that were cherished, commingle those with all the emotions of happiness you can muster. The dreamer needs to feel that this ideal life is in the present, with all the associated blessedness. It will be a lucid dream, so realistic that the dreamer doesn't realise they are actually in Dreamworld.

Objective: The dreamer wakes into a dramatic false sense of security and for a wonderful handful of seconds believes all is blissful in their world, until reality strikes a crushing blow and punctures their heart that it was all a cruel, premeditated dream, leaving them deeply hurt and cheated by their animated and callous mind.

Story 2 – The DEATH scenario. A picture of how life is now. Remind the dreamer of their heartfelt loss and the beautiful life they once knew. Sprinkle the dream with all the dreaded emotions they have already suffered, with a heady mix of loneliness, despair and an acute sensation that they were directly to blame for the current circumstances. Include images of people that no longer exist, show them in dying, decrepit forms, crying for forgiveness and making the dreamer believe they weren't ready to leave their life behind. Ensure all the people mutter incomprehensible, miserable phrases. They must all call out the dreamer's name in frustration, anger and/ or melancholy.

Objective: The dreamer wakes under a shroud of depressed feelings, unable to function past the debilitating sensation of solitude and gloom, entering the fierce world of regret and attempting to decipher the ambiguous phrases, whilst blaming themselves for the deathly demise of the people concerned.

It was the cruellest story. Each second, every scene creased another frown into Ash's distorted face, as the sedation drugs battled on the frontline of his battling brain and kept the unfolding events firmly in no man's land and far from his conscious mind.

'Come here, Ash, come to me, my lover. Come to me and let's make love.'

Jolene had that distinctive look in her eyes, the one that melted Ash's heart and remodelled it to beat uncontrollably. Ash recalled the feverous rush that enthralled his deepest, inner ardour the very first moment he had encountered the brazen allure of Jolene's eyes.

The appeal was instant, one esoteric, lingering stare that captured his sexuality unaware, and hooked him like a helpless fawn, drawn to its mother, barely able to stand on its rickety legs but knowing it was home, safe and precisely where it belongs. Ash received an instant, electrifying message, which typed indelible words into his uplifted mind and erratically beating heart,

'She is the one. You are home. This is the woman you have been looking for. Take her. Take her now. She will make you happy. She is all you've been waiting for.'

From that indescribable moment Ash was void of restraint and was incapable of any feasible action that didn't involve Jolene.

'Come here, Ash, what are you waiting for? Come to me, my lover. Come to me and let's make love. C'mon, Ash, I want you, I need you. Come here and make me whole again. Only you can do that. You always make my world complete.'

Jolene's moist skin glistened in the ray of sunshine that delicately caressed her provocative curves, as she beckoned Ash into their bedroom. His wanton body reacted accordingly and pointed firm into the direction of her stunning nakedness, weakening him at the knees, albeit they immediately acknowledged they were only allowed a temporary romantic weakness, for soon they would need to muster sturdiness enabling him to press the love of his life into their marital bed, with the anticipation of sexual ecstasy they always created.

'I'm coming, Jolene. I love you, Jolene.'

The sun expertly lit the darkened bedroom into which his gorgeous wife disappeared, as the sound of squealing bed springs called out to Ash, conjuring an image of Jolene's dampness craving to be impregnated.

'C'mon, Ash, I'm so wet for you. I need you. I need you inside me. Come here and make my world complete.'

'Jolene! Jolene! Jolene! I can't move! I can't move!'

No attempt was made to take any steps towards the bedroom. Ash already knew he couldn't move. There was no movement possible. There was no life in his body, as it flaccidly stood dead to the familiar floor of his home.

'Oh, Ash! That's gorgeous! Oh, Ash, you're so deep. I love it when you do that. Go deeper, Ash. I love you, Ash! Ash, I'm going to cum. You're making me cum. Oh, Ash, I love you. I will love you forever.'

'Jolene! Jolene! It's not me. I'm still out here. I'm still here! Jolene! It's not me, I'm here!

'I love you, Ash. Make love to me again and again and again!'

'Jolene! No! It's not me! Please stop, Jolene, it's not me!'

Ash cried unstoppable tears. His heart was viciously crow-barred from his chest, listening to his wife in ecstatic satisfaction, howling her orgasms through the membranes of his crippled body, as his mind took part in the charade and tortured him with phantasms of another man satiating his lustful wife.

'Stand firm, they're on the attack. Stand firm, men. The enemy will not cross no man's land. Not now! Not ever! They cannot and will not pass!'

The sedatives shouted the orders from the trenches. This nightmare escapade was never going to be victorious. Ash's conscious mind was unaware and blissfully ignorant to the barbaric onslaught of the remorseless depictions in his subconscious mind. Teresa glared at Ash's troubled face and wondered what today's Dreamworld was subjecting him to and placed her hand upon his to help support the heroic cavalry of drugs, battling to keep his shuddering dreams at bay. The battle had been won and Ash's face relaxed from the horrors of his ruptured world. Teresa removed the crumpled pieces of paper from Ash's hand and read for herself the profound words of his painful poem 'Black Dog', the misery of his own mental imprisonment and only true friend, depression. The bleakness of Ash's sad musings veiled the brightness of day, beating it into submission with a hefty bat of apathy but light can overpower night and control the gloom, as the second piece of paper behind 'Black Dog', shone bright and muzzled the pensive howling.

Teresa's clouds separated as the words outed an ounce of optimism.

Chapter 12
Glowing for ME

Death, patiently you wait for me,
My friend in black, I know you can see
Cowering in the corner, lingering until life will flee.
You count my days, the tick of my clock
When will I say goodbye? When will I open the lock?
Death, you stand so close to me, my only feasibility.
I rely on you. Your coaching skills will get me through
When I'm done this sacred living, you will stay true
And begin my darkest journey, leaving life behind me
I have faith in you.
In the quagmire you will help me see
You will be my eyes, in the murkiness where I will be.
But as a friend please take this warning,
My days are crawling and my life is fawning
You are my only saviour in my all-time low
Only with you I am willing to go.
But stand back, stand back there is a distant glow!
In this broken crumpled discrepancy
Could there be a light to set me free?
I have an ounce of belief in this sad life so frail
A key to the kingdom, to keep me from your jail,
A tiny gust of wind that could set my sail.
Soon, I decree my eyes will close and I will die
And you Death will breathe in my final sigh
But for a few moments more please let me adore
A meagre glow for me. A distant door
I'm hurt, I'm wounded. All my seconds are a chore
But the disquiet of my mental din
That punctures my heart with the mess I'm in
Is shouting over my grief and agitation
With one crowning definition of elation.
Death, be patient, I really won't be long
I still don't trust my calling song.

Glow for me,
Glow for me, release me from the reaper's infamy
If you are sincere, come here and take my hand
Although I have nothing, not even a stand
I will open my heart and gratefully greet,
Knowing with you I can stand on my feet
Glow for me, glow for me,
Please glow for me and barricade this drowning tide
Before I accept death's woebegone and pitiless ride.

From the misery of the gutter, as low as the vermin plaguing the streets, there was a sprightly fissure, an emerging ray of light peeping through the hopelessness of Ash's life.

'If you want my professional opinion, and I've seen hundreds of traumatised patients suffer in the same way, Ash's mental well-being is deteriorating beyond reach. It is my understanding he will never recover from the tragedy he has been through. There is absolutely nothing that will compensate for the loss he witnessed, his life is overwhelmed by the trauma, exhausting him emotionally, diminishing his self-esteem and creating a permanent dent in his everyday ability to accept life without his losses. Simply put, it is manic-depressive illness, with elongated bouts of depression and slight lapses where his mood is marginally elevated, albeit still highly irritable. His mental state will not allow him to think happy thoughts because in doing so, he will feel disloyal to the people that have died. His symptoms are classic psychosis, his only reality is focused on the past with no outlook for the future. I'm afraid, Teresa, Ash has given up on hope.'

'But Dr Sommers, something tells me he will recover. Something tells me there is hope deep inside his heart. It's just a matter of time. I understand his illness but I cannot accept it is the end of the road for this patient. I know something glows for him, even though he may not know what it is yet. It's there and it's trying to fight through the sadness. I can't pinpoint it but there is something very different in Ash, something I've never seen in other patients suffering with this form of traumatic psychosis.'

'Teresa, Teresa, Teresa, my dear. You're simply too attached to this patient. Writing a poem does not mean he is recovering. Far from the truth, my dear. Many patients who are suicidal will demonstrate momentary emotions of elated behaviour but they soon slip back into their dark and daunting worlds of despair. Now, you understand he can't stay here forever, I'm afraid he will have to move on from Teers House and go to where he belongs, where they are qualified to look after him and tend to his needs. We've tried rehabilitation and it just hasn't worked. He needs to be where he is no longer a danger to himself and, most importantly, to others. I will authorise the transfer to begin at the end of this month. It really is the only solution.'

'No, Dr Sommers! You're going to lock him away in a mental institute! How will he ever recover there? They will leave him to rot. He needs help to recover and I know he will. A straight jacket and a padded cell is not the only solution. What you mean is it's the only solution *you* can see, whereas I can see hope. Please don't commit him to die. I just know if he leaves here, that will be the end of his life!'

'Teresa! Ash is already dead! He died months ago when his family died. He has nothing to live for. Our work with Ash is done. We have to do what is right and give our attention to those we can help, not those that are hopelessly lost with no future. We can't just take a leap of faith when we feel like it. You need to separate yourself from your emotions and accept defeat with this one. We tried all we could. Move on Teresa! Move on! It is your job to move on.'

'No! No! No! My job is to save lives! Not just to write people off! I did this job to give people hope and I promise I will make a difference; give me six more months and I will fulfil my job description of helping Ash survive. I know I can do it. I just know he will get through this and return to a normal life.'

'Right, Teresa, and undoubtedly I will regret my decision. You have three months and if I see no tangible signs of long-lasting recovery, Ash will leave Teers House Hospital. Now, get out of my office!'

Chapter 13
Ghosts

'Alright, love? You look like you've seen a ghost!' Startled by the abrupt announcement, Teresa wondered how dour her expression was to the outside world of strangers.

'Thank you, I'm fine. I've just had a difficult day at work today.'

Her smile was clearly reluctant and unconvincing, dismissing the observation from a passing porter as she walked out of Teers.

'Well whatever happened, don't let anyone upset you. You have a pretty face, love, it was made to shine and light up the world. No one ever went blind looking at the bright side. Go home and relax, and life will find a reason to make you smile.'

With a perplexed frown, Teresa's smile became more convincing. A rare compliment, unbeknown to the stranger, was more powerful than he could ever anticipate. A random ounce of oxygen in her empty tanks of air were adequate to make her float and breathe again.

'Thank you. I will do. That's a lovely thing to say and I really appreciate it. Goodbye.'

'My pleasure, gorgeous. No one has the power to make you feel bad. Only you hold that power. So get lost, you ghosts! This woman is not scared of you. Goodbye, love. You take care now!'

It was the adrenalin injection Teresa's body and mind craved. There was a blindingly dazzling side to the anxious melodrama that her life had become, she had three whole months to disprove the hindering, orthodox views of Dr Sommers. The poignant words from the porter cavorted through her mind in a frenzy of optimism,

'No one ever went blind looking at the bright side'
'No one ever went blind looking at the bright side'
'No one ever went blind looking at the bright side.'

Ten words that individually stood for insipid nothingness but combined in a precise order, shone a glistening ray of hope, unbound exhilaration and sureness. Teresa could see through the tedious mist and was convinced Ash would show signs of recovery from the desperate isolation he was wandering alone in. Her helping hand was determined to hold his until he was bewitched with life once again.

'You look pleased with yourself, Madame. Is it catching, because I'd like some, especially if it brightens my face like your beautiful smile?'

'I'm very pleased with myself, thank you. After all, no one ever went blind looking on the bright side.'

Teresa chuckled inside and out in wonderment at the transformation in comments from strangers, from projecting thoughtful melancholy to confident friskiness, from the helpful advice a porter gave to the enviable flirting from a handsome waiter. Content that stopping for dinner at a French bistro on her way home was adding to the sprightliness of her evening, Teresa beamed as her second glass of Bordeaux titillated her already heightened vivacity.

'And, Madame, no one would want to ever go blind if they had you to look at.'

'Thank you, kind sir. I bet you say that to all the ladies.'

Teresa caught a glimpse of the decorative murals emblazoning the walls behind the waiter, strange she hadn't noticed their velvety gaudiness depicting the splendour of the Moulin Rouge on her many visits to the bistro before. They appeared to transport her to the neon frenzy and idyllic romance of notorious Paris as the delicately spooning words, fake French accent of the waiter and the flowing red wine, further soothed her dallying mind.

'Of course, Madame, but can I please add? Only to the beautiful ones, which of course, you are one!'

The waiter's wink sealed the deal. Teresa had succumbed to his barefaced wooing and her alcohol flushed face went a further shade of pink. Luckily, he disappeared back into the kitchen because not only was Teresa lost for words and embarrassed at her acutely glowing visage but it gave her rarely complimented brain precious moments, to assemble some cute words and continue the flirtatious repartee upon his return.

'I see you're still a hit with all the men.'

The Battle of Paris. No hostile force had reached the city for four hundred years until March 30th 1814. The French Empire surrendered after one day of fighting with the Sixth Coalition, consisting of Russia, Austria and Prussia. Emperor Napoleon Bonaparte abdicated the throne and the map of Europe was subsequently redrawn. The trembling terror and unquestionable dread of the twenty three thousand individual deaths and casualties from the 'Battle of Paris' gushed through Teresa's bloodstream, in unison with her choking throat, as the last gulp of Bordeaux refused to fight with the voluminous gasp of air entering her lungs. Paris had fallen and Teresa was on her knees, her mind swirling in a futile attempt to make quick-fire decisions and a worthwhile response. War torn words stuttered from her bomb-shelled head.

'Oh my God! Simon. What are you doing here?'

'I always come to our bistro and I have always wished one day I would see you here and today my wish has come true. It's been a long time Teresa. It's good to see you. You look amazing.'

The words 'You look amazing' didn't correspond with the words Simon had blasted Teresa with in the past, the words with which he had obliterated her life with and left irreparable scars in her memory.

'You fat worthless bitch!'

'You are a pointless dirty whore!'

'You are a huge overweight mess!'

'You are a not a proper woman!'

'You are the ugliest woman I've ever known!'

'You could never make any man happy!'

'You are a disgusting fat hippo!'

These were more appropriate and recognisable as some of the many choice lines that echoed between Teresa's ears. A collection of painful taunts. The indelible ghosts from her past that still haunted her psyche and tormented her soul, which Simon had carelessly hammered to a bleeding pulp.

'I'm sorry, Simon. I just don't know what to say. You are the last person I expected to see. It's been a long time. I really don't know what to say.'

Paris was burning to an unrecognisable cinder. The French Empire dumbfounded at the swiftness of their tumble from greatness, as the sullen words of defeat whimpered from Teresa's trembling lips.

'To be precise, it's been eleven months, seventeen days and four hours since I last saw your beautiful face. I have counted every minute and regretted everything that happened. I'm so sorry, Teresa. It was never meant to be like that. I'm not the jealous man you threw out. I've changed. I'm a new man now.'

The flirting waiter reappeared and vanished with a disgruntled smirk on his face. In the distance the cavalry drums were synchronised with the erratic beat of Teresa's pumping heart. The very one that had been ripped from her ribcage, squeezed until it barely functioned and the final bestial act when Simon's size ten boots stomped upon it and squelched its fibrous tissue until it was useless to anyone that believed in true love and passionate romance. It was scared and spooked by the unshakable ghosts of lovers' knives and their shameless acts of demolition.

'I still don't know what to say. You hurt me, Simon. More than I've ever been hurt before. I still hurt today. You just don't understand what you did to me.'

'Teresa, I do understand. I know what I did. I know what it did to you. I'm sorry. I've changed, I'm not the Simon you once knew. I need another chance. I love you, Teresa. I love you so much. I have always loved you and I always will love you.'

Patrons at the 'Le Petite Rouge' bistro honed into the developing drama on table four, smugly reaffirming their own relationships, as the crumbled remains of lovers past, fought with their final breath. There was a harmonious tingle in the atmosphere as the silent support for a romantic reconciliation, a happy ending, meandered a path to the forlorn couple.

'You didn't love me, Simon. Lovers don't do what you did to me. You killed me inside. The only thing you loved was yourself and the hurt you gave me. You killed me, Simon. You killed me!'

The Moulin Rouge was silenced. The unstoppable show, stopped, amidst a rousing can-can, the Parisian spectacle had been usurped. The insurgents and fallen heroes of The Battle of Paris put aside their fighting woes and anguish, as the war on table four captured the hearts and souls of the innocent bystanders.

'I have always loved you. I love you so much, I couldn't stand the thought of losing you and instead of telling you my feelings, I let it consume me and burn into a jealous rage, which made me belittle and destroy you. I know I should have built you and coveted you, made you stronger, so you would have loved me for the man I was. I was weak and pathetic and felt control by damaging you. I now know how simple it could have been. I now know, all I needed to do was to hold you, love you and make you feel special, make you the centre of my world. All I needed to do was be there for you and be a part of you, instead of fighting you, I should have embraced everything about you. Please, Teresa, you have to understand, you have to listen. I have to have you back. You are my world and I cannot live without you.'

Collectively hearts came to a grinding standstill, captivated by table four. Bistro customers, waiters, paintings of the illustrious French capital, legions of fighting armies from The Battle of Paris all impatiently waited and imagined the outcome of the boisterous articulation between an estranged man and his scorned lover, as a multitude of questions highlighted the unfolding melodrama.

'What did he do to her?'

'Will she forgive him?'

'Does she still secretly love him?'

'How did he kill her inside?'

'Has he really changed?'

'What is she going to do?'

'Quiet in the courtroom! Everyone, please quiet in the courtroom. Let's hear the summary and conclusions from the prosecution and the defence in the case of Simon Driscoll, before the Teresa Grace jury deliver the verdict!'

For the prosecution: A battered heart and broken confidence.

'Hereby the conclusion for Teresa Grace, the jury, to pass a verdict in the case of Simon Driscoll. This man who appears to be unashamedly innocent and is on his knees riddled with regret, overflowing with remorse and humbled by his distasteful past is no more than a humongous mockery of all that is passionate, caring and loving in the human soul. His heinous crimes of the heart have made a life-long enemy of Mother Nature and her beautiful camaraderie of emotions, nurtured since the beginning of human time. She will not forgive him and allow his hideous kind entry to the heavenly garden of amorous bliss again. His feline spots, albeit presently scarce, will refuse to change; on the contrary, they will rapidly blot the landscape of devotion and drown all in his circle of heartfelt influence. This man should not be allowed to freely roam the delicate garden of human relationships. Banish him to a life of loneliness, where he can suffer the torment of lost passion and upon his dying day finally realise the value of true love, through its lifelong deprivation.'

For the defence: A future of devotion, learnt from the regret of colossal mistakes.

'Hereby the conclusion for Teresa Grace, the jury, to pass a verdict in the case of Simon Driscoll. Look at this feeble, pitiable excuse for a man. Yes, he committed heinous crimes against the heart, yes he broke the rules of compassion and yes, he showed little remorse when he pulverised the self-worth and backbone of someone that freely offered him the greatest creation of man. Love! He is worth nothing, he is the decomposed remnants of a once maleficent human being who miserably failed the game of compassion. Nevertheless, those depraved misdemeanours have taught more than they destroyed. He has returned from the clutches of Satan with the ultimate education and perquisite of a perfect love, simply that 'the greatest thing you can ever learn is to love and be loved in return.'

Let him back into the garden of love and he will fight to the death to keep it from weeds and it will remain forever, evergreen.'

Simon Driscoll, his gravelly square chin, devilish dimples and perky cheek bones constructed a face of creased anguish. Teresa stared into his chocolate brown eyes, the same melty eyes that less than a year ago filled her with trepidation and were acutely focused on terrorising her life.

'Simon, I don't have to understand. I don't have to listen. I don't have to have you back. I don't have to do anything. You tore out my heart! You knew exactly what you were doing, you were only ever happy when I was crying! You just hadn't realised that I would escape your clutches and start all over again. You left my life in tatters, stripped of all my confidence and bleeding from your knife twisting words. You took all of my emotions and left me void of any feelings and a heart that barely worked anymore. No! No! No! I don't have to do anything! I own my life now and it does not need validating by a man! Especially by a man like you!'

'I'm sorry, I'm so sorry. I understand. I've only got myself to blame. You deserve so much better than scum like me.'

Teresa's rock solid resolve caught her by surprise, her confidence and self-esteem cheered and applauded her boldness, considering how much Simon intimidated towards the end of their torrid relationship and how brittle and nervous that had made her. Nevertheless, their jubilations were cut short, as they felt the familiar vibration of Teresa's emotions welling to fracturing point. Simon had tears in his eyes. Teresa hadn't seen any soft emotions in all the time they were romantically embroiled.

Her inner confidence hollered at the height of its voice.

'Oh no! Don't do it! Don't break! Stay strong! You can do this, Teresa! The man is a fraud! He will only hurt you and break you again! Please don't give into his lies. Please, Teresa, please don't do it. Run while you can!'

'Cry as much as you want, Simon. It's about time you cried. It's your turn to be fragile and destitute, to feel stupid and unwanted.'

'Bravo! Bravo! You've done it, girl! You've sorted the evil bastard out! Now get out, before you change your mind!'

'I'm done here. Goodbye, Simon!'

Teresa, listened to her inner confidence, threw her napkin onto table four and charged out of 'Le Petite Rouge' with the victorious omnipotence of the Sixth Coalition at the surrender of the French Empire.

It was 1814 again and the celebrations began. The Moulin Rouge reopened for business and Teresa's emotions danced the Can-Can in merriment. The map of Teresa Grace had been redrawn.

Chapter 14
The Torch

'What was I thinking? Why do all my roads meander to the same destination? I didn't need a map, it was easy enough to close my eyes and time after time, after time I would find my way to the same smile. The same smile that emblazoned the same face. She was my eternal torch, my forever flame.'

In all my darkness and plight
Through the mist and cold of night,
This torch I clutch is my guiding light,
It illuminates my soul, when days take their toll.
Goodness you were such a knave and yet,
It's you I crave
Life is meant to be free and yet I am your slave.
I forbid you to enter my dreams
But you don't let me sleep
So quietly into my thoughts you daily creep
Must I admit, I'm still into you so deep?
You always seem to plunder my direction
Okay, okay, it's for you I have my affection.
I surrender to your glorious memory
You're the only one that can set me free
So, I will hold this torch high
Come back to me now lover, show me how to fly.

A tumultuous evening could only be calmed by a few pages of 'Make My World Complete,' Teresa's eternally romantic bible. Once again she entered the world of romantic passion as Sitara Kai Khusa's masterpiece stole her senses to the world of deep, long-lasting passionate love. It was the only thing that could calm her trembling body and mind that had just witnessed a bizarre ghost from her tortured past.

But tonight there was a distinct flaw in her thoughts. Was it the Bordeaux still sparkling her blood? Was it the trauma of meeting

Simon after eleven months, seventeen days and four hours? Or was it the adrenalin boost from the outstanding courage her confidence had injected into her body that firmly pushed Simon, the monster that annihilated her life, back into the darkness from where he had surprisingly transpired? Teresa read Sitara's chapter 'The Torch' again, and again the same ridiculous thoughts troubled her mind. She clasped the book hard in her hands until the blood in her veins showed as redness attempting to burst from her sensitised skin.

'No, no, no, no, no, no, no!' Stop, Teresa! Stop it now! Stop! Stop! Just stop, you crazy fool. Stop! Please, please STOP! This is madness! You must stop!'

Teresa's conscience screamed in strained agony, her discerning voice of judgement, spewed reason after valid reason questioning her rationality. It was suited up for battle, as the onslaught of enemy thoughts, equipped with bitter firearms and fearsome resolve to the hilt, made their headstrong advance through Teresa's befuddled mind.

'Nearly a year! Nearly a year! Nearly a year! Nearly a year!'
'Alone! Alone! Alone! Alone! You were always be alone!'

Teresa's conscience was no more the stalwart figure, so brave and productive in pointing her away from the misadventure of her thoughts, its futility bolstered the oncoming forces as their chanting deafened Teresa's acumen and obliterated her sanity.

'Nearly a year! Nearly a year! Nearly a year! Nearly a year!'
'Alone! Alone! Alone! Alone! You were always be alone!'
'You haven't had sex in nearly a year! Nearly a year! Nearly a year!'
'Retreat! Retreat! Retreat! Retreat!'

Teresa's conscience was wise enough to know it was poorly rigged in the face of the enemy avalanche, intent on genocide of any common sense and history, so it backed down and cowered behind the miniscule remnants of sensible thoughts and helplessly watched the carnage begin. The alcohol trickling through her blood vessels glowed, as it joined the ecstatic rush around her body caused by the increased heartbeat as Teresa's brain transmitted lurid reminders of the passionate and explicit sexuality shared between her and Simon. There was no thin line between the two barefaced sensations, maybe for other people it resembled a fragile tightrope from which they could easily stumble onto either side, one labelled pleasure the other labelled pain. For Teresa the distinct pain was overshadowed, locked into a minute space at the rear of her brain, as ninety five percent of her cerebrum bowed down to the authoritarian command of pleasure. The pleasure over pain syndrome forged the trademark of the torrid eroticism between the dysfunctional couple. Simon possessed an astonishing, magical touch with Teresa's body. Her lovers before him were clinical and contrived, the same engineered routine, the same executed process, every single time. Teresa could almost set a stop-watch timer on their interchangeable procedures and often endured the rigidity of their methodical, unremarkable performances by narrating the four standard scenes of intercourse into a witty melodrama within her mind whilst they lethargically performed upon her body.

Scene one. The Foreplay – Duration: Four Minutes
Lover fumbles into bed. Strokes Teresa's curves with a swift sweeping hand still freezing cold from the bathroom, making her bed-warm body shudder from head to toe, causing reluctant goose-pimples over her skin and a cheeky hardening of her nipples. Lover mistakes the pointedness of her cold alerted breasts for sexual arousal and twists the pert pinnacles with a radio-dial tuning motion, whilst simultaneously pursing her lips apart with a moist, mischievous tongue carrying the fresh mint taste of the toothpaste used during his pre-bedroom ablutions.

Two brazen fingers head south and perform a piston motion into her body, bluntly oblivious to the lack of moisture within her womanly entrance.

Scene Two. The Entrance – Duration: One Minute
Slightly moistened fingers are;
     a. Placed in his mouth or
     b. Pushed into her mouth or
     c. First procedure 'a' followed quickly by procedure 'b'
If route 'a' or 'c' is performed, then it's followed by 'You taste very sexy.'

Scene Three. The Darting Tongue – Duration: Five Minutes

There is a tidal wave of moved air as the cumbersome quilt is flung away for the grand entrance of the darting tongue, in a symbiotic escapade of 'I'm doing you a favour and I hope you do the same to me once I'm done.'

The slurping noises are exaggerated as the lover's broad tongue rasps snake-like in and out of the saliva-soaked vestibule, barely hitting the glorious clitoral, button of joy, one percent of the time throughout the fevered activity. The only method of stopping the masticating attack is to sigh loudly and imitate sensitivity with a squirming together of the thighs. Teresa is relieved, her timely intervention works on cue, as the lover finally removes his inexperienced tongue from between her stubble-grazed thighs, blatantly wipes his mouth with the back of his wrist and plumps down facing the ceiling upon his pillow, with the slumping demeanour of a dog-tired coal miner returning from the dark and lonely depths of a coal mine, sweating with the satisfaction of a hard shift of grafting, knowing it was worth the pending payment for his gruelling exertion. The lover's silent voice whispers without uttering a word, into the sexually aromatic, dampened air, 'I will lie here with my aching jaw, until you engage your mouth upon my wanton implement that I'm delicately fondling, in the hope, I will present your tongue with the hardest treat I can muster.'

Scene Four. Seven Minutes to Blast-off! – Duration: Seven Minutes

'I can't take anymore. I can't take anymore. It feels too good. I can't hold back.'

Within two minutes, the lover's hopes are dashed as Teresa's reply 'Ok, I'll stop', suggests it's not appropriate to gush into her skilful mouth, once again shattering every male lover's boyish fantasy, of hearing the woman's throaty gulp, as the masculine deliciousness is discharged with volcanic ferocity from his body.

The lover pins Teresa to the mattress and hulks his disappointed semi-hardness into her body. Chug, Chug, Chug the freight train is on the track and relentlessly follows the programmed route, with exuberant hoots of 'Is that good?', 'Are you enjoying it?' and 'I'm nearly there!'

Five exceptionally lengthy minutes later and with a symbolic 'I'm coming', 'Come with me', or 'C'mon, darling, I'm coming', the pent up steam is released into the disinterested receptacle and the comically short, journey to the rattle of contented snoring begins.

In contrast, Simon wasn't a cumbersome freight locomotive, cluttering and plodding to its scheduled destination and returning on time, partaking in the basic role it was intended for. Simon was a high-speed, stealth train, there were no tracks, no direction and nothing conventional. He was a fanatical rollercoaster, with a crazed, psychotic driver, trundling into every possible direction, except the one Teresa expected. She was whiplashed with desire, he had rekindled an ancient fire deep within her physical being which erupted with ferocious geyser-like anger, converting her feminine moisture to pure heat agonising to escape from her sexually awakened body, drowning the dull memory of her listless lovers in her steamy wake. It was an exercise in futility, ignoring the craving explosions in Teresa's body. The landmine memories of the deranged, unpredictability and vitality of their carnal sojourn were littered in every thought she was thinking. The brief unexpected liaison at Le Petite Rouge clouded Teresa's reminiscence and dulled her conscience into silence, as her towering sexual urges veiled the evil dominance of Simon Driscoll and the sheer malicious, destruction he had showered upon her life. She could no longer quell her hankering reflections. Teresa had no option but to close her eyes and concede to her irresistible compulsion and relive her debauched relationship with Simon Driscoll.

Her oesophagus involuntarily opened to the warmth gushing into her throat. The swallowing motion forced it into her stomach as her gagging reflex ignored the bitter sweet taste filling her mouth and thickly coating her tongue, which barely had time to decipher the taste and decide whether this liquid was appetising or foul. The quantity was endless, spurt after spurt, swishing between her gums and teeth, their tongues embroiled in the bloody dance, further stretching the intended wound where Simon's front teeth had pierced Teresa's lower lip, causing it to profusely bleed into her cavorting mouth. Their lips were pasted together with the heated redness, splurging from their wet orifices onto their faces. They licked and kissed in a rabid frenzy in the mayhem of lust, almost child-like, avoiding the melt of a strawberry lolly on a hot summer afternoon, regardless of the ensuing mess, dripping and drooling in harmony, lost in the rich crimson taste. The division between pleasure and pain was severely breached, a punctured lip, oozing blood ordinarily would require medical attention to curtail the bleeding and alleviate the throbbing discomfort but whilst Simon and Teresa were interlocked in a consuming kiss combined with the raw grind of manly movement between Teresa's legs, the sharp sting from her lip was a bleeding orgasm, zealous as the blistering shaft of Simon's charged membrane, stimulating the awkward angle of her cloaked, vaginal hot-spot.

'Do you want me to fill you with my boiling cream?'

'Yes! Yes! Yes! Simon, do it! Please do it! Please!'

Simon stopped moving his body and in that stillness, expanded and contracted his blood engorged manhood. Teresa screamed in unison as the flexing vibrated and shook her drenched walls.

'No! Not yet! You can wait. I will make it worth the wait. I will give it to you when I'm good and ready and I know you're not ready!'

Teresa's body convulsed with the ripples of pain and pleasure as Simon teased her wounded lip, sucking the blood into his mouth. Each suck numbed Teresa's face but hardened Simon's firmness, almost bolstering its supply of fiery veins with the blood he was stealing from her. Red blood cell platelets were rushing to the scene to heal the gash and slow the bleeding, their attempts were pointless, as were the attempts of the white blood cell soldiers fighting on the frontline, rapidly building barricades against the gathering germs to avoid infection. Teresa's mind colourations mashed into a blurry blob of colour, she was in a hallucinogenic state, her nerve receptors were buzzing in a trance of unrelenting climaxes. Her brain was a swirling kaleidoscope of erupting fireworks, magnetising to a central location of confused but roaring ecstasy.

'Teresa, darling, this is your brain calling. If you are intending to die soon, you should do it right now. There will never, ever be a better time to die, you will never feel this elated ever again. Dearest Teresa, this is the ultimate pleasure, when you can no longer diagnose yourself, you can no longer make sense of anything. All of your bodily cells are cheering you and each cheer is a pin-prick of luxurious joy. Choose wisely dear, this is your perfect moment! The perfect moment to wave goodbye!'

'No, no, no, no, I don't want to die. I don't want to die. I want you, Simon. Don't let me die. Please don't let me die, Simon. I don't want to die!'

'You're not going to die love. Far from it. You have a little bite on your lip. You won't die. I won't let you die. Do you want me to stop the bleeding now? Do you want me to soothe your lip with some very soothing cream? Do you, Teresa? Is that what you want? Do you want me to soothe away the pain? I can do that, I can do that for you.'

'Yes, Simon! Soothe away my pain! Put some cream onto my lip. I want you to rub cream into my lip. Yes please, Simon. Please do it. Please, do it now. Please, Simon! Please, Simon!'

'Of course, my darling! Anything for you, my sweetheart!'

Simon gripped his palpitating, slippery excitement firmly and squirted all the cream he could squeeze from it over Teresa's massacred face.

'You need this in your mouth too, love. A little of this cream inside you will also help soothe away the pain.'

'Yes, please help me. I need it to be in my mouth too. Please put it into my mouth. Please, Simon. I need it in my mouth!'

His tube of cream finally emptied and Teresa's face was unrecognisable, she was an extra in a cheap zombie production, a macabre abstract of gooey redness, bleached with the sticky whiteness of the cream Simon had kindly administered. They wrapped their arms around each other as Teresa slipped in and out of heavenly delirium, her body had been blissfully desecrated, torn apart, shredded into strips of joy and agony, overlapping each other, creating a single insane, tingling sensation, bleeding in part and gorged with euphoric blood in others. The distant memory of Simon Driscoll and their animalistic sex had been reanimated. Teresa fell asleep and had simultaneously been reawakened, with her rapturous, all-consuming thoughts.

Chapter 15
Why?

Teresa arrived at work early, her customary routine, to visit Ash ten minutes before her shift started. He had no visitors and within Teresa's mindful, caring landscape, entering the ward off-duty was fulfilling the role of a visitor, whilst sparking the day with a friendly diagnosis of Ash's state of mind. Ash was asleep, with his ragged copy of 'Make my World Complete', his trustworthy bedside companion, as was often the case. Normally, Teresa woke him with a friendly stroke of his hand but today she refrained and consciously registered her unwillingness for their uplifting, sunrise banter. Her reluctance troubled her, asking herself what the problem was, worryingly, there was no answer forthcoming, simply a passing wave of indifference in a mind otherwise cluttered with Simon Driscoll. Teresa awkwardly left Ash's bedside with a sense of relief that he didn't wake, shuffling away with his waste paper bin, as per her daily routine. The amount of rubbish in the bin usually indicated the level of Ash's insomnia, the night before. Last night he was clearly restless, the bin was overflowing with scrunched up sheets of white paper, Ash's frustrations in writing, emblematically discarded to ward his burgeoning thoughts. Accompanying each footstep, Teresa battled with her addled reasoning.

'Why? Why? Why didn't you wake Ash? Why can't you shift Driscoll from your mind? What is your problem? Why is nothing making any clear sense this morning?'

Teresa's eyes separated themselves from her confused thoughts, their focus retuned her brain into a lightening flash, second of fated bizarreness.

'WHY?'

The word jumped up and demanded attention, slapping Teresa's cheeks awake. The letters were scribbled in black pen on the scrunched paper at the top of the bin Teresa was carrying. It was a scrawling from Ash. Teresa stopped in the middle of the ward, placed the bin on the floor and removed the partly crumpled paper.

Why are you so blind? Why can't you see?
Why am I drowning in my own misery?
Why do you ignore me? Why don't you set me free?
My heart is cornered in this kingdom lost
And I dare not envisage the ultimate cost.
Why are all my dreams just nightmares?
Why are you the only one that cares?
My life is wrapped around you wondering why
My prison is uncertainty, locked and making me cry.
Look into my eyes and be curious
All you will see is fiery and furious.
Enraptured mind, puzzled with sighs
My existence is frazzled insanity, shrouded with
Whys.

The words of 'Why' filtered through Teresa's reflections and shone upon her face. How could they mean so much? How could Ash have scribed such sentences that captured her timely imagination, piercing through her bewilderment? Her barrage of questions weren't answered but Ash's screwed up words perfectly summed up her erratic mind.

'Teresa, quit your daydreaming and come into my bloody office!'

Teresa snapped out of her whispering daydreams with the bellow of Dr Sommers' rude voice, echoing down the corridor.

'Yes, Dr Sommers. I'm on my way!' She pushed Ash's poem into her pocket and hurriedly trundled into the doctor's office, still carrying the bin.

'Please, tell me. Why on earth are you carrying a bin and why were you stood in the middle of the corridor, rifling through its contents?'

'I was just emptying Ash's bin and found this poem at the top of it and decided to read it. Here, have a look. He's quite a talent. He must have his dad's talent for writing.'

'Why indeed! The only why I have is why on earth I allowed you three months to rehabilitate him, when I know it's a waste of time. These words are the ramblings of a potential, neurosis case. I don't

66

understand why you're the only one that can't see that. Nevertheless, I caved into your lack of experience and I will allow you that time. Undoubtedly, I'm the one that needs committing for giving into you!'

'Dr Sommers. I disagree and I will prove it. He is not insane. He just needs care and attention and he will recover. His writing will be part of that recovery. It really is brilliant and emotional. I know you don't understand, I know you need results. So, I'm grateful again for the chance you've given Ash and of course for the trust you have put into me too.'

'Yes, yes, yes. I'm sure, Teresa. You two will be the death of me but although I don't hold much hope, I'm sure you will give him your best shot. Your three months started yesterday and I will not renege on that. Now, Teresa, may I ask you a question?'

'Of course, Dr Sommers. What is it?'

'What the bloody hell have you done to your lip? Looks like you've had a punch in the face. It looks a mess!?'

'Um, um, I'm clumsy. I, um, walked into a door'

'Yes, I'm sure you did. I can actually believe that. Well, go and clean yourself up, it's still bleeding!'

Dr Sommers had pulled the cord on a chainsaw, its whirring clatter seared through Teresa's brain, shaking and effortlessly dismembering millions of individual brain cells into activation, she could hear all of their voices hollering the same word over and over again.

'Why!? Why!? Why!? Why!? Why!? Why!? Why!? Why!? Why!?'

The distinctive sound of a stone bouncing off the window and the perpetrator of her illicit, lustful memories was staring up from the pavement below. Teresa's dismissive departure from 'Le Petite Rouge' with her uncharacteristic bravado was barely enough to ward the evil of Simon Driscoll from her door. His one final attempt to woo Teresa back into his life worked more amazing than a perfect dream. The reality far outweighed all the desired scenarios that rushed through his mind as he ambled towards the flat they had shared for so many months. Teresa's inhibitions and righteous conscience had been crushed into oblivion, with her craving for passion and the yearning she had for Simon Driscoll to manipulate and dominate her body again.

The ten millimetre stone that Simon had thrown transcended through the pane of glass and melted into her skull, forcing any iota of common sense from her mind as she pressed the electronic button that not only opened the entrance door to let Simon into her home but metaphorically blew open the gateway to the vile underworld she had escaped from.

She heard his footsteps climbing the stairs, each plod bringing hell closer to earth. There were no words. The fire between them roared out of control as their tongues, bodies and fluids entwined into a twisted helix of depravity and a shameless outpouring of pent up gluttony for carnal sex. Teresa had sent an open invitation to her nightmares and welcomed them with wanton open arms. Her throbbing lip remained a reminder for the rest of her shift as she walked around in a bemused daze, gradually piecing together the perversion of the night before.

'Why did she let it happen?'

'Why did she let Simon Driscoll back into her peace?'

'Why had she so stupidly jeopardised her own life?'

'Why did she smile inside, every time she saw her damaged lip in the mirror?'

Chapter 16
Intoxicated

Meander and rush through my flowing bloodstream
Devouring my senses into a heated dream.
I am intoxicated with wanton lust and desire
My veins are glowing rich with burning fire.
What is this poison that I have devoured?
It clings to my pumping heart, ripping my arteries apart
There is no release from the power it possesses
Creasing my body with its heavenly caresses.
I'm waving my white flag, I can resist no more,
My resolve is crushed, mangled and dying on the floor.
I have become blindly drunk on this deadly hemlock
Lead me astray, floating away, far from my dock.
This is my new world, tingling with expectation
Fulfilling the needs of God's loving creation.

Intoxication rippled through Teresa's befuddled mind as she hurried home after her shift. It was another poem from 'Make my World Complete', exploring the drunken effect of lustful love cavorting through mind, body and soul. Teresa's usually methodical thought processes, one plus two equals three, were clumsily undexterous and her simple sum was simply not adding up. Simon had destroyed her life. She battled against all common sense and let him into her home and her body again and now to completely unbalance her systematic thinking, there was a craving thirst brewing within her, an ill-starred yearning bubbling through her veins that had barely filtered the alien contamination from the night before.

'Simon, Simon, are you still here!? Are you still here!? Simon!'

There was an offbeat desperation in her voice as she unlocked her front door and scurried up the stairs that were once overjoyed at the prospects of never feeling the footsteps of Simon Driscoll ever again.

'Of course I'm here. You didn't think I was going to leave after last night did you?'

'The enemy is arriving prepare to fight. Weapons ready! Prepare to fight!' Confirmation of Simon's presence created a tidal wave of emotive barricades. Teresa's rationalising was in an eruptive state as the volcanic scenario sparked a steaming battle within her. The traditional fight between heart and mind was not in presence, this noteworthy war had both elements of her psyche split into conspicuous and opposing corners.

Dear Teresa,

This is your heart sending out a plea. Simon is a cancer. He will disease your blood, eat your body one cell at a time, leave you decayed, broken and an unrecognisable woman. The remains of Teresa Grace will have to be incinerated because what will be left will infect others with the same misery and sadness; for once I do believe I have an ally within you. Speak up mind! Speak your mind!

Dear Teresa,

This is your mind calling. Yes, I am in agreement with the heart in a monumental treaty, unheard of in human terms. For the first time in humankind history this mind accepts the reasoning of the heart, except I can visualise the horror of what lies ahead. Whereas the heart is tampering with the truth, attempting to create an ounce of goodness, for that's what hearts are created for, all I can see is vile annihilation, carnage and ultimately your death. Teresa Grace, I can feel the heat as your body will move through the crematorium of your wretched life, converting your battered bones into forgettable grey dust!

'Hurry up, darling. I've been waiting for my gorgeous woman all day. What's taken you so long? This patient needs his beautiful nurse. I'm waiting in bed for you. I have a painful growth only you can deal with. Hurry up! Hurry up! I'm about to explode!'

Simon's voice menacingly echoed from the bedroom. Teresa's confused head, awash with equal amounts of contempt and admiration, dizzy with the aroma of man, inebriated with preconception, sycophantically magnetised towards the bedroom door.

Dear Teresa,

This is your collaborated heart and mind calling. We remain in historical agreement that you are on the cusp of extermination. I, the heart will be ripped from my beautifully protective ribcage and Simon will jump upon me, from a height splattering my delicate tissue, bleeding me until my beat is obliterated, beyond the ability to sustain your existence. I, the mind will not fare much better, with the sharpest razor blades, Simon will score and slice through my membranes until I am in ribbons of massacred thoughts and memories, a fragmented jigsaw with integral pieces missing. I will never be whole again, I will be a forgotten picture of what once was reality. You will be blacked-out, another historical example of epic misogynist murder. We fear a lamentable fate frowns upon you. We are drowning in your intoxication, your blood is cheapened and defiled. We are helpless. Our conflict is futile against the gushing force of your sexual desire. Teresa Grace, we gracefully concede, no longer the stalwart defence, no more the spasmodic reasoning, erring on the side of precaution. Your heart and mind throw their arms upwards and bow down to the superiority of your cumbersome lust. Come and swathe us in your creaming lechery, break down our walls and rip out the memories we have embraced and held so dear, fill us to the brim with euphoric dreams of what life will be.

Our fight is over. We will commingle with your wishes. We will march as one. We will open our protective doors and willingly let Simon Driscoll pounce into heart and mind with pleasure and promise. Come on, you bastard! Come on, Driscoll, you evil bastard! We're all yours! We are ready and waiting for your rampant disease, your feared religion of inhumane assassination, your aversion to the power of love and the love of this woman. Goodbye, world! Goodbye, prudence! Goodbye, saneness!

'Simon, you're here. You're in bed. I don't know what to say. I don't know what to do. I'm, I'm... I'm just all mixed up. I'm all over the place. I was hoping you would still be here.'

'Don't be confused, baby. I have everything you could possibly need. I couldn't leave. I couldn't go away. I've realised how much I've missed you and after last night I never, ever want us to be apart ever again. Come here. Come to me. I've been waiting for this moment all day.'

'I'll just get changed, Simon. I've been in these clothes all day. Let me just get changed, have a shower and I will come and join you, then we can talk about things, sort things out properly.'

'No! Don't get changed, Teresa. Just come here. Come to me. I need you. I need you right now. I don't want you to shower. I don't want you to change. I just want you to come here and be close to me.'

There were no footsteps from the open door to the bed. Servile and limp, Teresa's uniformed body, hypnotised by Simon's assertiveness, floated to his side.

'Your lip looks sore, sweetheart. I wonder how that happened. Were you a naughty girl last night? I hope you didn't waste all that ointment I lovingly supplied to heal you?'

'Yes, it's been hurting all day. I'll just go and see to it and I will be back in a moment.'

'Don't worry about that, my love. I have something you need. I have something delicious for you that will help you forget about your silly little lip.'

The swish of air as Simon flung back the duvet, coupled with the simultaneous clasp of his hand on the back of Teresa's head made her heart and mind cower with apprehension and delight, as they pumped blood through the reopened wound on her lip, abruptly caused by the fierce piston motion of Simon's excitement engaging with Teresa's anxious mouth.

Chapter 17
Alarm Bells

The 7am electronic din rattled Teresa's slumbering brain. Surely, it wasn't morning already, surely that wasn't the conclusion of another night. All questions in Teresa's lethargic head were answered with the flashing display on her trustworthy bedside companion, her persistent alarm clock.

A scorching pain in Teresa's face woke her soporific mind, blood had crisply dried around her mouth, which felt inflated to the size of a bouncing beach ball, ready to burst. Unfolding herself from the tousled quilt she dizzily stumbled to the bathroom, her reflection shouted at her in frustrated disgust.

'What have I done?! This is not my face! Is this a dream? Am I even alive!?'

Tears came to rejoice at the waking calamity. Teresa's face was the mangled horror of an inexperienced boxer that had lasted the full twelve rounds with the heavy-weight champion of the world, in the presence of a blind referee who simply hadn't noticed the unbearable battering being relentlessly administered. Her carefully applied eye make-up from twenty four hours earlier had artistically metamorphosed to stage make-up, converting the fresh faced and lively Teresa from yesterday, to the war-torn, mess of a corpse this morning. Behind her cracked reflection she saw Simon moving under the duvet, as she recalled his voice from the night before,

'I'm not finished yet. Let's go one more time. I've missed your body.'

'Don't go just yet. Stay a bit longer then you can get changed.'

Teresa remembered seeing the time on her clock as Simon's droning snores and heavy arm pinned her down onto the bed.

'I'll wait a little longer then sneak out of bed to wash, eat and get a drink.'

Then it was suddenly the boisterous alarm and she woke still partly clothed, smothered in blood, make-up and Simon's musty rampant smell. Exhaustion had overpowered her, the pain from her wound and the rumble in her empty stomach. Teresa's limbs were aching, she wasn't particularly flexible anymore. Her stretched joints were out of practice and didn't take kindly to the heaving weight of Simon and the contorting to satisfy their mutual lust. 7.30am and Teresa was showered of the sexual mustiness and a cosmetic miracle, camouflaging the drained expression on her ashen face, her beige façade barely covered the moist scabbed and bruised lesion on her lip. Teresa's routine had been restored. 7.40am and she was drinking coffee, crunching through a bowl of cereal and reading her bible on love, romance, sexuality and relationships, 'Make my World Complete'.

Her usual concentration of the magical words was unintentionally adulterated with abrupt palpitating reminders of the night before, nonetheless the distinct power of her daily read immobilised her thinking and honed her into the fantasy of Khusa's masterpiece and once again aimed an arrow through her discombobulated heart.

'Alarm Bells
The ringing of the bells matched the beating of my heart
Vibrating through my tissue and shaking me apart.
You sounded when my brain was asleep, you cheered
When my emotions overflowed and dived in deep.
Your rattling keeps me awake
And in silence makes me leap.
You are a friend and you push me against the wall
And you defend my vulnerability from the fall.
Ring, alarm bells ring, and illuminate my beginning
Ring again when my determination isn't winning.
You forever keep me on the road to fruition
And make me stumble before my demolition.

'I knew deep inside my heart there was trouble ahead. The question I had to ponder and answer was, was the almost guaranteed anguish worth it, or do I pay heed to the eternal racket in my head and respond by running away? Dearest alarm bells, if only you could speak instead of shouting.'

'What's that you're reading?'

74

Simon was stood in the doorway, wrapped in the creased white quilt, decorated with splodges of blood from Teresa's mouth.

'It's called Make my World Complete. It's brilliant. All about love, passion and romance.'

'Ha, ha, ha, must remind you of us then, all that romance we shared last night. Nothing can compare to the love we shared.'

'Kind of, but it's more about deep psychological aspects of love, exploration of the emotions and ultimately finding someone that will actually make your entire world complete.'

'In that case, it really does sound like us. I mean, look at all our emotions. Look how we have changed since last time and surely we wouldn't have got back together if this time it wasn't going to be forever. Do you agree, Teresa? Do I make your world complete?'

'Well, kind of, Simon. We've only been back for two days yet. It's hard to say what will happen between us yet.'

'Come on, Teresa. You make my world complete. Otherwise I would have never returned to you. I always knew you were the one. I was just too immature to realise it last time but this time I'm not going to make the same mistake again. This time I know it's for real. This time I'm not leaving you. This time it's the real thing. Now put that silly book down and come here and give me a hug and let me make your world complete before you go to work.'

Unusually Teresa placed the book into her shoulder bag instead of leaving it upon the glass coffee table, where it had rested since it arrived and hypnotically strode over to Simon. The quilt dropped to the floor like a theatre safety curtain and Simon squeezed Teresa's body into his firm warmth.

'I will make your world complete. Look at how you affect mine in your sexy uniform.'

'I haven't got time, Simon. I'm already late for work, save it for tonight.'

Teresa's words were simultaneous to Simon's rapid action, his forceful hands had already fumbled underneath her hospital skirt and yanked at her underwear.

'Time! There is always time for love, Teresa, and you'll think of me all day with this warming inside you.'

Teresa's clothes were dishevelled, her face contorted with a mixture of pleasure and discontent as the alarm bells rang out

75

deafeningly between her ears. The cereal and coffee sloshed around violently within her stomach and struggled to remain contained as Simon bent her forward over the velvety sofa, attempting to make her world complete with the force of his dominant body vigorously sliding into hers. With every weighty thrust Simon roared his gratification.

'See, I can make your world complete! See, I can make your world complete! See, I can make your world complete!'

Chapter 18
Rose Petals

Fragranced, fragile and free, delicately floating.
My heart is a rose petal, compact with promise,
quietly gloating.
There were unwanted emotions
And heavy baggage weight,
The misery of past romantic battles
And historic freight.
Scrapped, demolished, extinguished into oblivion,
The fools that deliberately shackled me
Have now set me free.
My heart is a rose petal but handle carefully
In time it will gush the blood of romantic affirmation
Fiery enchantment and resolute elation.
My heart is once again open to a loving creation.

Every scintillating word from 'Rose Petals' gleefully punctured hurt from Teresa's pin-cushion heart, it was uncontrollably fluttering, remarkably without the burdensome memories that had laden it with acute hopelessness. Sitara Kai Khusa's poem shone a beam of hope into the darkness that once existed within her battered emotions. One week had frisked past. A mere seven days ago, Teresa could never have imagined Simon Driscoll back in her life, living in her home, with the drained quiver in her knees caused by the heart-fainting romance that he had forced back into her spurned reality. The barrage of questions that remained unanswered had been muffled, 'How can the man that destroyed you be adorning your bed again.'

'Has he really changed?'

'Why aren't you controlling your feelings? This man is a snake, he always will be, don't you think he will do it all again!'

'Why aren't you protecting your fragile heart?'

'Make my World Complete' had struck countless disconnected chords in Teresa's life, from the heartsick yearning for true romance and the rock-like acceptance that Simon Driscoll was a destined nightmare that had demonstrated the necessary baneful angle of love, to the comical acknowledgement of the very same man fulfilling her fleshy desires and hunger for poetic, starry-eyed true romance. Khusa's journey shouted out Teresa's life. His words mingled through every strand of her love-besotted soul from the utter assassination of heartfelt sentiment to the architecture and elevation of the greatest freedom known to man, love. With a lengthy sigh that reminisced the night before, Teresa replaced her personal bible of romance into her locker and floated into another shift at work, begging the hours to fly by so she could be back home with the renewed and amazing man that a week ago she despised with a doleful frenzy. Eight hours dragged, as every hospital chore became a dawdling bind. Teresa remained glued to her watch, on occasions comparing its time to the ward clocks, just in case it was functioning below par and dropping minutes of time.

Finally, the greatest tick of all-time pushed itself to the finish line and Teresa was treading the pavement departing from Teers, even before a full sixty seconds was complete, brushing past all her regular pleasantries with colleagues, who had to satisfy themselves with the feisty gust of air as she whisked past them with the wanton urgency of a fire alarm drill.

Cupid bombarded her with his doting arrows as she climbed the steps to her flat. The tips were lovingly sharp but sugar coated, blessing her blood with sweetness at each step she took. The stairs were covered with crimson rose petals, adorning the air with their delicate aroma, commingling with her senses, creating an aphrodisiac which pumped her heart and mystified her mind. Cupid had clearly whispered to Simon about the poem Teresa had read before work, the words of which had bubbled and boiled under her skin throughout the whole day and there they were, an abundance of soft, aromatic rose petals under every footstep she took. She unlocked the door as Cupid shot another cannonade of his amorous arrows into Teresa's sensitised and tingling body. The light struck her eyes, besieging her pupils with its raw intensity seconds before the waxy scent wafted into her nose. There were no less than thirty candles of assorted sizes billowing a combined heat and illuminating glow, flickeringly stunning in the otherwise dim room. Teresa could feel the glimmer on her face, flourishing her natural blushed radiance as she honed in on the coffee table, where lay a carefully arranged bunch of roses, scattered in a beautifully erratic formation, with a hand written card as the centre piece of the thorny red and green masterpiece.

My Dearest Teresa,

I'm not always the best at saying things, so I thought I would write down my feelings, in the hope you will understand and cherish my words.

The last seven days have been a massive revelation to me. I have realised many things and finally come to my senses and it's only fitting that I share with you my thoughts, as every single thought is about you and you only.

I have changed, Teresa. You have changed me. When we first met the change started but I didn't know how to handle it and instead of accepting my overpowering feelings, I fought them and ultimately my fight caused me to be possessive and jealous. Those emotions were only fit for one purpose. Destruction. I know I destroyed you but in doing so, if there's any solace for you, I destroyed myself too, into a bitter and meaningless nobody, nothing less than I deserved for what I did to you. For the eleven months we were apart I changed again. Each day I sank deeper into the depths of self-mutilating depression as I beat myself up daily, about the damage I had caused you and how my pathetic insecurities ruined the only worthwhile thing I had. Us.

I changed again to realise and accept what a weak, inadequate imbecile I had been and understood I was compensating for my deficiencies by being so mean to you. I hate myself for it but my strength was coming from being nasty and derogatory to you. I can't change that now but I have learnt from it.

After you rightly kicked me out of your life, I came obsessed by what we had. It's very true that one only realises what they had when they no longer have it. That was me through and through. I will admit to you, I had followed you for weeks until finally I drew the courage to follow you into 'Le Petite Rouge', in the hope that I could once again be part of your life. Not a day passed that I didn't think about you or wish you back into my life but I had to grow first, I had to become a better man before you would even consider looking at me, let alone having me *back. When you rejected me in the restaurant and I don't blame you, I was compelled to give it one final chance. I just knew that couldn't be the end of it. I just knew there was something in your eyes that said you still held a small torch shining just for me. I will thank my lucky stars that I followed my instinct that day and followed you back home. I just wasn't prepared to throw my feelings away without one more try, living a life of regret and loss. I just had to try. Then came the ultimate change. In seven days all my yesterdays have come together and made sense and I can now share with you that I have changed for the better. From the moment you let me step back into your life, I was determined to make this work, determined to be the best thing that ever happened to you, determined to help you forget what I did in the past, determined to give you the life, companionship and support you truly deserve.*

I can't change the things I did before but I have changed the man that was responsible for them. I now know why I did it and I now know why I will never be that man ever again. You, Teresa, have proven without a doubt, that you are an angel beyond comparison and I will be eternally grateful for the second chance you gave me. I will prove I am the man that my mother brought me into the world to be. I will make you proud of me and I will do all I can to ensure you never, ever regret letting me back into your life. Teresa, you make my world complete. If I do the same to you, please come into the bedroom where I'm waiting in anticipation to make love to you, the woman I adore and the woman I want in my life forever. After, we've made love I want to read to you from your favourite book, until you blissfully drift to sleep. I bought it and read it in the last few days, since I realised what it meant to you. Yes, Teresa. I will 'make your world complete'.

    Forever yours,
    Simon.

A million thoughts parading as fearsome dodgem cars at the local fair cavorted and raced through Teresa's dumbfounded mind. Bump! Bump! Bump! Bump! They bashed and collided with each other. Bump! Bump! Bump! Bump! As they bounced, retreated and bumped again. Round and round and round they circled, aimlessly clashing and smashing headfirst into a whirlwind mass of speeding, flashing blurs of bright colour. Teresa was hypnotised by Simon's letter, the twinkling candlelight and the sensual bouquet of burning lust in the air, her slow paced walk was synchronised with removing items of clothing, as they seductively slinked to the floor. Teresa was naked in body, soul and inhibitions as she floated into the bedroom.

Chapter 19
Blurred Lines

'Now what does he want? Sometimes I wish he would just leave me alone. I haven't got the time for another meeting. It's only been two weeks since the last one. He must enjoy wasting my time with his pointless drivel!'

Teresa's irritation at the email from Dr Sommers requesting a meeting, conjured images of more droning monotone from her irrepressibly tedious boss, as she wondered what inspired words of wisdom and criticism he was going to impart today. Naturally, it wasn't the attitude to enter his office with, particularly as his greeting was a tad more curt than usual.

'Morning, Teresa, I'm not a happy man. Two weeks ago you were thirty minutes late for work. You told me it was a one-off. You even apologised for your tardiness. That was Monday. Then woe and behold, you repeated your dreadful time-keeping on Tuesday, Wednesday, Thursday and Friday. You were increasingly late every day of that week. Then last week, you were late on three days out of five. That's eight days of lateness in two weeks and the two days you did make it on time, it was with seconds to spare. What on earth is going on, Teresa?!'

'I'm sorry, Dr Sommers. I really am sorry. I don't know what to say. I really don't, except that it won't happen again.'

'I'm sorry, Teresa. That's simply not good enough. You have never been late before, in fact you have always been early. Then suddenly you've changed. I need to know what the problem is. I need you to tell me what's going on. You apologised two weeks ago and your lateness only got worse. Your change in behaviour is not normal, certainly not from such an organised and methodical person. So tell me. What's wrong?'

'There is really nothing wrong. Life is good. Work is good. There is nothing wrong. I won't be late again. I promise I won't be.'

'I told you, that's not good enough. Something is wrong. As your employer, I need to know. There are unwell people that rely on you being here on time and being here mentally and at the moment you are not achieving either. So, tell me what is wrong?'

'I don't understand what you mean, Dr Sommers. What do you mean I'm not achieving either?'

'You're simply not with it, girl. You don't seem engaged to your role. Your lateness is inexcusable but when you're here you seem detached, almost as if you don't want to be here. Others have noticed too. Also, looking at your time-card, not once in the last two weeks have you done any overtime, you have left this building precisely on time, let alone making up the time for your lateness. Since when has your role been a nine to five position? Well to be accurate, with your lateness you haven't even managed that, have you? I need to know what is going on in your brain and in your life!'

'To be honest with you, Dr Sommers, it's none of your business. My personal life is just that. It's personal! And no concern of yours or any of the busy-body gossips that work here! I've told you I will improve my time-keeping and I will! Now, can I please go? I need to get my work done; as you said, there are people that rely on me and I need to see to them!'

'You can start by lowering your voice, Teresa. That's not the attitude I expect from a brilliant member of staff as you are. It *is* my business, when you begin to let people down! In the last two weeks you have become a concern, not only in your time-keeping and the worrying impression you give, that you'd rather not be here but your whole appearance has changed. You're just not the Teresa we knew no more than a few days ago.'

'I'm sorry, Dr Sommers. It just makes me angry that my colleagues are gossiping about me. Of course I am present mentally. I love my job, it's always been so much more than a job to me. It's part of me. So when people criticise that, it really makes my blood boil. Haven't they got better things to do, than talk about me? And what about my appearance? That's really insulting! I suppose they have complained about that too. What's wrong with my appearance?'

'Listen, Teresa. I'm afraid it's not your colleagues. In fact, they haven't passed any comments whatsoever. It was a handful of your patients that have been troubled by your demeanour, particularly Ash who has been worried about you and actually asked to speak with me because he is genuinely concerned about your welfare. As for your appearance, you only need to look in the mirror. You're looking tired. Your hair isn't as tidy as it was before and even after weeks your mouth still looks sore. You're looking run-down and bedraggled, Teresa, and certainly not a patch on the vivacious and sprightly Teresa we all know and love.'

'Oh no! I had no idea it was Ash. I don't know what to say. I didn't for a second think that my patients were troubled. I didn't think for a second my life was affecting them. They are all I care about. They are the reason I love my job. Caring for people was the only reason I became a nurse. I can't believe my troubles have overlapped into my work. I have always drawn a line at the entrance to this hospital and left my personal life on the other side, irrespective of anything going on.'

'Dry your eyes, girl, there's no need for tears. I am convinced we can sort this out. Otherwise you wouldn't be the outstanding nurse that you are. Teresa, you mentioned troubles. What troubles have overlapped into your work?'

'Oh, Dr Sommers. I don't really know where to begin. I don't really know what to say. I don't really want to talk about it.'

'Teresa. Firstly, you really need to stop crying. Ash only mentioned what he did because knowing you as well as he does, he's simply worried because he clearly cares for you and it's blatantly obvious something isn't quite right. You seemed to have lost your focus, not only on your work but on the way you look. For all the time I've known you, you've never had a hair out of place, you've always been beautifully made up and not dishevelled in the slightest. Secondly, I think you need to talk about it because whatever your troubles are, they are obviously affecting your work and your patients that you love so much.'

'I can't stop crying, Dr Sommers. I care too much about my patients. I care too much about Ash. I can't begin to tell you how much this has hurt me. I can't begin to tell you how much this has bothered me. I can't begin to tell you how much this has shocked me. I really can't.'

'I understand your disbelief, Teresa, especially as Ash is so close to your heart. However, what you can do is tell me about your troubles, at least as your employer, someone who cares about your future, someone who has to take all the patients into your consideration, someone who also cares for you as an employee, I can begin to understand your challenges.'

'I don't think you really understand how much that has hit me. I never ever wanted to blur the line between my personal life and my professional life. I really thought I was coping with it but I was clearly disillusioned. I will tell you, Dr Sommers, and I will also sort myself out. My ex-boyfriend has moved back into my flat just over two weeks ago and it's just been a whirlwind of change for me. I never ever expected to see him again and here we are living together. That is all. That's all that has happened.'

'I appreciate you sharing that with me, Teresa, but how has that affected your time-keeping and your appearance so adversely? Surely you're happy with him being back in your life, otherwise he wouldn't be living in your home. Surely you wanted that to happen. I really do not understand how you've changed so much and unfortunately changed for the worst.'

'That's just it, Dr Sommers. That, in a nutshell is the foundation of my troubles. I don't understand either.'

Teresa was tired. Two weeks of the torrid exploration of her body that had been uncharted territory for almost a year, felt ravaged and yet deeply satisfied. Both evenings and mornings had been welded together with red hot lust, sometimes replacing dinner and bolstering breakfast but always relentless long treks of carnal, animalistic activity. Simon's appetite was infinite, smudging the intrepid boundaries that fenced Teresa's life into normality and detonating colossal explosions of chaos throughout her landscape, which today had abruptly broken her most hallowed commandment about professionalism at work. The sheet of paper that Teresa clutched as she skulked away from her boss's office brought her reality into the unclouded limelight. It was a formal disciplinary warning demanding excellence in time-keeping and general awareness. Dr Sommers' words barbarically echoed in Teresa's ears as she attempted to deal with her disappointment and contemplate the improvements required.

'It really bothers me to take disciplinary action against our most valued employee, however I have zero alternative options available to me. If I don't see a marked improvement in your time-keeping within seven days of today's date, we may have to consider more serious action against your employment here at Teers Hospital. I don't expect to be sat here with you again Teresa, having this same discussion because I know what your role means to you. Now go and sort yourself out. Your patients desperately need you.'

Once a minute a pounding cannonade bombarded the jam-packed compartments of Teresa's brain. 'Boom! Boom! Boom!' Her headache was relentless, splattering the colours in her vision into black and white blurs. Today, marked a catastrophic landmark in her valued career, engraved into her chronological mental curriculum vitae. She had fallen to the ground-level of her qualified pilgrimage, she had achieved an all-time employment low.

Barely two hours ago, Teresa had left home drenched with Simon's morning excitement inside her beleaguered body, tittering to herself at the sight of little plastic buttons, from her pretty white blouse pinging forcefully off the bathroom wall. 'You know what white lacy blouses do to my body.' He had materialised behind her as she peered into the mirror applying the lines of her make-up, his two hands visible in the reflection tore her blouse apart and slipped his mauling fingers underneath her bra.

The cheek smear from her freshly pasted foundation on the mirror, the mess of clothes in the wardrobe as she fumbled for a freshly washed and ironed blouse, Simon whispering, 'That'll teach you for looking so sexy in your see-through top' as he nakedly returned to bed smugly satisfied, were the blissful images in her mind as she dreamily waltzed out of the house.

One hundred and twenty seven minutes later, three cumbersomely bitter tranquilising sedatives were cascading down her throat to calm the butchering head pains and blistered thoughts of deficiency, as she reluctantly marched towards Ash's ward.

'100mg Sedation — Violent nightmares / abusive behaviour.'

Ash's medication clipboard, hanging from the foot of his bed, explained the deep sleep he was clearly in. On his bedside table, sat on 'Make my World Complete' was a white sealed envelope.

'To my Angel, Teresa.'

Chapter 20
Crowded House

Welcome to my crowded house.
Space is annoyingly tight, dimmed is the light
But I crave your presence and the flowers you clutch.
My visiting inhabitants they seldom leave,
Packing the rooms with their stench,
Sticking around to receive.
Their contributions are scarce and greedy
Their lives so miserable and needy.
Their defecation is becoming my creation
I can't breathe, my senses are in sedation.
But this is my house, I cannot ask them to depart
For they too are my sturdy friends
And they curve my mental trends.
We will clear a corner for your glorious charisma
It'll charm, excite, delight
And defend us from the fright.
I have my own secluded room in my crowded house
I've locked the door and I crawl along the floor
I don't want to make a sound and attract more people
But if you gently knock, I will gratefully let you in
And together we will plot and calm the lonely din.
It's bursting at the seams even infiltrating my dreams
But this is my crowded house
And it's become a part of me.
I can't spread my wings, I can't set myself free.
This is where I belong, this is my destiny.
So come soon, come and meet the crowd,
Come to my house, and feel the weight of my shroud.
The crazy hustle and bustle of my crowded home
Where in my room I cower alone.
I hear the people, their incessant hum,
They holler and call my name

Reminding me of all my misdemeanours and shame.
I await your arrival to give my broken picture a frame.
My walls are bare but there is no one to care
But with you here we will establish a homely lair.
Please don't be late, please don't hesitate
For I fear without you,
My crowded house will become my mortal fate'.

The perturbing words of Ash's letter temporarily quietened the racket inside Teresa's head. His agitating musings were crying out for Teresa's attention. From a shambolic occupational low instigated by the disciplinary grilling from her boss to the heart-rending letter from her pre-eminent patient, she slipped down another rung lower on the ladder of career disenchantment and personal restlessness.

'Hello, Teresa. When did you creep in? What's that you're reading there?'

'Oh hello, Simon. I didn't realise you were here. I thought you were still out. I've only just returned from work and it's been a shocking day.'

'Why? What happened? And what's that you're reading?'

'I don't know where to begin. It's just been awful from beginning to end. It started with a warning about being continuously late. I've been given a week to improve and then I've had a non-stop banging headache all day. I just cannot shift it. It's just been one of those days. I can't wait for it to end.'

'Screw them, Teresa! You're allowed to be late every now and again, especially considering how much of your life you've dedicated to that hospital. They should be grateful you turn up at all. They couldn't survive a day without you. You still haven't told me what you're reading. What is it?'

'Oh, this. It's just a letter from a patient that's all.'

'Oh, ok. Since when do patients write to the staff? That's a bit odd, isn't it? Who's the patient anyway?'

'I don't think it's odd at all. I think it's very touching. Although I could have done without it today. It's a little deep.'

'Touching? What's touching about it? Deep? Why's it deep? Who's the patient?

'It's someone called Ash. I've been given three months to help rehabilitate him, otherwise he will be put into a mental institute.'

'Mental institute? What's mental about him?'

'I didn't say he was mental, Simon. He's suffered major traumatic shock, ended up disabled and just needs to recover, and I know he will. It's just a matter of time. I will not let him go into an institute.'

'Why not? He's just another patient, isn't he? Surely, if they think he needs to be in a mental home, then he does! Why are you so protective over him? He's obviously just another loser who's lost the plot. The world is full of them!'

'Simon! I don't need this! He is not a loser and he has not lost the plot! Don't be so bloody mean. He is a wonderful man and a very talented one too, so please leave him alone!'

'Why are you getting so angry?! It's not my fault you've had a bad day, is it? It's not my fault you're dealing with a loser that you obviously cannot cope with. Anyway, what the fuck is so talented about being mental and disabled?'

'For the last time, Simon! Ash is not a loser! And he is not bloody mental! He is suffering severe traumatic shock. He lost his girlfriend and father at the same time and can't get over it!'

'Why? Where did the mental loser lose them? He's probably just forgot where he left them. Ha, ha, ha, ha!'

'He didn't bloody lose them! You bloody well know what I mean! They both died on the same day! It was the only family he had! And please stop calling him a loser! Ash is not a loser!'

'Oh well. These things happen. It's not my fault they died! So don't fucking take it out on me! Death is hardly serious, is it?! It happens to all of us! But that doesn't explain why you're so protective over a loser that can't accept death!'

'For fuck's sake, Simon! Stop being so mean! Of course death is serious! How would you know anyway?! You've never lost someone close, have you?! Ash can't accept it. He hadn't seen his father for ages and crashed the car that killed his bloody girlfriend. Now, please leave me alone! It's been a bad day and you are not helping!'

'Fuck off, Teresa! This isn't about me! How dare you suggest I should lose someone close to understand some pathetic loser that you can't handle and to make matters worse, no wonder the arsehole can't get over it, he fucking murdered his own girlfriend. He's a murderer too!'

'No, Simon! You fuck off! I did not say you need to lose someone! Ash is not a loser! He is not mental and he is not a murderer. Stop arguing with me! Why are you trying to hurt me? Why are you acting so jealous about a patient? Just leave me alone and grow up!'

'Jealous! Jealous! Fucking jealous! I'm not jealous of some disabled, mental murderer! He's a loser just like you are! You've always been a loser and you always will be! Have your pathetic retard! I couldn't give a fuck about your stupid patients or your stupid hospital! You've just caused an argument for nothing. None of this is my fault, you nasty little bitch! I hope your precious Ash knows what a selfish, nasty little bitch you are! It's a shame he didn't murder you! Oh but there's still time if we're lucky! Give me that stupid letter you bitch. I'll show you who's jealous!'

'Give it back to me! Give it to me you horrible bastard. I knew I shouldn't have let you back into my life. Give me back that letter! Give it to me, Simon. Give it to me now!'

'You want it do you, you little bitch? You want your loser's letter back, do you? Well you'll have to come and get it! Let me into your life? I should have remembered what a nasty little, pointless bitch you are and should have left you to rot alone with your mental losers!'

'Just give me the letter back, Simon! You've said enough now! I think we all know who the loser is! I think we all know who the sad pathetic little man is! You know you couldn't stay away! You know you stalked me! You know it's you that couldn't live without me! I think we all know who the real mental loser is, don't we? Now for the last time, give me back the letter, you pathetic, jealous little man!'

'Right, you bitch! You've asked for this!'

The breathing motion of Teresa's oesophagus wanting to let air in, whilst trying to comprehend the rude intrusion in her mouth, stretched her brain activity to its farthest dazed reach. Buzzing messages were travelling at lightening velocity through her senses, attempting to decipher the potential threat to her wellbeing.

'Throat! Throat! Throat! Don't let it in! Don't let it in. Keep tongue curled back. The threat will cease. Hang on in there! Nose do your thing, breathe hard! Breathe hard! Breathe harder! Throat!

Whatever you do, do not choke! Stop gagging! This is not the time to choke! You cannot choke! We need more air! Emergency! Emergency! Emergency! Air! We need more air! Nose! Where are you? We need more air! Breathe nose, breathe! Nose, you must keep breathing! You must breathe! We are fifteen seconds to shut down! C'mon, everyone, we need to get through this! Throat do not choke! Nose give us air! We need that air! We need it now! C'mon, everyone, we need to get through this! We need to win! We need to survive! Too late! It's too late! It's too late! We are officially in hysteria status! Everybody! Stay on high alert, I'm shutting her down. We don't have enough air to continue and her body is at maximum stress! Five! Four! Three! Two! One! And Close!'

Teresa's eyes rolled upwards as her body went into temporary shut-down, gasping for oxygen. Simon stopped forcing Ash's screwed up letter into her mouth.

'Are you happy now, you little fucker? You wanted the loser's letter, now you've got it! I hope it tastes good. Next time you'll know better than to take your bad day out on me. Don't pretend to faint. It doesn't work on me. I know your type, just going for the sympathy angle. Oh! I know your type just trying to make others feel bad. Well, here's news for you, Teresa. I do not feel bad! In fact, I feel nothing other than relieved that you have your stupid letter back. Now let's see what you're really made of. Let's see if this jealous little man can wake you up in the only way you know how, in the only language your body understands. You keep your letter in your stupid mouth, you keep your eyes shut and leave everything else to Simon.'

Five seconds of bliss as Teresa woke. Five seconds before her waking brain disentangled the riddle and slipped her uncomfortably back into comprehension mode and repainted the catastrophe of events.

She didn't quite vomit, although her throat reflexes gagged as she removed the soggy letter from her mouth, leaving behind the bitter taste of black pen. She was naked. Her body quivered as her mind recaptured the last stored image in her memory, the inhumane red anger in Simon's eyes as he spluttered insults at her and pushed the crumpled letter deeper into her asphyxiating mouth.

'Morning, sweetheart. I was wondering when you were going to wake. You wouldn't move so I went to bed. You need to get sorted and get to work. We had a little argument last night but it's all better now. I'm sorry for my part and I forgive you for what you said to me, although you were really nasty. It doesn't really matter now.'

'Why didn't you wake me up? Why did you leave me naked on the floor? At least you could have covered me in a blanket!'

'I tried to move you, honey, but you were a dead weight. I didn't cover you because I thought you would wake and come to bed. Anyway, the argument is over and done with, I've said sorry now, so it doesn't matter anymore. Here, have hot cuppa. I got up early to make you a cup of tea. See, I'm not as bad as you think I am.'

'But, Simon. You tried to choke me on Ash's letter. You tried to hurt me!'

'Don't be silly, Teresa. Don't you think if I wanted to hurt you, I could? I just got angry after you insulted me but I wouldn't hurt you. I mean it's not like you were innocent. I've still woke to make you a cup of tea. I'm not even angry anymore. So, I don't think you should be either. I have said sorry, which is more than you've done!'

'Sorry! Sorry, Simon! I didn't do anything wrong. What have I got to apologise for? But you. You tried to choke me and then left me naked on the floor all night. I don't understand what I need to apologise for.'

'Why do you want to carry on arguing? I've said sorry for everything that happened. I really am sorry, even though it wasn't all my fault and anyway we made love to make up. So, I really don't understand why you're still so angry with me. I've even woke early to make you a cup of tea.'

'What do you mean we made love? Are you trying to tell me you took advantage of me whilst I was knocked out and whilst this letter was stuffed in my mouth?'

'I did not take advantage of you, Teresa. We were both angry and the best way to control anger is to make love. That's hardly taking advantage of you is it. I actually did you a favour and calmed you down by doing what we do best. Of course, in that moment of passion I completely forgot the letter was in your mouth. I'm sorry. What more can I say? I'm really sorry!'

'Simon! You raped me! I did not consent. I was not conscious, therefore you raped me!'

92

'Teresa, you're being very dramatic. This is ridiculous. As if I would rape the woman that I love. It's beyond me that you can say such a horrible thing. No one would believe you and everyone would understand that we are a loving couple. You're just upset and later you will be sorry. I'm really sorry you feel this way towards me. In fact it's really upsetting me that you think I could be so evil and harm you in that way.'

'Who cares about everyone else!? I know what you did! I don't need to prove a thing to anyone because I know what you did. You attacked me, tried to choke me and then raped me. There is no other explanation Simon. I think you need to leave. I think you need to leave right now!'

'Look, I'm really, really sorry. I'm not sure what came over me. I don't think I'm coping too well and being accused of being a rapist is not helping. I'm totally shocked that you can think of me like that. I know you don't want me to leave and I know you don't really believe I'm that bad, nowhere near as bad as you're making me out to be. All I can say is sorry and you've got to believe me. I am really sorry!'

'This is getting nowhere! You know what you did and your intentions were only bad. You wanted to hurt me and you did and there's no return from that. I need to get to work because that's also been fucked up since you reappeared in my life. Now get out of my way and make sure you're not here when I return. Just be gone, Simon! Getting back together was a bad choice and you've just proven that last night; I can't get over what you did. Don't keep saying sorry because it simply doesn't count. There are some things you just cannot apologise for. What you have done to me is not repairable. You have broken me and us beyond repair!'

Chapter 21
Love is Dying

The requiem of my contaminated heart
Passion and empathy blown apart.
An obituary bitter with disillusion,
A horde of promises bleeding in confusion.
Conceived for infinitude so carefree and fluttered
Numbing my senses, emotions cluttered.
You were pain waiting to proceed
Knowing how comfortably I would bleed.
Artistically contrived, my euthanasia calling
Utterly impervious to my desperate falling.
Byron, Keats and Shakespeare!
Your dissertations on love misleading and unclear.
Futile musings, callous poets were blatantly lying
Goodbye heart, emotions are abortive
And love is dying.

'Make my World Complete' bled the appropriate words from its pages. Love blossomed, love lived and love died. All the seasons of heaven's stimulating emotion leapt from its contrived chapters and relentlessly punctured Teresa's heart as she replaced the masterpiece into her locker and prepared for her shift at Teers. Incredibly, Sitara Kai Khusa's book never failed to capture whatever emotion Teresa was currently swaddled in. She had sulkily opened it for some sympathetic solace and languished through the chapter 'Love is Dying' in which Sitara criticised and lamented about the advent and subsequent departure of the almighty conviction of love. Her heart too felt contaminated, she had been fooled again by the omnipotence love had flagrantly impersonated. She had been persuaded down a familiar alley, long, winding and knowingly treacherous but she was safe holding onto her lover's hand, until the darkness of this unknown, uninhabited place, scared him away, leaving her to be ravaged by the fearsome wolves of jealousy and possessiveness. Pillaged, forlorn and somber her face refused to let her make-up cover the cloudy despondency her bitter blood was bubbling with. Romantic love was dead and buried. Only the weary aches of her tiresome limbs remembered the depravity of Simon's crude and sleazy actions from the night before. Teresa was no more than a discarded plastic shopping bag being effortlessly carried by the wind, controlled by an outside force, not aware where the landing was going to happen, simply floating on the gusts that unreasonably blew her way.

'Byron, Keats and Shakespeare. Your dissertations on love misleading and unclear!'

The repetitive whirlwind in her addled mind shouted out the derisory line about her favourite writers, surpassing the surprise that her top three beloved wordsmiths had been immortalised in Khusa's poem, belittling their futile musings about love.

Teresa scuttled around doing her ward duties with only one patient in mind. Her entire focus was on Ash, she felt a sense of betrayal towards him, attempting to remember the words of his 'Crowded House' poem which she almost swallowed and which had set the repulsive scenario of Simon's demented behaviour.

'Will she really be here today? I hope you're right. I have really missed her. We have so much to catch up with.'

The voice was familiar. It was Ash. Teresa felt a sense of uplifted delight knowing that Ash had a visitor. Daily interaction was vital in his rehabilitation process. She hurriedly skipped around the corner of Ash's ward to see who he was talking to.

'You were right. You were right. Thank you. Now do you mind leaving us alone for a while we have much to catch up with, it's been a long time.'

'Hello, Ash. How are you today? I've really been looking forward to seeing you. Who were you talking to?'

'I'm so pleased you came, Teresa. Dad said you would come today. Yes, it was dad I was talking to. He's just left, so we have some time to talk in private.'

Teresa's heart thumped in desperate defeat. This was another shocking blow against Ash's rehabilitation. She knew Ash was talking himself into the institute.

'Ash, you poor thing. Dad wasn't here. You're probably just missing him. You're probably wishing him to be here. Now, what else do you have to tell me?'

'You silly-billy, Teresa. I know Dad doesn't physically exist but his spirit is here and he talks to me every day. He really likes you and hopes you are enjoying 'Make my World Complete."

Ash's medicine was clearly affecting his demeanour. Teresa had already been warned about his violent nightmares, which had resulted in his increased sedation to help control his erratic thinking. This delusional behaviour was a documented side effect of the drugs he had been prescribed.

'Oh, Ash. I'm so sorry I haven't given you the attention you deserve but you must tell your dad to go away. You must stop talking with him. It's not good for you to be talking into thin air. I will help you and visit you more often.'

'No, Teresa. Dad is here to stay, he told me so. He never wants to leave me again. He even knows why you've been so busy lately.'

'Ash, your dad unfortunately died. He's not here. You're just imagining his presence into being. What else do you have to tell me? It really has been a while since we had a good natter.'

'Of course he died. I know that but he is still here. In fact, he's right there beside you. He's smiling at you.'

'C'mon, Ash. Let's get on with our day. We've got a lot of checks to do. I also need to take your blood today.'

'No, really, Teresa. It's Dad that wrote 'Crowded House' because he said you needed to know and you needed to understand. Did you like it? Did you like the words?'

'Yes, Ash. 'Crowded House' is a lovely poem, I loved it. I loved your words.'

'They weren't my words, Teresa. Dad wrote them for me to give to you. He wrote them for you and will write more.'

'Ash, we need to sort this out. You dad is not alive. He is not here and he did not write those words. You're suffering temporary delusional trauma and we will work together and make you better. We can do this. We can make you better. Together we can achieve what we need to.'

'But dearest Teresa, I know we will work this out together and by 'together', I mean with Dad. The three of us will make me better.

Since Dad returned and told me things about mum and all the things that have happened, I feel so much better. I can now see a way through our challenges, I can now see the path we need to take to get my life sorted out.'

'Okay, Ash. Let's move on with your checks. First, blood pressure.'

'Teresa, don't you believe me when I tell you Dad is stood right beside you, because he truly is. Right there.'

'I believe you, Ash. I believe you, Ash. I've just had a very bad night and I'm all over the place at the moment. Not that I should be telling you that, considering I'm the nurse and you're the patient. If you can see your dad, then I'm very happy for you but you need to understand not everyone is going to be happy the way I am. Some will most certainly use that against you and try and tell you you're not very well and suggest you need to be locked away, just because you can see what they can't.'

'I understand, Teresa. I really do and so does dad. We both know you are my saviour and we both know you will do all you can and don't worry about talking about yourself, I already know what has happened. We can also help you.'

'What do you mean, you already know what's happened? What do you know, Ash?'

'Dad told me to say sorry about last night. You didn't deserve what happened. It wouldn't have happened had he not wrote what he did and I'm sorry too for using the pen that I did to write 'Crowded House'. A more expensive ink wouldn't have bled into your mouth.'

Chapter 22
Reasons

Isolated and disorientated, Teresa was wandering alone. A crushing boulder of loneliness, weighed its gravitational force upon her. Benumbed and barefoot the dewy grass clammy on her feet as they squelched into the firm, chilled morning ground and she disjointedly galumphed forward. The moistness of the mist was glued to her face and restricting her vision. There was no direction, no shortcut, simply forward movements with no particular destination planned. Her mind addled with Ash's words, even more sharp pins piercing her already perforated pin-cushion brain. There was no escape from the solitude and frustration of bewilderment, as the erratic jigsaw puzzle of Ash/Khusa fell to the floor and amalgamated with the lost pieces of another hundred anomalous jigsaw puzzles.

'Are you ok?'

'Yes, yes, I'm fine. It's just been one of those strange mornings that make no sense whatsoever.'

'Ah yes, we all have those from time to time. By the way, my name is Dee. I take it you're a nurse here?'

'Yes, I am. Ha, ha, did the uniform give it away.'

'It did indeed. You've been sat there for fifteen minutes, just staring into space. I just wondered if you were ok.'

'Yes, thanks for the concern. I'm great. Just recovering from a bad night and a bizarre morning. I'm assuming you're a visitor here?'

'Yes, just visiting an old friend. I was once a nurse too. Not in this type of hospital though. I have the utmost respect for what you people do in these places. Some of the patients here wouldn't have anywhere to rehabilitate if it wasn't for these hospitals. Oh, I'm so sorry to hear about your bad night. Whatever it is don't let it get you down and don't let go of hope. Hope will always show you the way.'

'Thank you, Dee. You are right hope does always show you the way, even when you feel lost and lonely. There is always hope to get you through.'

'Well, Teresa, I assume that's your name on your badge. Let me tell you something. Many, many years ago, it was only hope and the kind words of another that got me through my darkest days. If it wasn't for hope and those encouraging words, I wouldn't be here today telling you. I better go and see my friend, you, my dear, need to smile and keep that hope shining bright in your heart!'

Dee's chair screeched backwards on the grey tiled floor, as she pushed it back and rose to leave. There was a gleaming, ray of warmth from her enraptured smile, undoubtedly the sunshine Teresa needed to burn through her clouded befuddlement.

'Thank you, Dee. I will fight through this and I will get there. Hope your friend is well. It's been lovely to meet you.'

'The pleasure was all mine my dear. Nothing can stand in the way of relentless hope. Keep smiling and have a lovely day and never, ever forget everything and I mean absolutely everything happens for a reason, albeit the reason isn't always apparent to begin with.'

Teresa watched Dee walk out of the canteen and somehow could tell she was once a nurse. There was always a caring glint in the eyes of a nurse. The sparkling star that twinkled with kindness for other human beings, a sincere rosiness that comforted the underprivileged in health and eminence. Ash's emblazoned words within Teresa's thoughts had been replaced with Dee's parting comment.

'Absolutely everything happens for a reason, albeit the reason isn't always apparent to begin with.'

Teresa scuttled aimlessly from duty to duty, pondering the reason behind Simon's actions and what good could possibly come from it. Hope, sprinkled with a dash of well-prepared reasons baked a cake full of overwhelming conclusions as Teresa's shift ended and she reluctantly made her journey home. There was no doubt left in her mind. There were no more questions concerning Simon's disgraceful and humiliating outburst. Teresa's unimpeachable theory was faultless. Ash's poem 'Crowded House', Simon's peevish reaction to Ash's condition and his abusive repartee were all a huge pre-warning and wake-up alarm signalling Simon's dazzling true colours. His colourfully blighted contempt for her as a woman and the magnificent exposure on his acute jealousy and stifling possessiveness was everything Teresa had forgotten in the haze of her loneliness and their animalistic lust and magnetism. Cold-bloodedly choking her and subsequently defiling her body whilst she was unconscious was no more than an intimation of the future, a distasteful glimpse of what was ahead.

'Absolutely everything happens for a reason. Absolutely everything happens for a reason. Absolutely everything happens for a reason. Absolutely everything happens for a reason.'

Teresa's thoughts were a swirling kaleidoscope, as Dee's most welcome sentence circulated her mind in dazzling technicolour. An identical swirl of stress hormones was maliciously grinding in her stomach, as she peered up from her front door wondering if Simon was going to be there or as instructed rightfully departed.

'So tell us, Teresa. Do you really want him gone? Or are you going to forgive him again? C'mon, Teresa, what do you really want? Was it a tad dramatic last night? Do you really hope Simon Driscoll is no more? Are you happy being lonely again? Are you going to miss him being around? Are you going to miss the torrid love-making? Well are you? What do you really, really, really want? C'mon, Teresa, we need to know!'

With each step up to her flat, Teresa's conscience was fire-bombing biting questions at her, churning her stomach with vomit inducing force.

'You're not sure, are you? You just don't know, do you? You don't want to lose him, do you? You don't want to be lonely, do you? You want to forgive him, don't you? You want Simon Driscoll in your life, don't you? Teresa!!! It's not like he really raped you, did he? You did ask for it, didn't you?'

The bludgeoning muscle of a full swing sledgehammer smashed square into Teresa's disorientated forehead, the ripple effect of the pain vibrated through her frazzled head, awakening the slumbering voice of reason as two distinctly carved images materialised and appeared to echo her thinking. Time was too limited to ask herself the obvious question, 'Why were Sitara Kai Khusa and the friendly woman she met in the canteen only hours ago, prominently featured in her debating mind? What was their role in her dilemma with Simon Driscoll?'

A surge of cerebrum chemicals besieged her negating conscience and doused the contemptible questions that were pummelling her judgement. Every quandary in Teresa's brain was savagely belittled, instantly answered and duly rejected in precise nanosecond agility. Her mind was made up as it relished the renewed vigour that engulfed it.

'Yes, I know what I want! Yes, I know how I feel! Yes, I want him out of my life! No, I won't be lonely! No, I don't need him! No, I won't miss the love-making! I am one hundred percent sure! I cannot and will not forgive him! I don't ever want him in my life! No, I didn't ask for it! Simon Driscoll is an evil, manipulative rapist and I want him gone for good!'

Teresa aggressively turned the key in her lock and was prepared to enter the ring and win the fight as she commandingly shoved the door open.

'Simon Driscoll. God help you if you are still in my home! Simon! Are you here!? Simon!'

Silence. Teresa's emotional pandemonium took its last churn. Her stomach ceased its washing machine motion, from chugging back and forth, to an almighty spin to a sudden standstill, just waiting to be opened and have its tousled clothes removed and unravelled. More unanswerable questions gyrated in Teresa's hectic head, she could hear the audible sound of cheering from the two bizarre guests ensconced in her mind. The din was excruciatingly raucous in comparison to the deadly nothingness in her home. In the welcome absence of Simon Driscoll, Teresa expected a letter, albeit she would have preferred nothing, except the final remnants of his manly aroma, contemplating their escape once she opened the door and windows for fresh evening air to waft in and start the necessary removal process. Expectant but still mildly disappointed to see his handwriting staring back at her, scrabbling off the ivory page to speak his barefaced words.

Dearest Teresa,

I know what you're thinking and I know how you are feeling. You're thinking 'here we go again', more Driscoll bullshit and you're feeling you wish there weren't even words left behind to remind you of me.

Honestly, I don't and cannot blame you, I've brought this upon myself, so I did as you asked and have left your home and once again left your life in peace without the misery I clearly rained upon you. In the drawer next to your bed, I've left a sealed brown envelope, only open that if this letter compels you to do so and I stress the importance of this with all my life, only if after reading what I've got to say, otherwise simply throw it away without ever opening it. I sincerely thought my anger, jealousy and possessiveness was under control and God only knows how hard I tried to keep the old Simon away from you. I know there is no room in your beautiful life for an immature, dishonourable arsehole like me. You're a kind, worthy and gentle woman who just doesn't need a monster destroying the goodness that you are. Today, I finally realised that and against my own heart, against my own feelings and with the utmost respect for what you asked me to do have disappeared from your home and your life and I will not darken your doorstep again, that's a promise.

In these last few weeks my passion and love for you has escalated beyond measure, I'm not even sure I have the words to explain to you how you've made me feel and how you have captured my heart and made it your own. I know I've now lost the one person that made my life complete, well there's no one to blame for that, except myself. I will walk this earth regretting what I have done to you and live the rest of my life with my dismal empty ribcage because I know, I will never feel this way again for anyone, ever. Maybe, that's a good thing. Maybe that simply means if I don't find love, then I can't destroy anyone and my unstable emotions will stay intact and within my own head where they should be, incarcerated forever, until I die a sad and lonely man, which is nothing less than I deserve. Teresa, I don't ask anything of you, except I just need you to know something. I need you to know I have no control. I thought I did but I was so wrong. My love for you made me lose any sense of good judgement, which is why I hurt you the way I did. I am an ogre. I am a despicable nasty, crude man. Everything in this world has an explanation and a reason, even when something seems so wrong, there will always be an explanation that will make some sense. I know I've ruined our relationship and I know there is never, ever going to be a third chance, I truly understand and respect that. I know how much I hate myself, let alone how much you must hate me. Teresa, my sweet love, if you need a little explanation behind this pathetic, broken man then you can open the brown envelope. If on the other hand, enough is enough and you really cannot care less and I do understand if that's what you're thinking, then please discard this one and the brown one without opening it.

I'm history from your life anyway, so it ultimately doesn't matter to me, in fact I won't even know if you looked in the brown envelope or put it in the bin, where it probably belongs. My heart just told me you deserved an explanation, my head tells me you don't give a damn after what happened last night. Either way Teresa, goodbye my love. I just wanted to thank you for giving me a second chance and for once in my life experiencing the beauty of true love and happiness, for that I will remain grateful until the day I die and in that final moment of life, my parting thought will be you, the regret of hurting you and a hope that you did find someone that made you as happy as you deserved to be. Goodbye my darling Teresa.

Simon

P.S. 'Make my World Complete', inspired this poem I wrote for you, in the hope that one day in the far, far distant future you may just look back, remember me and have one tiny favourable memory of the hateful man I have become.'

Chapter 23
Hate

Razor sharp, slicing through my jugular vein
The steely cut has stopped blood to my brain.
I wholly deserve this heart-stopping pain.
There are no words left to describe my remorse
I'm bleeding me dry, dwindling this life force.
The redness of my warm blood is cold and black
Tarnished corpuscles damaged with disgrace
Curdled with my self-loathing, wretched face.
Beats from my dwindling heart gush
With rhythmic fate
Poisoned with grievance, hostility and hate.
This parting gesture, the final smile,
Acceptance of a person utterly vile.
Clap and rejoice, this world
Is now free of my adulteration
As I float into the abyss, raise a glass in elation.
Goodbye accursed fiend, blemish in God's creation.
Your revulsion is my compulsion
As I hang my hat in defeat
I am a loser, a liar and a dishonourable cheat.
I hate myself with endless infatuation
As I crumble into eternal sedation.
Sorry is my terminating word,
The epilogue to a man so absurd.
Go forth and set yourself free from this
Contemptible personality.

Intense and almost at an unbearably hot temperature, the sharp streaks of glistening water from the shower tap, bounced from Teresa's skin as it steamed and flowed over her curves. She was attempting to wash the defilement from her tired and abused body. Simon's self-pitying poem of personal repugnance filtered into Teresa's water soaked membranes and epitomised the disgust she felt for herself and the epic contempt she felt for the maniac that had knocked her cold and raped her. Teresa needed Simon Driscoll out of her head. The thought of him cutting his own throat with a sharp knife filled her with caustic glee but he was still in there lingering, threatening like a colossal black cloud, terrorising with its menace to rain. The infuriation pounded within her skull, lightening apocalyptically gathering its commanding surge to burst from the bitterness of the foreboding sky.

How could she have been fooled again?

What on earth was she thinking to let him into her life after the way he destroyed her the first-time around?

How could she have been such a pathetic idiot?

Why was she so desperate for sex that she let a monster ravage her and hurt her inside and out?

How was she ever going to recover from the car-crash he had left her to die in?

Her torrid anger was blossoming as frustrated tears poured from her eyes and mingled with the steaming shower spray.

'No! No! No! No! No! No!'

The water in Teresa's hair splashed upon the walls of the shower cubicle as if she was a dog shaking its hairy coat dry.

'No! No! No! No! No! No!'

It was making her head dizzy and disorientated as she continued to shout 'No!' and violently shake her head from side to side, uncontrollably in the steamy hot water.

'I hate you, Simon Driscoll!'

'I hate you, Simon Driscoll!'

'I hate you, Simon Driscoll!'

'I hate you, Simon Driscoll!'

The glass of her watery containment vibrated but stood firm and strong as it was forcefully pounded. With each scream of 'I hate you, Simon Driscoll!' Teresa smashed her forehead into it. The pain seared through her skull and numbed her face, each blow was a bolt of electricity, fierce and desensitising, crushing and colliding her grey matter until it slushed into submission and accepted the fate of releasing her enslaved rage and resentment. Her crimson blood painted an abstract pattern that dribbled down the pane of glass, further blows forced more redness from the bruising tear on her pulverised forehead.

'I hate you, Simon Driscoll!'

'I hate you, Simon Driscoll!'

'I hate you, Simon Driscoll!'

'I hate you, Simon Driscoll!'

Her brain function rattled and gathered its forces to eliminate Simon Driscoll from Teresa's thoughts as the ferocious pummelling raised the alarm of potential permanent damage. There was only one way out considering the glass was not conceding. Teresa's mind went blank, the switch was flicked to off and she collapsed as her decimated frame melted to the floor, crumbling into an embryonic curl as the scorching water continued to douse her debilitated body.

'Wake up! Wake up! Wake up! Teresa, you need to wake up!' The concerned words were smooth velvet brushing over her face, comforting her watery slumber, recognisable vocal chords signalling safety and contentment, she smiled and snuggled restfully into the softness of her familiar, condoling pillow, descending into a deeper sleep.

'Wake up, my sweet woman. I need you to wake up. You are not asleep, you've passed out in the shower. Please wake up. You really need to shake off this blackout!'

'Why do I? I just want to sleep. Please let me sleep. I'm so tired. I've done so much. All I want to do is sleep. Please let me sleep.'

'You can sleep, my darling woman, but this is not sleep. You are out cold and your head is bleeding. You're drifting further away. You only think you are asleep but you're not. I need you to wake up and be safe.'

'I am safe. I'm always safe when I'm alone in my own bed. This is where I am always the safest. Anyway, I can't wake up. This sleep is too deep. I really needed it. It's what I really want!'

'Come back, Teresa! Come back! I demand you come back! Come back for me. Please come back!'

'This is the best sleep I've had in ages. I'm floating on air. I'm sure I will be ok in the morning. I really did need this rest. My bed is so comfortable.'

'Teresa! You're floating away from life. You are disappearing into death. You have to return. Do not float away. This is not sleep. This is the peacefulness of death. You are leaving your life behind. Wake up! Wake up! Wake up! Teresa, wake up! If you don't wake up, you will die. Death will take you away from life!'

'I can't. I can't move my body. My eyes are open but I can't move. Can you help me? Can you help me move? I don't want to die! Please don't let me die. Please help me! It's getting so cold. I can't feel my body! I don't want this anymore, please get me out of here!'

'Hold my hand, Teresa. Put every thought in your mind towards my hand. Grab my hand and don't let go!'

Teresa felt the compassionate refuge of the tender voice transform into a rock-like clench of her hand. It was kind hearted and supple, a warming ray of delightful sunshine on a drizzling, bleak day.

'Ah, thank you. I can feel your hand. Please don't let go. Please don't let me down. I trust you. I will come with you. I don't want to die. Promise you won't let me die.'

'I won't let you down, Teresa, and I won't let you die. Please don't let my hand go.'

Teresa moved unintentionally. Cosily gliding to sanctuary, the warm voice echoed through her body as its reverberation was an escalator effortlessly transporting her to an alternative safe haven.

'You can sleep now, Teresa. Sleep. You are safe. You are not going to die. Stay here and you will be alive again.'

'Thank you. Thank you. Thank you. You didn't let me die. I feel safe now. Please don't leave me, please stay here. I'm scared. I don't want you to leave me alone!'

'I have to go now, Teresa. You are safe, nothing can harm you now. You need to sleep. You need to rest.'

'I want to see you. Let me see who you are. I can't see you. Please let me see you. Who are you and why did you help me?'

'You can't see me, Teresa. I'm here in spirit. I'm not visible to you. I need to go now. I need to go, now that you are safe.'

'Who are you? I know that I know you. I recognise your voice. Please tell me who you are. I need to know who saved me from dying. I need to know why you saved me.'

'My name is Sitara Kai Khusa and I saved you because of the compassion you've shown to my son; you are the only saviour in my son's life and without you he would have perished. That is why I saved you because you have saved my son. Now sleep, Teresa. You need to sleep.'

'I knew from the first second I heard you but I wasn't sure because you are dead. Is this magic? Is it a miracle? Did you come from heaven?'

'It's not magic, Teresa. It's not a miracle and nor am I from heaven. I am no more than a manifestation of life from beyond this physical world. I am only alive in the psyche of people who keep me mortal within their subliminal thoughts. You have done that you have kept me alive and you have given me the energy to return by keeping my son alive.'

'I will always help keep Ash alive. He will survive and I will help him live his life again. I will be there when he falls and I will be there when he laughs. I will be his light when he's in darkness. I will be his smile when he has sadness and I will show him the way when he is lost. I will do that. I will do that for you and I will do it for Ash. I will never let you down. I will do everything I can.'

'Sleep now, Teresa. Sleep now. You need to sleep. Close your eyes and sleep and always remember you have all the power you need to make your life complete. It's all inside you and it's only you that can do that, only you, Teresa, only you.'

Chapter 24
Only You

Upon your life there is a weighty scourge
Battered rocks on a windy shore,
Troubles queuing at your door.
Crying remains in crushed cars,
Bottles smashed in brawling bars.
Bloated hunger pangs in warring countries,
Dying children no one sees.
You are stumbling into your day
And braving your night
There is an abundance of magic out of your sight.
Your candlelight flickers in a typhoon of melancholy
There is no rescue party coming to set you free.
Look into your mirror and discover your saviour
The hero that will bludgeon the enemies
And beautifully colour your behaviour.
There is no helping hand,
No friendly Samaritan to meet
Let the winds change your direction,
Let the rain drench your volition.
Only you can stand up on your own two feet.
Rejoice you have found your liberator,
Only you are the creator.
Only you can make your life complete.

'Well what do you think? Do you like it?'
'I love it, Ash. Thank you. You have such a talent for words. In a strange way this is exactly what I wanted to hear. It's so true and so obvious in my life at the moment. Ash, this is genius, thank you!'

'I'm so glad you like it, it just came to me last night. I'm sure dad puts the words into my mind.'

'Thank you. I love it. I better get on with my duties, I was almost late again this morning. See you tomorrow, Ash.'

'Bye, Teresa. I hope your head feels better tomorrow and try and be more careful, we need you here. In fact I need you here.'

Teresa walked away from Ash's bed, maintaining a forward glance as the words 'Only You', the title of Ash's latest literary offering, pounced from the lily white paper and squeezed through the gauze covered wound on her forehead.

Chink! Chink! Chink! Chink! Chink! Chink! Chink!

Seven letters weightily punched into the antique typewriter, embedded their inky shape into Teresa's befuddled head, pounding it with a thumping pain of realisation.

Her blood soaked pillow, the steam filled bathroom, the shower head gladly spraying water into the cubicle and above all the returning lapse of memory reminding her with the hefty smack of an angry, insulted palm across the face that her hero was Sitara Kai Khusa. He had woken her self-inflicted slumber and coaxed her into bed. The clarity of happenings between entering the shower and dizzily waking rushed for time in the morning was a windscreen wiper effortlessly gliding the millions of rain droplets and clearing the restricted view.

'Sleep now, Teresa. Sleep now. You need to sleep. Close your eyes and sleep and always remember you have all the power you need to make your life complete. It's all inside you and it's only you that can do that, only you, Teresa, only you.'

The landscape was visible again, Khusa's words shone through her foggy memory and yet clouded her sanity into a convoluted maze of craziness where every turn was another dead-end, with an impossibility of escaping.

'Oh my. What have you done to your head, my dear?'

Teresa returned from her meandering puzzle as the familiar voice in the corridor averted her baffled attention.

'Oh hello. It's Dee, isn't it? Ah yes, I'm afraid I had a fall in the shower. Well, it's just me, I'm such a clumsy clot. I take it you're here visiting your friend?'

'You poor thing. You really must be careful. Don't you know that people here need you? Yes, I'm here to visit my friend again. Take care, take things slowly and don't have any more accidents. See you again, Teresa.'

'I won't, Dee. Yes, see you soon. It's lovely to see you again.'

Teresa recalled Dee's words of wisdom from their inaugural meeting in the canteen;

'Absolutely everything happens for a reason, albeit the reason isn't always apparent to begin with.'

It didn't help Teresa's comprehension. Her brain was tender and nervously sat upon a ticking time-bomb, she could feel the weight and tension of its latent power. An almighty detonation moments from exploding. Teresa had registered she was a single 'tick' away from a dynamite reaction in which the ability of her brain to cope through the blast was questionable. The deadweight upon her thinking and taut pressure between her ears throbbed relentlessly as zero explanations were materialising or forthcoming. There was a missing link but it was lost in an ocean of agitated waters as Teresa's hormones gushed between desperation and crouched anxiety. The only reaction she could muster was a deep sigh and determination to get through another disorientated and obscure day, knowing that people needed her here.

Chapter 25
Detonation

Tick! Tick! BOOM!

The detonative mechanism was unstoppable and instigated the threat it had forewarned. Teresa's head smothered the inevitable destruction of a full convulsive punch to the softest and most vulnerable part of her body. Her brain. She flopped, face-first upon her bed, in which the springiness of her mattress was suppressed with the force of her cumbersome plunge. The eruptive explosion burnt the tears from her eyes. There was no crying as they were evaporated into a 'can't handle any more' vapour. The fierce combustion spread like a torched barn full of thirsty, parched hay as it scalded the living membranes of Teresa's mind. Thoughts, memories were left shrivelled and lifeless as the crescendo that caused the final and fatal tick of her time-bomb, shrouded her history and sapped the life-force of preceding episodes that had made her head their congenial home. Two words remained in the fruitless battlefield. Victorious and eminent as they rose from the ashes and carnage they had caused. Parading around Teresa's now cavernous head, they demanded attention as all before them bowed down in defeat, blemished and discredited by the almighty cannonade. The only sentence in the hulking force of the two words that Teresa could brood over was 'Absolutely everything happens for a reason, albeit the reason isn't always apparent to begin with.'

The two words stood firm and stared at Teresa from within. Glued to her eyeballs they knew the conquest to take control was complete. Teresa could not see past them. The only thing within her depleted vision were the words 'Simon Driscoll.'

The final countdown to detonation had been triggered by Ash's poem 'Only You', Teresa was following her routine with prized possessions and placing it within her bedside drawer. Detonation happened as she discovered and unsealed the forgotten brown envelope left by Simon in the same drawer, when he departed.

Intuitive Beat

Bleeding grazes, bruised wounds, blistering burns,
The forgotten lacerations of my heartfelt churns.
That traumatic moment, my immortal celestial beat
Intuition, preconception,
Divination these assurances I cannot cheat.
Douse the pain, quench the bygone, repress and bury
My destiny is hollering, deafening me with its resolve
And overwhelming my vision.
From this ultimate palpitation
To my consecrated collision
My breath is interrupted, my days are suspended
Life is circumvented until my forewarning has ended.

'I simply couldn't breathe. All my dynamic living senses were concentrated into a compelling gut-reaction and in the face of that authority I had no right or probability as a human-being to resist my enduring sixth-sense. The commanding dominance funnelled one hundred percent of my intellectual transmissions into taking the only computable action that was going to settle my demented heart. Silenced was my mind, there was simply no competition as my heart destroyed it into total submission. David had cutely and stealthily floored the giant in the past but today, long before he managed to develop his slinking strategy, Goliath thumped down his behemoth foot and crushed David into oblivion and audaciously slugged forward with his tunnelled, single vision. I have no alternative plan, no big idea to change my mind. I have to pursue my heart with an unrelenting passion, otherwise my heart will simply wither away and die a fruitless death. Hearts are to be followed fervidly. Intuition, the selfish, fiendish and irresistible stimulus is the narcotised sign post, directing the infrastructure of life itself. Goodbye common-sense and learned behaviour, you have served me well and consistently slung me a helping hand when I've been drowning and remorselessly shone as my beacon of goodness and command but intuition collaborating with my heart, is greater than all the combined firepower in the world, an invincible titan, crushing the bones of education and sound judgement.'

2am and Teresa's steadfastness was in tatters. 'Intuitive Beat' pulverised her resolve in the only way that 'Make my World Complete', without fail, always managed. The cyclopean giant stamped with little procrastination upon her insignificant David-like thoughts and continued to heinously squelch any murmurs against the clarity of her innate perception. 'I don't know how you do it but I appreciate you do. I know you watch over me, even though I probably don't deserve a guardian angel but that's exactly what you are, Mr Sitara Kai Khusa, you are my guardian angel. Thank you for once again pointing your words in my direction, so that they may direct my life. Please don't ever stop your wonderful guidance!'

One more read of 'Intuitive Beat' and Teresa galloped out of her home and started a journey she would not have imagined in her scariest and most bizarre nightmares.

Chapter 26
Limitless Love

You have me bound with bone-crushing ropes.
You have enlightened me with undying hopes
No movement, no power, resistance is futile.
My broken pieces are glued into infinity
You've travelled so far, even an extra mile.
Hypnotised and bewildered, I've fallen from a height
Still floating above the ground, I will never fight
For this is a gift, an eternal shift,
This is limitless love stitched into my life-force
And you are the cause.

Emotions strong and thick as old twisted rope bundled her together and chaffed against her skin, squeezing together the rips and slashes from past belittling encounters. Hope gushed and gathered as gallons of water flowing into a reservoir for the future, the necessary sustenance through potential days of arid drought and dryness. The segments of disorientated and mismatched jigsaw pieces melted into a mesmerising landscape of stunning sunsets, sunny green pastures and glimmering, sparkling seas, a picture of perfection with no joints, just one distinct icon of staggering, irradiated art. Teresa was uplifted, lighter than air, wallowing in the clouds and peering down at the world with a more superior and positive vision than she had ever been blessed with.

'But I actually raped you. Abused your body while you were knocked out, if anything I deserve to be in a police cell. I deserve to get the beating of a lifetime. There isn't an excuse in creation that makes my behaviour acceptable.'

'I know, Simon. I know what you did. I know how I felt about what happened but I also know I want to forgive you and start again, even though I would never have thought a third time was ever possible.'

'I cannot live with what I did to you. I have even contemplated suicide because I know how wrong I was to hurt you in such an evil way. I understand how you feel but Teresa, you need to know, it doesn't change anything for me. I am an evil, cruel bastard and nothing can change that. I am what I am. You do not deserve scum like me, you deserve someone proper and decent, not someone that raped and hurt you!'

'Simon, I came here because I knew I was doing the right thing. We are simply destined to be together. We can sort this out and be happy forever, I just know we can. No one has ever made me feel the way you do. No one has ever made me feel so fantastic. I know deep down I love you and I also know you love me too. It doesn't matter what happened we can sort this out. We have to because I cannot be with anyone else.'

'Look! See these pills. They are sleeping pills, the strongest ones on the market. See that bottle of vodka. That was my destiny, that's what I had planned tonight. My final cocktail. All these pills and all that vodka and if you don't believe me here's the goodbye letter I wrote to you. Here read it!'

Dear Teresa

I am now somewhere where I can no longer be harmful to anyone, somewhere where I should be getting the judgement I deserve. The world is now a better place without me in it.

After the way I behaved, I knew there was no way back into your life and I knew life wasn't worth living without you. I don't want forgiveness and I don't want any sympathy, I am a pathetic example of a human being and a disgrace to the goodwill of God and the people within his world. Goodbye, Teresa. You were the only light in my life and I will love you eternally.

Simon.

'Don't cry, Teresa. You've shed enough tears for me. I just wanted you to know. I think it's time to leave now. Turn your back on me and never, ever look back.'

'I'm not going, Simon. I'm not leaving without you! You belong in my life. We belong together. We need each other more than ever. We are one and we will get through this together as one!'

'I'm not going to tell you again Teresa! You need to leave! Please leave. This is hard enough as it is, without making you suffer more. You deserve better than Simon Driscoll! Now please turn your back on me and go and live a happy life. Forget about this unworthy rapist!'

'So you want me to go? You really want me to go so you can take your own life. The only way I'm going to leave is with you by my side. If you're not coming, then I'm not going either. We will both end it here, we will both take our lives. It's your choice come with me or let's say goodbye together, forever!'

'Is this all a game to you, Teresa?! Do you think that's the solution? Do you think that's acceptable? Now go, before I throw you out!'

'No! It's not a game, Simon! I mean it. One way or another we are leaving tonight. In life or death, we are leaving. I'll show you who's playing a game. I am willing to die with you right now, if you don't leave with me and come home!'

'You'll have to do just that, Teresa, because I cannot have you living with the man that callously raped you and left you choked on the floor. I'm not coming and that is final. Either you go or you carry out your threat. Whatever happens I am not letting the woman I love live with the man she should hate forever!'

3.30am - with a swift, fluid movement both unexpected and bizarre, Teresa grabbed the bottle of sleeping pills from the wooden shelf where Simon had put them back, unscrewed the jolty lid and rattled a mouthful of pills past her teeth and into her throat, Three of the feisty little contenders swam down into her gullet, excitedly anticipating the sleep they were going to induce, the other three stubbornly sat on her tongue and she spluttered them into her hand as the bitter taste rapidly dissolved.

'You stupid woman! Give me those pills! What on earth is wrong with you? Give me the pills right now!'

Simon angrily snatched the bottle from Teresa's grip as the three successfully deployed sleeping pills arrived in Teresa's adrenalin filled acidic stomach and surveyed their new surroundings, mischievously contemplating the work they were intended for. Deep sleep. They had never travelled in a threesome before, life was usually about being solo but this project seemed to be very different, unique and interesting, as they started to rapidly disintegrate and filter into Teresa's blood, knowing they will be on a one way journey to her brain.

'I told you I would. I will take these three in my hand too, if you don't come with me and let me look after you. I love you, Simon. We will get through this. You are forgiven for what happened, it wasn't your fault. You weren't really being yourself. I can forgive you. I already have. Now please come with me or I'm going to die right here, right now! I will love you forever and together we will get through this and have the life we both want, in each other's arms.'

'I give in! I do love you and if you have really forgiven me, I know this will work out. I never ever wanted to leave you but I knew life wasn't worth living if I couldn't have you. I've been so miserable with everything that has happened that I simply lost hope. There was nothing left for me in life and I know I didn't actually deserve anything either. One way or another I was going to die, so I just thought today would be the day. I don't believe it, you have already saved my life by coming here tonight. You've already saved me, Teresa. You really are my eternal angel. I don't know what I've ever done to deserve you.'

'Don't cry my love. Don't cry, Simon. We will get through this. I will get you through this. I always knew you were the love of my life, the only one I wanted, the only man for me. We will get through this and one day we will look back and smile at what we did.'

Tears flowed together mingling in their saltiness as the entwined bodies became a singular twisted mass of anarchic passion. Clothes were flung around the room as two people on the edge of destruction realised the essence of life existed when their fluids mixed into one explosive concoction and they blissfully drifted into a sexual haven of togetherness.

Chapter 27
Drowning

Deliciously smitten green. Sparkling with delight
Abandon ship. My senses drenched.
Crushing the fright.
Ripples of sultry euphoria embrace my skin
I have no volition. Hypnotised, I'm overboard.
I've dived right in.
Swimming deep in your eyes.
I'm adrift, bewildered and mesmerised.
Captivated, enticed, bewitched.
Saturated by your allure. This is my cure.
I'm drowning. Breathless. Deluged.
Hankering for more.
Relentlessly floating in your endless ocean.
I'm reluctant to touch the floor.
I cannot fathom tomorrow,
While today is through your sight.
I don't want salvaging. No rescue operation.
Nor liberating fight.
Deeper and deeper. I'm fervently falling
Breathing in your velvety waters. This is my calling.

'That's beautiful, thank you. I love that book. What time is it? I need to get home and get into work.'

Simon's recital from 'Make my World Complete' whilst sat on the edge of his bed, stirred Teresa into the magical five seconds of waking life when the scattered pieces of reality lay dishevelled. 'Morning sweetness, it's only seven. I didn't realise you had to go into work today, otherwise I would have woken you sooner but you were so blissfully asleep, I just didn't want to disturb you.'

'That's fine, Simon. There's more than enough time, thank you for waking me, I could have slept forever. I'm not in work till nine today. More than enough time to get home and still be on time.'

'That's good. I just wanted to gently wake you with a poem from your favourite book, particularly as you have green eyes too. I didn't know you did night shifts at work.'

5, 4, 3, 2, 1, Teresa's magical five seconds collided full speed into a juggernaut as her scattering of reality rushed around the room and forced a picture as she jumped out of bed with a synchronised heart attack through her pounding chest.

'It's the evening! Fucking hell! I've slept all day. How the hell did that happen?! Why the fuck didn't you wake me up?! How did I manage to sleep all through the entire day? I don't believe this is happening! I just don't believe it! When is my life ever going to get any better?!'

'Stop screaming, Teresa. You really need to calm down. I tried waking you but with three sleeping tablets inside you, you were completely dead to the world. It was impossible to wake you up! I really did try but those tablets are industry strength.'

'Fuck! I forgot about those. I can't, I cannot stop screaming. There will be hell to pay at work, Sommers will not let me off lightly for this. I am fucking doomed! This is it, there is no way round this. I have missed a complete day at work and not even an explanation. He will go mad. There is just no possible way I can explain this. He will not accept anything. I'm done for. I have finally drowned!'

'I'm so sorry, Teresa. It's all my stupid fault. If it hadn't been for my pathetic life this would not have happened. I'm a failure and I've failed you yet again. I actually need drowning because however it happens I cannot stop ruining your life.'

'Don't be stupid, Simon! Dry your bloody eyes. This is not your fault in the least. I'm a qualified nurse, I should have known better than take those stupid tablets. It fucking serves me right for being so ridiculous and dramatic. I guess I need to put things into perspective. It's only a job and nothing compares to what you're going through. Who cares? We'll just have to see what happens in the morning. I will have to take this one on the chin and anyway, everything always happens for a reason.'

Chapter 28
Besieged

Blood, heartbeat, thoughts, my normality fought,
Conquered, overruled, commissioned.
Shamelessly caught.
Romeo did that stare, his realisation
Of the ambrosial snare
From humdrum tranquillity,
To inescapable vulnerability.
Juliet his weakness, his wanton fragility.
An audacious aggression, beaming with little heed,
Planting life's eternal, adorable seed.
Unrepeatable, unconditional, the latent force.
This is love and its true spine-tingling course.
That exquisite second, that gripping moment,
That thrilling day,
Love's abusive virtue,
Whisked in a whirlwind far, far away.
The past has been trashed,
The future has been besieged,
Emotions brawling, time crawling,
Involuntarily falling.
This is love. This is utopia. This is dreamland calling.

Even the latest literary offering from Ash posted to her pigeon hole could not blow away the grey clouds colluding to submerge any uplifting kindling of Teresa's already dampened nerve. She shuffled the poem into her handbag and reluctantly walked the death march to her line manager's office, anticipating his utmost wrath.

'Well, well, well. We certainly weren't expecting you back!'

Dr Sommers barely raised his eyes from the paperwork upon his desk as Teresa stood in the doorway of the office she had begun to dread, as every conversation that happened in this authoritarian cubicle seemed to drag her career backwards.

'I can explain, Dr Sommers. I really can. I've had a nightmare. I'm so sorry. I promise it'll never happen again. I promise you with all I have, it'll never, ever happen again.'

Dr Sommers looked craggier than before, the weather ravaged, battered rocks on his seashore face, creased and contorted with each disinterested word that emanated from his mouth. 'Teresa, I do not want or need an explanation. Save it for your hearing. You are officially suspended from all duties at Teers Hospital until further notice. Furthermore you are forbidden to make any contact with the patients at this hospital, until a conclusion of your gross misconduct has been reached by the disciplinary board.'

Dr Sommers' words echoed around his office, ricocheting off the performance chart emblazoned walls before locating their target and piercing through Teresa's head, forcefully puncturing her already vulnerable waterworks. A waterfall deluge sprung from her eyes as disconnected words rambled and spluttered from her mouth.

'No! No! No! I beg you, Dr Sommers. It will never happen again. I need to be here for my patients, I need to be here for Ash. You can't do this to me. I was drugged on sleeping tablets. I slept through the day. I didn't know what I was doing. I cannot be held responsible for being in a sleeping coma. Please, Dr Sommers. Please try to understand. Please understand I was in a state of overdose, I didn't know what was happening! I didn't wake up till the evening. Ash needs me, I'm the only one that can look after him. This is ridiculous. You cannot do this to me. You just cannot do this to me. I need to be here. Please, Dr Sommers, I need to be here!'

'Teresa! Will you please pull yourself together and leave the building now! You have just admitted to having a sleeping tablet overdose as the reason you were absent for a whole day. You are not helping your case! Please leave now! As for Ash, he has become increasingly volatile, your absence yesterday did not help and he spent the whole day talking to himself at times disturbing the other patients. I am having him transferred to an institute where they can help him with his deteriorating mental condition, we can no longer be of service to him at Teers. Now goodbye Teresa, please leave the building and we will notify you of your disciplinary hearing in due course.'

Dr Sommers' damning sentence savagely rammed the remaining wall in Teresa's barricade as it pounded her already adrenalin besieged stomach. The malefic crush to her abdomen sucked her tears back into her face instantly drying her dripping eyes and crunched her words into incomprehensible rubble. Her landscape was barren, with the bleached bones of past victories callously strewn, jutting sharply from the ground. Deathly, tortured nothingness was all that remained. No words. Dr Sommers refocused on his paperwork. Teresa turned around and subconsciously marched, against the protocol Dr Sommers had just articulated, towards the only direction her stomping feet and her sentiments could carry her. Directly to Ash.

'Hello dear, Ash was just telling me before he nodded off, all about you. He's just told me he wrote you a poem. How charming.'

Leaning over Ash's inclined bed was the friendly, enchanting Dee. Teresa's disconcerted brain didn't have a moment to compute, that Ash was the patient Dee regularly visited the hospital for.

'Are you okay, dear? You look like you've had a bad morning already. Do you need to see young Ash? Do you want me to leave? I'm sure he will soon wake. He just had a very restless night and was feeling really tired.'

'Dee, I had no idea you knew Ash. No, I'm not okay. I'm far from fucking okay. I'm in hell and I just don't know how to escape it and this time Dee, I cannot and will not be able to work out the reason why. There is no reason why. It's just me, it's just my life. I'm a walking disaster. That is the only reason why I can think of.'

An amiable person, the despairing thought of Ash being sent to an asylum, the distinct possibility of her nursing career coming to a brusque end, was a gutsy medley to spark Teresa's unrestrainable and frantic crying.

'Now, now my dear. Stop that crying and tell me all about it. You can't do that here. Let's go elsewhere. I'm certain we can work it out. I'm a good friend of Ash's and I will do anything for the people he cares about and for you dear, well for you, he has a huge soft spot.'

Chapter 29
Dee

'This is a lovely restaurant. Let's get coffee and you can tell me what's been going on. I already know you're a wonderful person and that's aside from the affection Ash has for you. As I said at the hospital, I will do anything for the people Ash cares about, absolutely anything.'

Le Petit Rouge. Ravaged by the plethora of emotions secretly embedded within its walls. Memories created. Promises forged. Differences expressed and futures formed. Teresa's weary head barely recollected her last liaison in the French bistro. The reluctant fall of Napoleon Bonaparte and the reclamation of her clandestine passion and basic need for emotional and intimate fulfilment.

'My world has just fallen apart, Dee. There is nothing you can do. Everything I have touched has turned to shit. I don't know how I can continue. I don't know what I can do. I literally have nothing left.'

'Teresa, there is always a way. There is always another door just waiting to be opened. You can't always see it but it is there. I can help you find the door. I can help you open the door and I will be waiting on the other side to welcome you into your renewed world. Here, take my handkerchief and wipe your tears and let's work this out. I know we can do it.'

The perfectly crumpled white cotton willingly soaked up the despair from Teresa's eyes and wafted its soothing floral aroma into her body. Blooming, spring fields in the hazy mid-morning sun, a sense of comfort in a broken, hectic world.

'But Dee, I'm about to lose my job, my career will then be doomed. The patient that I pledged to help is about to be committed and I have a partner that is terminally ill. I just don't know what else can go wrong.'

The handkerchief reached sodden breaking point as the torrent of saltiness drowned its delicately woven fibres.

'Your career will not be doomed. I'm sure you will get through this episode at work. Whatever happens with Ash, I'm here to help, I will not give up on him, his life means more to me that you can ever imagine and as for Simon, I'm convinced he will get through this and will recover.'

Every white thread rejoiced as Teresa's tears froze and shuddered with anticipation as they cowered behind her next blink. Lines of confusion spread across her forehead, eagerly awaiting the question poised on the tip of her tongue.

'How do you know Simon's name? I've never mentioned his name.'

'You're right, my dear. You have never mentioned his name but Ash has. Ash told me all about Simon and his health issues.'

'I'm really confused, Dee. I've not mentioned Simon's problem to anyone, not even Ash. How could he possibly know?'

'Well, my dear. Ash has a very special talent, a talent that makes him look insane but he is far from insane. He talks to his late father, Kai. Almost as if he is in the room at the time. It is Kai that told Ash about Simon'.

'I'm sorry Dee but I can't take this in today of all days. I cannot have Ash's delusions to worry about alongside everything else that is happening in my life. I'm sure he does have a special talent, it's just not something I can cope with at the moment but why don't you start by telling me how you know him. What's your connection with Ash?'

'Ok, my dear. My connection is very simple. I'm an old friend of his mother's, Rebecca. Our lives crossed long before Ash was born. We became very close and after she passed away I lost contact with Ash's father and then recently found out he too died, so I came looking for Ash. That's how I ended up at Teers and that's why I will help you because you're helping Ash.'

The soft embroidered wallpaper adorning the walls of Le Petite Rouge absorbed yet another unfolding drama. This particular story fed no familiarity to the usual and commonplace relationship melodramas that regularly bounced through the air of the French bistro. There were no awkward infidelity revelations, beautifully timed chemistries signalling enchanting preludes or ignoble connections disconnecting. This was a story of unyielding cliff-hangers and breath-stopping discoveries that fluently washed the ingrained anecdotes clean off the impregnated walls.

'But this will be a great help to Ash. You need to tell him your connection to his mother. It may help him mentally recover which could be the key to him staying away from an institute that will do nothing but wreck his poor life even more!'

'I'm sorry, my dear. I made a pledge to Rebecca that I would never reveal our past to her son. He knows we were friends but he does not know to what degree. He can never know the truth behind his mother. The truth will not set him free. The truth will do nothing but damage him. I will tell you the story one day but it's suffice to say Ash's mother was the most amazing woman to have ever lived and she certainly changed the course of my life for the better.'

'I don't know what to say, Dee, I just thought it might help him. I really want to do whatever I can to make sure he doesn't suffer anymore, he doesn't deserve the pain he is going through and then have the threat of an institute. Dee, they will just lock him up and throw away the key. His life will end!'

'You need to understand, my dear. You are the key to his recovery. You are the only one that can set him free. You are the only one that can help him recover. You are the only one that can bring Ash back from the darkness he is in. If he knows you are happy that will help him. His recent volatility has all been centred around you and the fact that he is convinced your heart will break and your life is in dangerous turmoil.'

'I'm sorry, Dee, that does not make any sense to me. I am happy! Or at least I was until I was suspended this morning, until I had my life thrown into disarray. Simon isn't too well, that doesn't help but at least we're together now and I've made the right decision after a few rocky weeks with him and I will do all I can to help him through his sad episode in life.'

'What's actually the matter with Simon? What's happened to him?'

'It's hard to explain, Dee, so read for yourself. I'm sure he won't mind you reading his letter. Our relationship had ended for one reason or another. He had left me two letters but only told me to open this one if I wanted an explanation behind his behaviour. I opened it. We got back together two days ago and I promised myself, like I did with Ash, that I would nurse him back to health.'

Dear Teresa,

At least I now know you care enough about us to open this second letter. It doesn't mean you will understand but at least it gives me the chance to explain why I am so broken, volatile and unreasonable. Ultimately, it's still no justification for the things I have done but you will know why I haven't really been myself lately. I came looking for you because I realised life is just too short and that the things deemed important enough are always worth pursuing before it's too late. Six months ago, after weeks of unbearable stomach pains, I finally went to the doctor who subsequently sent me for a scan at Walton Hospital. The scan revealed ulceration of the stomach, painful bleeding wounds probably caused by intolerance to alcohol and spicy foods plus the agonising stress of losing you, the love of my life. After a month of medication, there was very little improvement, with the added discomfort and pain of persistent vomiting. I was sent for another scan in the Oncology unit at Walton Hospital and they gave me the worst news of my life. I have a malignant tumour the size of a pound coin in the pit of my stomach, near my colon.

Since then I've had treatment for it because it was discovered soon enough. Any later, then I wouldn't be alive to tell the tale now. I'm far from fixed. I'm booked for an operation at Walton because it has to be removed considering it continues to grow at a rapid speed. There is only a 40% chance that I will be rid of this cancer, therefore God only knows the days of life I have been granted. The medication I have to take eight times during the day has obscene side-effects from dizziness and sickness to depression and aggression. I didn't want to worry you so I saved the conversation about my tumour, until it was time for the operation, I now wish I'd told you sooner. I guess, I've been praying and living for a miracle to happen, to rid me of this horrendous nightmare I've been living with. It's made me into a bitter, twisted wreck. You have been the only sunshine to shine upon my life since the day I was thrown into hell with this never-ending pain and solitude. I don't expect anything to change between us because I've gone and you will never see me again. My only hope is that this letter has helped you realise I wasn't as evil as I seemed.

You made my world complete.

Simon.

'You poor dear. My dear, dear Teresa. I am so sorry to hear about this. No one deserves to suffer this way. I'm not sure how you even cope and what must be going through your mind. I know you will need all the support you can get. I am willing to, actually let me correct that, I will support you through this ordeal.'

Whoosh! The breakneck spinning of the lathe modelled a new creation at the expert hands of the operator. A block of unfashionable wood, speedily transforming into a delightful carving of solid substance, indistinguishable from the original, mundane lump that existed only minutes ago. A relationship sculpted from insignificance. An enchanting stranger unexpectedly etched into a presence and entwined into Teresa's cumbersome burdens, lifting a proportion of the deadweight that was attempting to crush her. A large helium filled balloon tied to her problems, separating them from her heart and mind, even if only for an inch of breathing space.

'I'm not sure why, Dee, considering I barely know you but I feel like I do, so thank you for your offer of support, I will welcome it with open arms. I'm not sure how I will cope but somehow I know you will be there for me. I just know it, Dee. I just do. So, thank you.'

'Some things, my dear, are simply meant to be, they are designed that way, already destined and already defined. In the same way Rebecca lifted my life, I'm now here helping to lift yours as a direct consequence of your association with Ash. Rebecca would be thrilled with this outcome. I already know how important you are to Ash, so being here for you will also help him.'

Chapter 30
Broken

At the deepest depth. My lowest ebb.
The floodgates are agape.
My head is above water.
There is lead around my ankles. Incapable of escape.
Every inhale and my lungs fill with liquid,
I'm cold. I'm sinking.
Eyes wide open. The sun is on my face.
My shackles are clinking.
Dragging me down as my life peers beyond,
Irreparable thinking.
Broken. Damaged. Soiled.
My belief in me is shattered,
Birth was a conundrum, days were a burden
But the future mattered.
I can't fight the fight that was burning inside me.
So desperate and damp
I gave it the shot of heroes, I battled on.
There was no greater champ.
Abide my time. Endure the test.
Smash in the face, I lost the race.
Built into my destiny, my crowning fate.
A damned locked gate.
I have no key, no force of mind,
My courage has fainted.
My impending life is tainted.
You cannot help me, you cannot lift me.
You just came too late.

Khusa's tortured life echoed in Teresa's broken thoughts. She was scattered, adrift, meandering from desperation to hope but 'Make my World Complete' glued her garbled thinking into stern boldness as the anger of being suspended from her job fuelled resolutions to create a brighter future and become the best nurse she could possibly be. Deep inside she also realised she was broken apart with dilemma after dilemma. All roads concluded with the same destination, the same torrid finale. All of Teresa's hopes and aspirations were clinging on with their fingertips to not losing her job. Teers Hospital was the linchpin of hopefulness and it was totally uncontrollable, there was little Teresa could now do to influence the stormy challenge on her weather-worn doorstep. Her head momentarily bobbed above water, albeit the drag of her weighted ankles and the forceful current below the surface was gathering an uneasy momentum, rocking her willpower. Helplessly, she searched Khusa's words for encouragement, for essential breaths of oxygen to push the gushing fluid filling her organs with despondency.

'You literally never put that book down do you? You read it day and night.'

'Simon. It speaks loud to me. It gives me direction. It has a power that I cannot explain. From the clarity it gives me now, through the lows I'm going through, to knowing it was the right thing to do to bring you back home. This book has changed my views on life a number of times. I can't begin to understand the power it holds over my days. It has a grip on me that I know I need and I know I can't do without. Sometimes I read it over and over again to give me the strength and belief in myself.'

'So, if it wasn't for that book I might not be here with you now. I guess I have to be grateful for such a masterpiece that is clearly attempting to save my life and there was me thinking it was your love and compassion that asked me to return home.'

'I know you're being sarcastic, Simon. No, that is not the only reason I brought you back home, obviously your letter was the main reason. This book has persuaded me to view life differently and not be so afraid of making some decisions and understanding love a little better.'

'Oh, I see. It's made you less afraid of me and helped you understand our love better. In that case I'm definitely grateful to Mr Sitara Kai Khusa.'

'C'mon, Simon. You know what I mean. You know exactly what I mean and where I'm coming from. It's just a fantastic book and I love reading it. Can we please just leave it at that?'

'I know. I know. I'm only joking with you. By the way, who is Dawn?'

'Dawn who? I don't know who you're talking about.'

'Well you should know who Dawn is. You left her hanky on the bed. You know the white hanky on the bed, you left it there last night. It has the name Dawn embroidered into the corner. So who is she?'

The lathe spun faster. Shavings of wood were randomly being flung into the air as the beauty of carving and shaving continued to materialise into an unrecognisable showpiece.

'Teresa, what's wrong? Where are you going? Who is Dawn? What are you doing?'

Returning from the bedroom, where she had dashed upon hearing Dawn's name, Teresa was mesmerised into silence.

My dear, dear Rebecca. I have no words to express my grief that you are no longer of this world, all I can say is without you, my world would have died before it had even started. You were my only angel. My only saviour and simply the only person alive that I would have gladly given my life for. You will forever be my heroine and I will die a happy woman, knowing that I once had the greatest person alive in my life. You allowed me to breathe. You gave me hope. All my love forever.
Goodbye Rebecca.
Dawn.

The ornate carving had been created. The lathe came to a halt and there it was in all its splendour ready to adorn life and give pleasure to any eyes prepared to look upon its delicate beauty. 'Dee' was no more than the letter 'D', an acronym for Dawn. The convoluted puzzle of the Khusa household had suddenly become more intriguing and yet clearer than before.

'Are you, anytime soon, going to tell me what is going on? Who is Dawn? What's that piece of paper you're clutching? And what's with the look on your face?'

'Simon, it's Dee. I mean it's Dawn. Dee is Dawn. It's just too much to explain but Dee isn't just Dee. Dee is Dawn, the very Dawn in Rebecca's eulogy. Rebecca is Ash's mother and Khusa is Ash's father. All these people are connected. It's no wonder Dawn is so close to Ash.'

'I've no idea what you're rambling on about but I do know it's the happiest I've seen you look in days. Teresa, I don't feel very well. My illness is going to be the end of me, I just need to rest. Maybe, you can explain what you're bleating on about tomorrow. I don't have the patience today. My life feels broken apart, so I can't concentrate on what you're so excited about. Sorry, Teresa. Goodnight.'

Chapter 31
From Dawn to Dusk

Beginnings conjuring the chain reaction of reluctant endings, ignorantly blissful that metamorphosis is imminent. Never quite grasping the conclusions that will be reached. There is change or there is finality, either way a beginning is an expiration in waiting. Human existence, the culmination of daylight. The pattern of the glowing sun, alive and breathing fire, so fresh and vibrant but always knowing the end is a matter of hours away. Death awaits on the doorstep, only to rise again and bring with it an altered universe, creating new patterns, another temporary incandescence. The commencement of the untidy rigmarole. The cycle of threatening death. Unwavering resolve, a daylight that has a secret. A powerful forceful secret that will never divulge the minutes, hours, days that are left on the ever-ticking clock. Teresa remained dumbstruck by her accidental discovery, the informality that Dawn always had in her eyes. The affection of her gestures. The sympathetic tones in her voice and the luscious lining of their developing warmth, embodied with the laureate words 'absolutely everything happens for a reason, albeit the reason isn't always apparent to begin with.'

Dawn was an adrenalin boost into Teresa's cowering bloodstream, an embracement of the gratifying affirmation that everything happens for a reason. No reason was apparent but for Teresa it wasn't necessary, a flaming approval at the forefront of her brain signalled the optimism of meeting Dawn, an abundance of reasons were tentatively awaiting to make themselves known, it was clearly a matter of time.

'Are you sure you don't want me to come with you, Simon?'

'It's fine, darling. Some things one just needs to do alone. It's only a routine hospital visit, I'll be back in no time'

'I feel so helpless. Even Dawn has offered her support. I know together we can all get through this. You've just got to let me in to help you through this, this is your fourth visit this week and I really want to be here for you.'

'Ha, ha, ha, Dawn as well. I'd love to meet her. Two nurses together, what a treat that will be. Seriously, I can do this. I just don't want you to see me going through all this. You're already a massive support. You are here for me, that's what's getting me through. You really have become my rock, I hope you understand that?'

'I do understand, Simon, I really do. By the way, how do you know Dawn is a nurse?'

'Oh! I'm so sorry, darling. She called on Monday, I forgot to tell you. You know how my medication affects my memory. You were asleep, so we had a little chat, its then she told me she was once a nurse. She sounds like a lovely, charming woman.'

'Simon! That was three days ago. You know how important Dawn is to me. I can't believe you forgot to tell me!'

'I'm sorry, Teresa. I've had a lot on my mind and on Tuesday morning I went to hospital before you even woke and by the time I returned, brimming with the disgusting potion they inject me with, it had completely skipped my mind. I'm really sorry. She did say she would call you back.'

'Ah it doesn't matter. I know you're going through a lot at the moment. I'll call her back today. Good luck at the hospital, can't wait to see you later.'

The injection of concentrated adrenalin rushed through Teresa's body with sparkling delight turning her blood into a fevered stream of bubbling champagne, tingling her veins with its effervescence whilst intoxicating her with its potent alcohol. She was exhilarated that Dawn had called and excitedly snatched her phone from the coffee table to return the call.

'Hello Dawn, I hope this message finds you well and happy. It's Teresa returning your call. I'm so sorry it's taken me until Thursday to ring you. Typical, useless man but Simon only remembered this morning, albeit his medicine hasn't helped his memory. I've been dying to speak with you all week after making an excited discovery on Sunday. Please call back whenever you can.'

Five minutes of anticipation passed. Teresa was pondering how to pose the obvious question to Dawn.

'Tell me about your eulogy to Rebecca.'

'What did Rebecca do for you that made you write such a touching tribute?'

'What was Ash's mother like and where did the two of you meet?'

'Why was Rebecca so important to you?'

The urge to know the story was blossoming with each moment that passed, adding to the drunkenness of the flowing chemicals lightening the density of her blood.

The phone screen lit up. Teresa didn't wait long enough to capture her own childlike excitement at seeing Dawn's name resonate and flash begging to be answered.

'Hello Dawn. I'm so glad you've called back. I really wanted to speak with you. How are you?'

'Hello, is that Teresa?'

'Yes it is. Is that Dawn? It doesn't sound like you on the phone.'

'Hi Teresa. It isn't Dawn. This is PC Trevlock. I'm afraid I have some sad news. I'm afraid Dawn passed away yesterday. I'm sorry to have to be the one that has to break the news to you.'

'This can't be true. Is this some kind of sick joke? Who is this? Where's Dawn? This isn't funny! Can you please put Dawn on?'

'I'm sorry, Teresa. It isn't a joke. This is PC Trevlock. Dawn has died and as you're one of the recent people she was in contact with, we would like to ask you a few questions. Can we visit you at home?'

'Yes, yes, yes! Of course you can. This is awful news. How on earth did she die? What on earth happened to the poor woman?'

'I'm sorry, Teresa. I cannot discuss this over the phone. We will visit you now, if that's convenient to you'

'Yes, yes that's fine. I just don't know what to say. I'm totally devastated!'

'I understand, Teresa. See you later.'

The amber glistening champagne turned to pallid white salt sludge clogging Teresa's arteries as another chapter of her twisted life burnt right off the page, leaving her in a smoky, haze of disbelief.

'Death has enriched my crippled days into life
My melodrama has been halted
From an existence utterly faulted.
Peace in the sky, another twinkling star,
Happiness that once seemed so far.

135

Nightfall has crept into my little worth.
Daylight pushed aside from my birth.
Goodbye melancholy and anguish,
You had no charm only harm without a wish.
Hello darkness and truth,
You are my trusting bedfellows,
My macabre youth.'

'Make my World Complete' was the only door yielding comfort for Teresa. Little else made any sense. There was no reasoning behind Dawn's death as her words haunted Teresa's garbled thoughts.

'Absolutely everything happens for a reason, albeit the reason isn't always apparent to begin with.'

'She always used to repeat that phrase like a mantra. It was her belief but there just cannot be any reason to die. Simon, I can't believe she has gone. Disappeared just like that!'

'These things happen. I'm sorry but you hardly knew her. You have no idea what her life was all about. Didn't the police say how she died? What was the cause of her death?'

'I know that but I really liked her. I felt stronger knowing I had her in my corner. No, they just said they were investigating her death but they wouldn't say how she died'

'What did they want to know then? Don't worry my darling, you have me in your corner and I will not let you down. I will always stay in your corner forever. You need to move on. I'm afraid you didn't know Dawn. Maybe she was ill herself. Maybe, that's how she died, through some terminal illness that you just didn't know about.'

'They wanted to know about the relationship I had with her and what I knew about her. They also mentioned she was once a nurse at Walton Hospital.'

'Hardly surprising, Teresa. It's the biggest hospital in the county. I don't suppose there was that much to tell them, considering you hardly knew her.'

'There wasn't, Simon. It's just been a very sad day. I just know she was going to be good for me. Good for us and now she's gone. I will never see her again.'

'I guess we'll never know, Teresa. I guess we will never know the truth. We will never know who Dawn really was or how she could have helped us but one thing I am sure of, using Dawn's own words, if everything does happen for a reason, then it's a big reason that she is no longer here and a reason why we didn't need her in our lives. I don't want to sound harsh on such a sad day but we clearly didn't need her, that's the reason, right there, we did not need her, we will do just fine on our own, you just watch and see, Teresa, just watch and see.'

Chapter 32
The Mire

Trudging through the viscous darkness,
There is a weakness in my stubborn knees
Grinding to a halt as
My weary bones crunch in desperation
My battered senses, bemused in sedation.
There are no clouds because there is no light,
Nothing to see, nothing to feel. Nothing to fight.
Isolation in abundance.
An unceremonious, deadly plight.
The roadblock is here, my journey has ended,
No more reasons, goodbye all you beautiful seasons.
I am stuck, weakened by the sludge, this putrid mire,
My burdensome days all so utterly dire.
Here I'll wait, with no more life to create.
My only solace, the breath I no longer want to take,
Is a dedicated whisper away
from giving me a break.

'That's lovely, Ash. Thank you. You have a real talent for words. Do you mind if I take it with me? I want to show your amazing words to the other doctors, to see what they think.'

'Of course you can. I know what they will say. I know what they want to do. I know you all think I'm crazy and I know you want to lock me away. When's Teresa returning? When's my Teresa returning? I want to know when she is coming back. I know you're going to send me away. I need my Teresa!'

'We're not sending you away. We don't believe you are crazy. I'm sure the doctors will love your words and be very impressed with you, why wouldn't they be?'

'Why wouldn't they be!? Why wouldn't they be!? Because you all hate me! I'm a burden to you! You don't want me here! You think I'm mad! When is my Teresa coming back? Why won't you tell me when Teresa is coming back? I demand to know when my nurse is returning!'

'Ash, you are not a burden, we don't hate you. Now stop being so silly. Of course we want you here.'

'Why won't you tell me about Teresa!? Please tell me about Teresa! Tell me about Teresa! Tell me about Teresa! I want you to stop being a bitch and just tell me. Just tell me when Teresa is coming back! I want to know! I want to know now!'

'Don't you dare speak to my nurse in that manner!'

Dr Sommers' usually heavy footsteps had gone unnoticed as he sauntered into the ward during his morning jaunt through the hospital.

'Now, what's the commotion? If you calm down I will answer your questions. What do you want to know?'

'She was being a bitch to me! She won't tell me when Teresa is returning! If she's a bitch to me, I will speak how I want to!'

'Ash! I will ask you politely to stop referring to my nurse in that way. She is only doing her job. She does not know when Teresa is returning.'

'Well who knows then?! Someone must know. Surely, someone can tell me when my Teresa is returning!'

'Actually, Ash, I know when she is returning. I can tell you when she is coming back but I'm only going to tell you if you lower your voice and ask politely.'

'Just tell me! Just tell me! Just tell me! Just tell me! Please! Please! Please! Please! Tell me! Tell me when Teresa is coming back!'

'Ok Ash. As you politely said please. I will tell you when Teresa is coming back. The answer is Ash, she isn't coming back. She isn't returning to Teers Hospital Ash. Teresa is not coming back. Not now. Not ever. That's the end of it Ash. There's nothing else to be said.'

Dr Sommers smiled at the nurse as his black polished shoe squeaked on the vinyl floor whilst pirouetting in a semi-circle towards the door.

'You bastard! You bastard! You've got rid of her haven't you! You little bastard. You did that. You got rid of the best nurse in this pathetic hospital!'

A semi-second ticked past as Dr Sommers reversed his rotation, in disgust at the blasphemous outburst. Simultaneously Ash, using the power of his arms and upper torso, powerfully pressed into the firm mattress and literally bounced upwards, rebelliously lunging forward, towards the unsuspecting doctor, who, with Ash's weight crashing into him, stumbled and fell on his back to the floor. Ash grabbed Dr Sommer's grey tweed lapels as he scaled his body, dragging himself on top of the doctor, until his face was level with the doctor's shoulders.

Anger and resentment, further fuelled by the smugness of Dr Sommers's wry smile to the nurse, catalysed the dormant exasperation slumbering within Ash's embittered blood, fizzing it into a raucous melody of impulses, which overpowered any logical thoughts he had left within his disheartened life. His quivering hands, powered by the effervescence electrifying his blood, circled Dr Sommers's neck, and with an almighty whoosh rocketing through his veins they squeezed his oesophagus as indifferent rage, spluttered the same sentence through is grinding teeth.

'Die, you bastard! Die, you bastard! Die, you bastard! Die, you bastard! Die, you bastard!'

Ash's grip remain locked, as the nurse screamed and attempted to pull him from the doctor with hard clenched punches directly to his head. It was futile. The beat from the impact echoed through the fibres of his mind. He couldn't feel the force of the repeated assaults as the ferocity of his wrath vigilantly defended him against the pain.

'Stop this, Ash! Stop this, Ash! You're killing him! You're killing him! Someone please help! Someone! Help! Help us! He's killing the doctor!'

'Good! I want him to die! He has to die! He must die! Evil must die! Evil must die!'

Every growled word tightened Ash's crushing brace. Dr Sommers's brain was in red alert stage, irretrievably attempting to ration the limited supply of oxygen left in his brain. His eyes closed underneath his hatred splattered glasses.

'You need to die! You need to die! Die! Die! Die! Die!'

'Ash! Stop! Stop! Stop my son!'

Ash froze. His clamping hands loosened. The nurse continued to push and pelt him with every swipe she could muster from her delicate body.

'Dad! You're here. This man has done evil, for that he must pay. He must pay for what he did to our Teresa. Dad, he must pay! We have to do what is right for Teresa. Dad, we have to!'

'Listen to me, my son. This isn't right. Please let go of the doctor. Give me your hand. Let me hold your hand. I will hold your hand. Please let go. We cannot do this. It is time to stop.'

'Yes, Dad. Hold my hand. Don't let go.'

Ash raised his hand into the air and smiled. The nurse took the opportunity to grab his arm as hospital security ploughed into the room man-handling Ash away from the doctor and forcefully settling him down with their knees deeply embedded into his torso.

'Dad! Dad! Dad! Dad! Don't leave me. Please don't leave me. Please don't leave me!'

'I'm not leaving you, my son. I will never leave you. I will always be by your side. I will always hold your hand.'

'This will help you calm down you little shit! This will help you. Just give it a few seconds and you won't know what hit you!'

The powerful syringed sedation pierced through layers of taught skin and happily oozed into Ash's blood, dissolving his anger rush into blissful calm, emancipating his engulfing angst.

Dr Sommers choked and vomited. Dazed and holding his neck, where Ash's hands had been destined to end his life, he stumbled from the ward, muttering to himself. The nurse hurriedly followed him, leaving the scene of human downfall, stepping on Ash's poignant poem, a once desperate plea, shouting out to the world to be understood and accepted by a society that was prepared to condemn him.

Ash had slipped into the fathomless mire. A ceaseless blackness of diminishing hope. Each metallic click of the steel hand and foot restraints the security guards clamped around his wrists and ankles, weighed down the possibility of ever escaping the opaqueness shrouding his future.

'What's that there? What's that writing? That piece of paper on the floor. What is it?'

'Oh, it looks like a poem or something. Called The Mire. I wonder if this bloke wrote it. I wonder if it's his words. 'Trudging through the viscous darkness, there is a weakness in my stubborn knees. Grinding

141

to a halt as my weary bones crunch in desperation. My battered senses, bemused in sedation. There are no clouds because there is no light.'

'No don't read it! No one cares what it says. No one is interested but one thing is for sure, this dude is certainly not going to see any light where he is going! Ha! Ha! Ha! Ha! Ha! Ha!'

Chapter 33
Closing Doors

Slam! Another door firmly shut and locked. A road once so obvious and uncluttered, now impossible to pass. A vision so clear, now clouded by immovable obstacles blocking the view that seemed so beautifully visible. A peerless sky with unlimited horizons, now blighted by an ugly, hindering ceiling.

'What are we going to do, Simon? I'm all out of ideas and hope. I have no fight left inside me. No courage to keep going and not an ounce of anything that can help us through. I had everything pointing me in the right direction. Now this crossroads has appeared and I just don't know which way to turn. In fact if I'm really honest, I don't even know if I want to actually find another way. I'm just exhausted!'

'Teresa, darling, you can't ever give up. This will all pass and we will look back and laugh at it all. We will survive this and we will survive it together. You are an amazing woman, you're a survivor.'

'Nothing seems right, Simon. Nothing is working out. Everything seems wrong. I've got no job, you're sick and there's nothing I can help with and Dawn is dead. Three parts of my life have all crashed landed onto my head, I just don't know which way to turn. I feel crushed. I really am exhausted. My mind and my heart have just both given up.'

'But you are helping me. You are helping me by just being you and being here for me. You're the greatest help I could ever want or need. As for your job, good riddance, you hated working for that creep, a much better job will come along. You know it will. As for Dawn, even she said you are an amazing woman and that you're a survivor and I totally agree with her.'

'When did Dawn say that about me? When did Dawn say I was amazing?'

'The other morning when she called. You know the call I stupidly forgot to tell you about.'

'I don't understand, Simon. Why on earth would she say that about me? What else did she say?'

'That was all really. That's all she said. It's no big deal. You are amazing and it's good that people recognise that.'

'That's fine and I appreciate it but I still don't know why she would randomly say I'm amazing, what led into that conversation. I really don't get it, Simon. What was she talking about? She didn't even know me to make that conclusion.'

'What's the big deal? Why don't you just ask her? Whoops! You can't ask her she's dead. So, you will just have to believe me when I say she said you're amazing. I don't know why you're making such a big thing out of it. What's your problem? You are amazing! There's nothing else to be said. Is there? It didn't take Dawn to tell me that. I already know you are amazing, in many, many ways.'

'Simon! I can't believe you're so cruel! That's an awful thing to say! Sometimes, you're so unbelievable. You know I'm upset about Dawn! Why do you need to be so horrible about her, knowing I'm so hurt? I don't have the problem! You're the one with the problem! You're the one making a big thing out of it. All this on the day I've lost my job, I'm feeling down and on top of all that I have to contend with you being mean to me!'

'I wasn't being mean! I don't have a problem. I know you've lost your job. I know you're feeling down. I was just trying to help you by saying Dawn said you're amazing. I am not horrible! And anyway who cares why the jailbird said you were amazing! The fact is you are! I wish I'd never had mentioned it, especially if I'd known you were going to be so ungrateful!'

'Jailbird! Jailbird! Why are you calling her a jailbird? Why the hell are you calling her that? What has got into you? What is going on? Why did you just call her that? Simon! Why?! Why are you being so horrible about her?!'

'Because she was a fucking jailbird! That's why! She was a jailbird! And before you ask me, like I'm the one to blame, she told me that during the same fucking phone call! So, in conclusion, good riddance to her. Good riddance to the pathetic jailbird. I'm glad she's fucking dead. There is no room on this planet for people like her. She was only a jailbird for doing something wrong! Which means there's no reason for her to live! Happy now? Are you happy now? Why did you have to cause another argument? Why are you so cruel to me, knowing I'm so unwell?'

144

'What? She told you she was a fucking jailbird! This is getting more fucking bizarre by the second! Why the fuck did she tell you that? Why the fuck didn't you tell me before? You said it was only a short conversation! Simon! What is going on? Are you just making all this up? Or am I just going mad?! Why are you doing this to me? Why are you treating me like this? What is going on in your head? Well! Did she really say that? And what kind of conversation did you really have and why haven't you told me this before? I need to know and I need to know right now! Fucking hell, Simon! You're driving me crazy! I just need to know the truth!'

'Teresa! Why are you making me out to be the bad guy? I haven't done anything wrong! I forgot to tell you! I just fucking forgot! Is forgetting suddenly a crime?! It's not my fault I forget things! It's not my fault my drugs make me lose my memory! It's not my fault your so called friend was a criminal! Stop treating me like I've done something so wrong. I don't know why she told me that! I can't remember the whole fucking conversation! I just remembered it just now when we started talking about the silly bitch! I really wish I'd never had mentioned it. I was only trying to help you!'

'Help me! Help me! How was that ever going to help me? How did you ever think that was going to help me? How was telling me Dawn went to jail and that your conversation with her was that in depth ever going to help me, knowing she is fucking dead! I'm in total disbelief at your insensitivity! I just don't know what to say! And what's worse, the worse thing of all! I will never, ever know if you're telling the truth or not because she is dead and gone. I will never know Simon. I will never, ever know because the stupid woman is no more, the silly bitch is dead!'

'I'm done with this conversation, Teresa! I'm sorry you lost your job! I'm sorry I'm such a sick burden upon you! I'm sorry your friend is dead and most of all I'm sorry you don't totally believe me! Goodnight. I'm not feeling well. I'm going to bed!'

Teresa, customarily sunk her head into her hands and sobbed loudly with the standard repetitive surge of emotions that never seemed to be too far away, carelessly rushing through her with their usual effervescence, fizzing and deteriorating her defences into a crumbling. 'When is my world ever going to be complete? When?

145

When? When? When? When will my world be complete? When will my world come together? When? When? When?!'

Chapter 34
Final Goodbye

'Well, PC Trevlock, I can categorically tell you now, I have never in all my days seen such a mess. I don't know where to begin. Someone out there needs serious psychiatric help. This is beyond any reasonable doubt the work of an absolute maniac. I have been a forensic coroner for thirty-four years and this is by far the most bizarre case I have ever studied'

'Thank you, Doctor. I understand that. What was the actual cause of death?'

'Poisoning, strangulation, internal bleeding. Take your pick officer. Although, the last breath as she passed from life to death was probably the ligature around her neck which ultimately asphyxiated her. That was likely to be her final goodbye. I cannot imagine the pain she suffered but I can tell you whoever committed this crime is likely to strike again. It was the sheer malevolence of a very unstable person. I suspect the person responsible probably felt it was the right thing to do, as opposed to perceiving it to be a heinous crime. I also suspect the victim did not at any time feel she was in danger, in other words the perpetrator was not an initial threat. Poor woman, if only she could have known it was to be her last day. Such is the tragedy of this fickle thing called life.'

Pinks, turquoises and a slither of orange. The sun gives birth to another day as its strengthening rays of dazzling fluorescence incinerate the cloudy mist and force au revoir to the departing remnants of another night. The womb of the cosmos pushes out the glimmering ball of warm joy, drenching the landscape with searing radiance, nourishing all that is caught within its sensational aura. Within hours of gleefully screaming its eyes open and viewing the world it begins to grow in strength and smoulder its presence to anyone that acknowledges the birth of this glowing deity. Obstacles are spewed into its path, their floating fluffiness coercing it to cower until they glide by harmlessly. Middle age approaches with glowing vulnerabilities and weakness emanates from its once dominant, overwhelming core of energy. Power is fading, brawn is diminishing. Fieriness is dwindling as the dreaded cloak of darkness ruthlessly advances, with its enormous hands ready and willing to choke the final breaths from a sun once so valiant and able-bodied.

Night has flourished over day. Death has burnt and relinquished the land of light, browbeating it back into intergalactic space, until the conjuring of creation beckons another extraordinary birth of a new day. There was a thin layer of dust on the slats of the wooden blinds, unmasked by the dusky sun sinking into oblivion as it waved a defeated goodbye to the world, beaming its parting glory into the gloomy living room. Her pupils were half rolled into her head, reflecting the rays that would have once made her squint, close the blinds and make a mental note to do the dusting soon. Not this evening though. This evening was different. This evening Dawn had a kindred spirit with the abdicating sun. She too had reluctantly waved goodbye to the day but unlike the temporary absence of sunshine, Dawn had migrated to darkness for eternity.

The crowning streak of sun dipped past the last slat of the blind and disappeared into the horizon, its parting glimmer shone upon the powdery, dried redness streaking a kitchen knife, which was awkwardly sat next to the silenced cadaver. Stuck to the sharp blade of the knife, a slowly shrivelling chunk of chubby pink flesh.

'This will stop you talking! This will do it! This will silence you! This will do the trick! Oh yes! This will most certainly do the trick!'

The assailant's angry words were still echoing in the lounge, along with Dawn's muffled protestations as he forced his leather gloved fingers into her biting mouth and grabbed her slippery tongue. Slash! He cut through it with the serrated blade of the kitchen knife, three swift saw-like movements and her throat gurgled with the out-pouring of blood from the roughly carved wound, easier to cut than a rare slab of beef and twice as bloody.

'Oh dear! Looks like I've also cut through your lips. Oh well! You won't really need those where you're going. You should learn to keep your mouth shut shouldn't you? You should have kept it shut! Now look at you! Let me just squeeze your tongue and let all its nastiness drip out! Here you go Dawn! Here you go! I can almost see the nasty words coming out! Can you taste them? Can you taste your words?

Can you? Can you taste them?! Good! They're fucking nasty aren't they? They're fucking nasty like you aren't they?!'

Droplets of blood rained down upon Dawn's choking face as he clenched the slithery piece of bleeding meat in his fist and squeezed the veins dry.

'Don't you dare try and swallow your blood before you taste your nasty words! Don't you dare, Dawn! Don't you fucking dare do that! Don't you dare! They're your words and you must savour them. Here, let me help you! Let me help you taste them before you drink them down!'

Throwing the segment of tongue and the knife on the floor, he untied the delicate knot in Dawn's scarf and overlapping his hands pulled it hard into a garrotting tourniquet.

'That's better! That's better isn't it! There you go now love those words. Love them and taste each one! You're only allowed to swallow when you know what it is you're swallowing!'

His arm muscles tensed hard as the crossover action used all his might to stop the vital supply of oxygen going to her brain. The gurgling stopped as her body jerked and convulsed into retreat and her eyes rolled backwards. Her life crumbled before his eyes. Dawn was dead.

'You fucker! You fucker! You fucker! Good riddance you fucker! You deserved to die! You deserved to die! You deserve this you nasty fucker! You asked for this! You asked for it! And you got what you deserved! Who you gonna tell now? Who you gonna tell, you bitch? Who are you going to speak to now? What are you going to do now?! Nothing! You're going to do nothing. That's what you will do! Nothing!'

His vitriol spluttered out, he coughed, he choked and he vomited onto her blood splattered face. A final parting gesture marking the demise of Dawn as he loosened the pull on her silk scarf. A scarf that once enhanced her look and now took her concluding breath.

Acerbic rage had been fought in Dawn's lounge. The uncontrollable urge to express an opinion through undiluted barbarity, where words were clearly incapable of expressing a view, therefore were transformed into savage severity, articulated by remnants of the victim strewn around the once serene room. A dissected slice of tongue that once spoke elegantly of the past, present and future, now dehydrated of blood, words and intentions.

Chapter 35
Whirlpool

Chicken, hammer, yacht, plastic bottle
Burning Ferrari, velocity increasing, full throttle
Seldom confused, my wandering brainwork
Ludicrous images, disconnected they lurk
Whoosh! Churn! Spin! Mix & Circulate!
Demented spinning whirlpool blending my fate.
Cracked pavement, blue cheese, Chinese man
Swirl! Coddle! Bubble! Ferment & agitate.
The hammer hits the man,
The chicken swallows the bottle
The Ferrari drives into the cracked pavement
And the blue cheese sinks the yacht.
Wait! In a second all those pictures forgot.
Squelched into my whirling mind to rot.

'I'm not sure what it's supposed to mean. This is all he does. Write, write, and write but none of it makes any sense. None of it means anything. None of it has any purpose. It's all he's done in the six days he's been here. I understand you were his nurse at Teers and you're also his only registered next-of-kin?'

'Yes, I was and yes I am, he doesn't really have anyone else. His father was a writer. Ash writes just what comes into his mind, doesn't mean he or his words are unhinged though. Just means he's quite creative. Some of his poetry is very touching and beautiful. I take it you're his nurse here. How's he been?'

'Yes, I am. Although no one has their own personal nurse here. I look after twenty patients. His writing might not be unhinged but his belief that he has an imaginary friend is very odd. When he's not writing he is talking but not to anyone here, he just talks into thin air, almost if there is someone there. It spooks us all out, like he's talking to a ghost. Other than that, considering he arrived with no notice as an emergency case he's been reasonably okay and the only conversation he has with anyone living is to ask where you are. Anyway, good luck with him, he's just down the corridor, in the fourth room to your left.'

'I already know. I already know, Dad. I know! Of course I know! I can just tell!'

The slightly perturbed voice was unmistakable. Teresa had forgotten the nurse's directions to Ash's ward and just followed his semi-shouting dialogue. A frail woman wearing a pink striped nightdress brushed past her, almost deliberately knocking into her arm. Teresa could sense the woman was now stood behind her just staring.

'You know what, Mr Khusa?'

'I knew you were coming. I knew you were here. Dad was telling me you were on your way.'

'Are you Teresa? It's you. You're Teresa, aren't you! He's been talking about you all week. Day and night. Day and night. Day and night. That's all he does, talk about you. Are you his wife then?'

The frail woman engaged herself into the conversation and then wandered freely out of the ward into the corridor.

'I've been waiting for you, Teresa. I've really missed you.'

Ash turned to face Teresa. The sun shone through the ward window onto one side of his face causing a shadow over his cheek bone, highlighting the curvature of his jaw line and the purple bruised landmarks over his visage.

'Ash what on earth has happened to your face. Did this happen at Teers? Did they do this to you? Did they hurt you?!'

Salt water knew the drill and swiftly welled in Ash's tired, puffy eyes demonstrating their angst the only way they knew how to. His face contorted with the burden of a million troubled emotions. There was an entire story unfolding without a single word being uttered from his inflamed lips.

'No, Teresa. This didn't happen at Teers Hospital. They were kind to me right to the end. This has all happened here. It's all from here. It all happened right here.'

The sun cowered behind a passing cloud, unable to witness the trickle of saddened tears flowing over Ash's bruises, its disappearance cinematically lowered the lights over Ash's face, revealing the full outrage upon his skin. Every soft feature was pummelled, crushed and coloured as dramatically as a boxer's face as he finishes a feisty bout and jokes, 'you should see the other guy,' but instead of pugilist hilarity and celebration, this face was crying out for attention. Broken blood vessels were still seeping openly under the dermis of his battered skin as bloodshot corneas rejoiced for Ash's tears that were soothing their soreness, all attempting to silently tell the tale of the last six days.

'Don't worry about his bruises, love. There's no need. He's in good hands here!'

The frail woman in pink had scuttled back into the ward and instantly embroiled herself into the conversation.

'What do you mean, don't worry. His face is a mess, I want to know who did this!? When did it happen!? How did it happen and who are you anyway?'

'Keep your voice down, Teresa. You don't want to wake his ghost do you? One question at a time love. My name is Gloria Bentworth and I've been looking after this poor abandoned sod.'

'Okay Gloria. But how did this happen? Who did it? Who has hurt Ash!? I need to know right now!?'

'Hurt! Hurt! Hurt! No one has been hurt love. Ash hasn't been hurt. He's been saved love. He's been saved. Don't you go around saying he's been hurt, when he has actually been saved! That's how rumours start love. You really don't want to spread rumours around here love!'

'Right! I will ask you one last time! Who did this to Ash? Who did it? I need to know right now!'

'It was me love. I did this! I saved Ash. I saved Ash from his Demons. I beat them out of him. I hope you're going to thank me. I don't do anything for free my love. I saved your little Ash from his Demons. I sent them packing and I did it all alone. Just me and my fists and I promise I will save him again tonight. They always come back at night and every night I save him. If it wasn't for me love Ash would have been dead now. Wouldn't you Ash! You'd be dead now if it wasn't for your Aunty Gloria looking after you! Wouldn't you Ash?!'

'I'm sorry, Gloria. Slow down. What do you mean you did this to Ash? These bruises, this mess! You did this?!'

'Well, of course I did you silly woman! You're not here to help are you? Who else was going to look after him?! Who was going to save little Ash?! Fucking Santa Claus! This is the thanks I get. This is how you treat someone that saved your little Ash.'

Ash cowered like a mischievous puppy that knew he was guilty just because raised voices were daunting and his canine vulnerability made him insecurely believe it was all his fault. The stinging waterfall took wilful advantage washing over his ravaged features. He sensed the volatility in the air, he knew this was a dangerous situation, as last night's memories of Gloria's clenched fists uncontrollably lashing him in a reign of violence reminded him this was not going to end with a pleasant walk in the park. The outlook was anything but pleasant.

'But this is abuse! You have deliberately hurt him! You are a horrible, insane woman and you will be reported. I will report you right now. You cannot do this. You cannot attack someone like this! Don't you dare touch him again! He does not need saving and certainly not by you, now go away and get out of my sight you cruel, nasty woman!'

Teresa and Gloria both turned around simultaneously, perfectly choreographed into stalemate, both angry, both violated and both striding into a mission of accomplishment.

'I'll be back in a moment Ash. I'm going to fetch the ward sister and I want you to explain to her what that witch has done to you.'

Ash gestured with the faintest movement, the slightest wag of a worried but approving tail, drooping his head downwards watching his tears circumnavigate onto the crumpled white bedding. Gloria stomped back to her bed with a dampened sound from the cushioned flooring and didn't look back. Scorned she stood glaring at the white wall emblazoned with clipboards adorning charts.

'Teresa!!'

There was a sense of slow-motion at lightning speed. The rumbling shockwave commenced at the very tip of Teresa's manicured toes and gathered immense momentum as it surged with atom-bomb ferocity upwards through every throbbing molecule of her alarmed body until there was a terrifying explosion in her cranium.

Two thoughts emerged from the combustion in her brain as they coexisted together.

Whose was the familiar but unrecognisable voice?

Stop and look back immediately!

There was no alternative, no time to elect a Plan-B, no volition to take any other action, no other option than to SCREAM!

'You bitch! You bitch! You bitch!'

It was already too late. Gloria had sprinted across the room, clutching a small pair of rounded metal scissors that she had removed from the top drawer of her bedside cabinet and launched herself into the air at Teresa's shell-shocked frame. Her eyes were bulging from their withdrawn sockets and were a descriptive testimonial to her clear intentions.

'I hate you and I'm going to kill you!' Pulsating veins throbbed the silent words. She was aiming for Teresa's face. Teresa's only defence to the onslaught of the crazed attack was her hands, both to keep the demented woman at bay and to protect her face from being slashed by the weapon she was wielding.

Relief, pain and blurred confusion interweaved Teresa's thought pattern. She had saved her face from being punctured but the brute force of a scowling, maniacal woman was adequate to perforate her hand with the blunt weapon, her blood, liberated, flowed down her raised wrist and was agreeably absorbed into the sleeve of her blouse.

Faced with an atrocious predicament, Teresa's brain retreated into 'what if' mode and within seconds began concluding the outcome.

'What if I die? Who will look after Simon?'

'What if I die? What will happen to Ash?'

'What if? What if? What if? What if?'

Gloria's scrawny weight was energised by her leaping momentum and raging anger, toppling Teresa with fluid ease. Crunch! Her head cracked on the floor and sent her internal bodily emergency services clambering to assist the jolt on the skull, as her body blacked-out and plunged into terrifying shock mode.

Chapter 36
Balance

'I don't even understand why we're having this ridiculous argument. I don't know why you're so angry! I don't know why you just don't understand. Why don't you tell me what the real problem is? Why don't you be honest and tell me what is really bugging you? Because so far you've done nothing other than be rude, unreasonable and just angry for no reason at all, especially after everything you know! C'mon! Tell me! Tell me what the real problem is.'

'No reason at all! No reason at all! You haven't listened to a word I've said. You are the problem! Of course there is a reason. You know what the reason is! Teresa, you're not that thick that you don't have a clue as to what the problem is. We both know what the problem is! Don't we?! We both know why we're having this argument! You should have just asked out of politeness before making such a massive commitment. I think you've just been selfish. All you had to do was ask, then we could have discussed it like two grown adults. That's all I wanted, a show of respect, to feel valued, to feel that I mean something to you, before you made such a huge decision!'

'Two grown adults! You are not acting like an adult! You're acting like a spoilt child that simply didn't get his way and now you're having a tantrum over nothing at all! You're turning into a pathetic man who doesn't even understand the most basic of things and prefers to argue than just step back for a moment and look at all sides of the situation! You damn well know if we had discussed this you would have disagreed and you would have wanted it all your own way, like you always do! It's no wonder I didn't ask you, you would have been against the idea from the outset! Wouldn't you!?'

'That's just bullshit and you know it! So you went ahead deliberately! You've just admitted you didn't ask me on purpose and yet at the start of the argument you said there was just not enough time to ask and that you had to just make an immediate decision! Now you're telling me you did it despite me and you never, ever had any intention of involving me! The thing is, you have no idea what I

156

would have said and now you'll never know because you were too pig-headed and selfish to involve me!

'Look, keep your voice down! There's no need to shout so much. You're wrong, totally wrong! I didn't have time to ask, that's right. I had to decide immediately but now on reflection, I know I did the right thing because you would never have agreed. I know that from the reaction you're already having! I know you hate the situation, I know you hate him but at some point you have to grow up and accept that I'm an adult too and I'm entitled to make decisions that affect me and my life! My life isn't all about you!'

'Oh we all know that, Teresa! We all know it's all about you and your selfish self! We all know it couldn't just be about me. It doesn't matter that I might be dead soon as long as you are happy with your pathetic little life and your pathetic little decisions. As long as little Teresa is happy the rest of the world can just go fuck itself! You really are a horrible woman, I thought I meant something to you but the only person that means something to you, is your fucking self!'

'Horrible! Horrible! How dare you! After all I've done for you, after all you put me through! I still let you back in my life! I still made room for you! And here you are living in my home under my roof, telling me I'm the horrible one, you should be ashamed of yourself Simon! You should be fucking ashamed! I have literally devoted my life to looking after you and you remain the ungrateful bastard you've always been! Why should I need to ask you? This is my house, this is my life! I do not need to ask you what to do with my house and my life and if I want to have Ash living here for a short time, then that is entirely up to me, it is none of your business what I do in my house, it is none of your business what I do with my life. My house Simon! It's my house! It's my house, not yours, it's mine!'

'I knew it would come down to that! I knew you would throw the 'my house' bit into it! I knew you would make me feel unwelcome again. I really don't care what you do with the fucking invalid, I don't even care if you fuck him. You can do what the fuck you want in your stupid house. I hope you're both happy together, just leave me out of it. I'd leave your house right now if I hadn't given up my fucking house to live here with you but now that you've made it so clear you don't want me or need me here I will find my own place and die on my own! I really don't need your pity anymore, neither do I want to be a burden on you, anyway you don't need me, not now that you will be living with the fucking invalid!'

'Simon! You know I care! You know I didn't mean you're not welcome here, I want this to be your house as much as I want it mine. I regard it as ours. Ash won't be here too long, just enough time to find him a better hospital that's all. You know I had no choice but to invite him here and you know I wouldn't put him or anything above you. You just know I wouldn't. You're not a burden, I don't pity you. I just care for you and I want you to get well and I want you to get well here. Here, in your house.'

'I don't care anymore, Teresa! Just do what you want. Live the life you want to live and be happy doing whatever you need to do. You're right, it's your house! It's your life! Now excuse me, I'm not feeling too well and if it's okay with you, I need to go to bed in your house and in your bed. I promise I won't be here long and soon you won't have to worry about me, I will find my own way. I will start looking for a new place to live in the morning, somewhere I can feel welcome and call my own. I will find my own house. You don't have to worry about me anymore. Goodnight Teresa.'

The customary slam of the bedroom door as the doorframe rolled its eyes and once again accepted the standard outcome of Simon and Teresa in freefall argument mode.

'Here we go again!'

Even Teresa's tears exclaimed sarcastically and commenced with the salty waterfall before her lambasted emotions signalled the tear ducts to begin their prescriptive actions.

The last twenty-four hours had been a mishmash of bemusement and fanatical tremors. The fragmented pieces were still scattered somewhere between the hospital ward, the habitual slam of the bedroom door, multiple bruises upon her torso, a searing pain in the head, a throbbing, bandaged hand and the fleeting notion that somehow Ash had saved her, purely by shouting her name and alerting her to the maniacal Gloria.

Absolutely everything happens for a reason, albeit the reason isn't always apparent to begin with.'

Absolutely everything happens for a reason, albeit the reason isn't always apparent to begin with.'

Absolutely everything happens for a reason, albeit the reason isn't always apparent to begin with.'

Dawn's deathless words, on repeat function, were carved deeply into the cartilage of Teresa's smarting skull.

'Someone please give me a reason. Please. I need a reason. Anything. Just anything. Anything. Anything will do, I need a fucking reason! I need a reason. I am desperate for a reason!'

The inquest of valid reasons ricocheted through Teresa's head, with each deflection the trouncing pain suggested a counter-argument of 'what possible reason can there be to feel this bad?'

All renderings of the confounding question and its conflicting debate relied on the only remedy that had become Teresa's calm, tranquillity and antidote to an increasingly spasmodic life. 'Make my World Complete', mutely sat on the coffee table, patiently and knowingly waiting to placate Teresa's tortured mind.

'Come here, my friend. Come to my rescue. Come here and make my battered world complete. Show me some light through this dark place I'm once again lost in.'

Balance
Equity, harmony, stability and symmetry
My antagonistic soul, will you ever set me free.
Contentious and fierce, belligerent at loggerheads
Battle beaten imbalance and instability
Fragmented disproportion and crumbling equanimity
The residue of abortive, barren exaltation
This is balance in an irregular formulation.

'My life was entirely out of composure, there wasn't an ounce of equilibrium. Nothing ever weighed the same. There was always structural indifferences in the basic building blocks of my fractured and dismembered days. Maybe, just maybe there was an unregistered balancing act, teetering on the tight-rope of the hand I'd been dealt to deal with. What if, what if the whole idea of evenness wasn't in direct physical equivalence but poised with the development of my personal thoughts and mental cultivation. Then, I have balance! C'mon, give me your worst, splatter my days with your best-shots but beware, beware of what you sow because I have the greatest weapon available to mankind. I have a weapon that is more omnipotent than the most threatening, domineering warheads that can be fired for total annihilation. Yes, I have the only weapon that I need, the only weapon that will have the virile horsepower to inflict permanent contamination to the ghastly imbalance. I have my thoughts. My colossal, vanquishing pictures of how I want life to be, the adamant anticipation and downright belief that I will prevail and victoriously tumble the asymmetry and hound the unevenness into the justified and balanced life I crave.

That was the moment, the very second, my onslaught upon imbalance began its earth-shaking journey of fulfilment. There is no such thing as natural balance, life will always be in a continuous state of lop-sidedness, one has to outwit the shortcomings with a breath-taking attitude of the way one wants life to be. That is the battle-bus that wins the vote and declares war upon the congenital inequalities we're all cursed with. Balance simply cannot exist, otherwise how would we thrive, grow and achieve the greatness and power we are all endowed with as our birth-right?

Love you have miserably failed me. You have attempted to quench my thirst for someone to share my bloodied heart with. You have ripped my emotions into shreds of unrecognisable scraps. You have deteriorated my emotions, chewing them alive, laughing as they screamed and spat them out as venom. I thank you! I thank you from the bottom of my bruised and reluctant heart, for you have instilled within every aching strand and fibre of my being a violent torrent, a gushing belief of romantic love and its imminent appearance and adored resolve within my life.

Teresa put her bible down and smiled. Khusa's classic always seemed to succinctly tune into her emotional waves, intelligently interact, weave into her thought patterns and create the desired effect. In this instance, the understanding that she needs to concentrate on the outcome, her dreams and aspirations, allowing such positive pictures of how she wants life to be, to counteract the caustic imbalance plaguing her brain.

'I adore you, your words and what I'm gleaning about your life, Mr Khusa, but you've just taken my whirling, churning thoughts

160

to a difficult, alarming disposition. You are absolutely right, there is balance to be sought from imbalance, through the tremendous power of the human mind-set. However, the uneven segments of my life centre around my relationship, segments which are supposed to be the happiest ones, therefore any opposing positive demeanour would suggest those have to be annulled to restore a contented medium'.

Teresa gradually slipped into a deep sleep daring not to enter her own bedroom fearing it would compromise her rest and the quietness since the door was slammed shut.

'Hello, my dear. You are right, you know.'

'Right about what, and anyway who are you?'

'You know who I am. You can feel who I am and you are right everything does happen for a reason and one day the reason will all become very clear.'

'It's you! It's Mr Khusa! It's you! What are you doing in my dream? Why are you here?

'My dear, Teresa. My dear, dear Teresa, I'm here to tell you all will work out, your life will become balanced. You will be happy and everything will make sense.'

'How, Mr Khusa? How will that happen? How will it all make sense? How? Please tell me how?'

'You will find out all in good time, my dear Teresa. All in good time. All in good time.'

'Please tell me, Mr Khusa. Please tell me the reasons. Mr Khusa! Where are you, Mr Khusa? Where have you gone, Mr Khusa? Where are you? Where are you? Where are you?'

Chapter 37
Home

'Hello, I guess you're Ash. No matter what you've heard about me, this is now your home. Whatever you want, whatever you need, we can help you with. I want you to feel at home, like this is your home. We want you to be comfortable and we will help you through this.'

'Thank you so much, Simon. I've only ever heard good things about you and how you make Teresa happy. Anyone that makes Teresa happy is a friend for life and someone I hold in high regards. She said you'd be back before her this evening. She should be back soon. She is a good woman and you're a very lucky man.'

'And Ash, my friend, you are lucky too. Teresa isn't just an everyday nurse, she has a rock-solid heart of gold and what she's doing for you is far beyond the call of duty, especially as she has no duty anymore, she has no job, she had no reason to help you, except just the kindness of her heart.'

'I know I'm lucky and I know I am special to her, we have an amazing connection and I can categorically say I would not have survived had it not been for Teresa's intervention into my wrecked life.'

'Yes things haven't been good for you have they? In fact you really are lucky to be here, I mean lucky to be alive.'

'I'm not sure how I've survived myself. Everything happens for a reason, except when it comes to death, there is no rhyme or reason for losing someone.'

'And worst for you because of the way your girlfriend died, I expect its not easy living with the fact you killed her.'

The bow had been stretched to full capacity and the vibrating twang as it was released signalled the speed, accuracy and potential of the arrow. Swoosh!! It hit its target and lacerated Ash's heart into two barely beating, bloodied halves. Shockwaves rippled through his skin and activated a gush from his grieved eyes, as instantaneous as water from a smoke penetrated sprinkler blindly spraying to quench the flames.

'It's not been easy. I live with it every day and I will do forever.'

'C'mon! Chin-up, my friend. You are where you are and you have to rebuild yourself. Sorry, I didn't want to upset you. I'll leave you alone and see you later, I've got some things to do. Anyway, it's good to have you here.'

'Thank you. No need to apologise. I deserve it.'

Turning away from Ash, towards the bedroom door that had been violently slammed only last night, Simon heard the excruciating screech in his head as he bit his jaw shut and his teeth grinded together.

'Amazing woman! Amazing woman! Amazing woman! I'll give you a reason! I'll show you how everything happens for a reason! I'll give you a fucking reason!'

The nondescript curved, three inch dent in the wall between the bedroom and the bathroom had maintained its calm mystery, regularly attracting Teresa's attention and always leaving her momentarily baffled, before the urgency to get to the bathroom usurped thoughts of irregular dimples. Simon and the dent had a closer relationship, they understood their individual perspectives and harboured no secrets, although the affiliation was strictly parasitic, the wall gave all it could and got little in return except to feel battered and bruised but that was the understanding they had from the outset and nothing had changed as Simon wantonly traipsed towards it, nonchalant to his surroundings and with bearish potency treated the waiting dent to all his might, as his forehead plunged directly into the lethargic but stout cavity, rigorously shaking its brick foundations, dislodging more plaster and widening the curvature.

'Amazing woman! Amazing woman! I made her amazing. I made her. I made her. She was nothing, I made her and I can put her back again if I want to!'

Simon's incandescent mutterings were absorbed into the submissive wall as pushed his head harder into it, the pain from colliding continued to vibrate through the entirety of his brain and syringed itself down to the small of his back, rippling down his backbone.

'Simon! Simon! Where are you?'

Brushing the powdery whiteness of his altercation from his brow, Simon leapt away from the wall and strode back into the living room, as his anger subsided back into the darker portion of his psyche.

'Sorry, darling, I didn't hear you arrive. How are you?'

'I'm good thanks. I take it you two have met?'

'Yes we've met and I told Ash we are here for him to help him through this.'

'Excellent. I just knew you two would get on. I'm so pleased. I'm taking a shower and then we can fix some food.'

Teresa dropped her handbag, removed her coat and smiled away into the bedroom, sucking the friendly atmosphere with her, leaving a floundering silence in the room. Simon was fixated on Ash's stare as he followed his eyes watching Teresa disappear into the bedroom.

'Simply beautiful, isn't she. I love her so much and I can't believe she's all mine. All mine forever.'

'As I said before Simon. You're a very lucky man indeed. She is a truly amazing woman.'

'I am, Ash. I am lucky. I am very lucky. You just sit there and listen to how lucky I actually am. I'm going to shower with her and give her what she needs, what she really needs, a real man and I'm going to give it to her hard, so hard that she will know how lucky she is to have me in her life. Just listen and imagine what I'm doing to her and how lucky I am. See you soon buddy. This one will be from the both of us. From both of us to an amazing woman. I know you can't really do much where women are concerned but at least you can enjoy it from a distance, especially as we both admire the amazing woman she is.'

The door closed behind him, leaking out the brief torturous noise of the pouring shower, as Ash watched him disappear into the bedroom.

Swirling, swishing and gurgling, Ash's emotions were spiralling down the plughole, emulating the water in the steamy shower cubicle.

Startled by the impetuous intrusion, only one word formed from Teresa's saturated lips 'NO!' hastily followed by a string of repeats.

'No! No! No! No! No! No!'

'I can't do this, Simon! I just cannot do this! Simon! I can't do this! No! Please get out. Please, Simon. I'm just not ready for this!'

A trio of clashing emotions cavorted with each other, hands held tight, unable to escape, entwined and awkwardly obsessed in a plaited symbiosis.

Ash, Simon and Teresa were connected in a brash whirlwind of rawness, with little interpretation of the essence, consequences or significance. Melancholy, melodrama and panic glued together this intense, perturbing moment.

Ash was in freefall descent as his ears crucified his imagination, leaving it bleeding profusely to a miserable death. Teresa's lengthy, muffled moans drew stark images of satisfied nakedness, heady delirium and animalistic fervour, immediately trouncing the inappropriateness of imagining Teresa unclothed and swathed in heated, wet lust.

'Stop, Ash, stop! She is not your woman! Why do you feel like this? She is your nurse! Teresa is nothing but your kind carer, banish her nudity from your head! How dare you! How dare you think of someone else's woman in this way, particularly one that has shown such kindness and heartfelt beauty towards your pathetic self-inflicted situation! She belongs to Simon! They belong together! Grow up! Grow up you pitiful freak! You should be ashamed of yourself! This alone proves you got what you deserved, you vile little man! Stop! Stop right now!'

Ash gritted his jaw tightly together and allowed his self-talk berating, calm the tasteless pictures in his addled mind. His concerted effort was futile and only served to concrete his understanding of his moral downfall.

'I can't do it! I can't do it! I can't do this! I can't stop myself. I know how awful I am. Yes, I'm pathetic! A pathetic broken, pointless little man but I can't stop thinking about what's happening!'

Ash's imagination fought back with heroic gusto and bombarded his well-intended self-talk with a volley of defeating impressions.

'Thud! Thud! Thud! Thud! Thud! Thud! Thud!'

Each heaving rhythmic bang from the bathroom, penetrated Ash's body with the throbbing pulse of the recipient as he conceded to the vicious onslaught from his determined visualisation.

Ash's desperate guilt was crushed into indifference.

'I'm done! I can't fight anymore! This is my life now. This is all I have left. This is all I now deserve. This is me for the rest of my days. I give up! I put my arms in the air and surrender!'

Ash's body reacted in the only way it knew how to, in the only way that was left. Uncontrollable tears.

'I wish I was dead!' I wish I was dead! I wish I was dead! I wish I was dead! Father please take me! I want to be there with you. You can see how low my life has become. I have no part in this world now. I only want to be there where you are. I can't live anymore. I can't live like this anymore. This life is no longer for me! I've lost everything I had and now I'm being torn apart by all the things I want but can never have. I don't need this lesson anymore. Please forgive me! I don't want to live anymore knowing what I want is never going to be mine. Father, I need to die! Please, please I need to die! Why have you left me when I need you the most? Why!? Why!? Why!? Why!? Father! Why have you abandoned me!? Please Father I only ask this one thing. Please release me of my burdens. Please take me! Please father. I will never ask another thing of you!'

The pounding from the steamy bathroom, beat in rhyme to Ash's sobbing appeal, eloquently dramatizing his peril.

Recognising the closing of the shower cubicle he had never seen but one that had already imprisoned him with unwanted images pelting his imagination, Ash wiped his face clean with his sleeve as footsteps wandered towards him. Dripping with droplets of lust, swathed in a fluffy white towel, Simon sauntered through the door, a beaming, crescent smile that barely squeezed through the gap.

'Mate, that was amazing. I know it's not something you can ever do again but let me tell you, it was just amazing. I really am lucky aren't I? I hope you didn't hear anything Ash, Teresa is always so loud when she is excited. Know what I mean don't you? Of course you do. I think she will be knackered after that performance.'

Simon chucked the verbal grenade and disappeared back into the bedroom, knowing the devastation it caused upon his captive audience. Without hesitation, the grenade discharged its habituated anarchy and tore through the already damaged and vulnerable membranes of Ash's boldness, with no consideration for the biting indecency of Simon's defilement.

Haemorrhaging violently, Ash was benumbed in a state of detachment, pushed over the edge, a rollercoaster dropping vertically after its frightening ascent, helplessly abducted by the inflexibility of momentum and the pull of gravity. He closed his eyes and surrendered to the marching decomposition of what was formerly known as life.

Chapter 38
Sleep

'**Y**our tiny head slotted into the crevice of my chest and there to the beat of my heart you would find your solace and no matter how you felt you would fall asleep. I would hold you for hours, knowing any movement would be an indication to you that I was about to put you down, you would always wake and with sleepy, silent eyes, look at me, your stare would simply say, 'don't let me go, Dad'!'

'But, Dad! You have let me go. You left me to suffer! You've left me on my own. You and Mum have both let me down. You have let me go.'

'I only wish I could be there with you son. Just know this I will guard you and guide you. You will smile again. I know you will.'

'Don't leave me. Don't leave me. Please don't leave me!'

The voice echoed to silence and with it the comfort that Ash only felt when he heard his father's soothing tones.

'Oh no! Ha, ha, ha, ha, ha! You poor sod! You poor, poor sod! Teresa, you better come and see what's happened. Ha, ha, ha, ha! Absolutely shocking!'

Any droplets of confidence that Ash had gripped onto were savagely syringed out, startled he woke to Simon's boisterous laughing as another curtain of dejection plummeted down upon him. The unintended puddle below his wheelchair was the slapstick scenario adding to Ash's distress.

Weeping, he attempted an apology.

'I'm sorry. I'm sorry. I don't know how I managed that. I don't know what to say. I'm so sorry.'

'Doesn't matter mate. It happens to all of us. You were probably excited at what you could hear last night. Eh! Eh! Was that it? Go on Ash, confess you pissed yourself with excitement. Go on mate, I won't tell Teresa. It was wasn't it! You dirty little rascal. C'mon, you can tell me, I promise I won't tell Teresa.'

'Won't tell Teresa what?' Teresa stepped from the bedroom, wondering what Simon was so ecstatic about.

'Oh, morning honey, that was just boy's banter, you don't need to know but look, look what naughty little Ash has done!'

'Oh, Ash! Have you been here all night? Don't worry it's just a little accident. C'mon, Simon, please show a little respect!'

'Respect! Of course I show respect. I'm only pointing out the poor sod has pissed himself. Heh, it can happen to anyone. Maybe he was just excited'

'Simon! Please show some sensitivity, it's an accident. Why on earth would Ash be excited?''

'Ha, ha, ha, ha! I'll let Ash tell you that. Anyway, you clean up this little accident. I've got things to do and places to go. I'm already looking forward to having another shower with you tonight. I think we should start to shower twice a day!'

'Simon! You're just being silly. Just ignore him, Ash. Let's get you sorted.'

Still amused by the drenched floor, Simon returned to the bedroom, muttering under his breath.

'I know this isn't easy, Ash, but I hope you're reasonably happy, don't worry about this accident, as Simon said, it can happen to anyone.'

If nursing had taught Teresa one huge thing, it was simply knowing, instinctively when someone was far from 'reasonably happy'. A learned curse that overrode all contradictory evidence and had an uncanny resolve in assessing people. Teresa's knack was never astray with its nimble, intuitive scrutiny. The greatest actor in the world, painting the falsest grin could not escape the instantaneous six-sense skill that bored peeping holes into the innermost psyche, plunging into personal depths of hidden agony and revealing the camouflage disguising them.

Teresa already knew the answer before she had asked Ash the inane question.

'Of course I'm happy, Teresa. I'm just embarrassed at this mess. If I could clean it up myself, I would. I'm so sorry. It won't happen again.'

'I do believe you, Ash, but I also need you to know that I'm here for you. We will follow this through, we haven't come this far to only come this far. I know you have some very difficult days, you've been through a lot. Most people would have crumbled with what's happened to you. So always know I'm here for you, no matter what and that's not just because I'm a nurse but because I've grown to like you and feel close to you. You're more than a patient, you're more than a friend. I won't let you down.'

Context is irrelevant to the ears that are already convinced, particularly when they're searching for guidance to support conspiracies. The only sentence that colluded with Simon's warped uneasiness pelted his insecurities with a remorseless volley of machine-gun fire.

'I've grown to like you and feel close to you. You're more than a patient, you're more than a friend. I won't let you down.'

A compilation of words that sunk their serrated teeth into Simon's flesh symbiotically feeding his deliberate return to the door and his defiant longing to listen. He was searching for a morsel of evidence that he didn't expect to hear, evidence that he didn't know existed but now the guilty words were gripping onto his freedom and fertilising his persistent uneasiness. They had caged him into an inescapable crater of instability as they whizzed around his brain, dizzying his thinking. He moved away from the door, the pain was too intense to analyse the full consequences in this reluctant bruised moment.

'Thank you, Teresa. That means the world to me, thinking that I'm a burden here in your household. I am happy being here but I'm just not happy to where my life has brought me. All I want to do is sleep. A long, long sleep. A sleep I never want to wake from. I don't think I will ever feel any different, I don't really have anything to live for. I don't see the point of my pointless life. I just want to sleep. That's all I want to do. That's all I want forever.'

'Ash, please don't think like that. You have so much to live for. So much life yet to live, even though you've been through some tragedies, you simply cannot give up. Life is too precious. The people in your life would be devastated to lose you. You will get better and you will live again. I know you will.'

'What people, Teresa? What people do I have? Everyone has left me. There's no one for me. No life and no one that will be devastated. I have nothing. I have no one.'

'But Ash. You have me. I will never leave you. You have me. We will always be together, we will always be close and I will look after you and nurse you to health. I care and we will always be together. I won't leave you Ash. I won't leave you!'

The warmth from Teresa's hand injected an ounce of hope into Ash's body as she held his deflated hand and squeezed it tight with her reassuring words.

'You will always have me, Ash. I won't leave you. I won't let you down. I will care for you until you're better. You will always have me. Sometimes people are just meant to meet and be together'

The temptation to listen was unavoidable and literally pushed Simon back to the door, to catch more battering words. Words that stood strong and tall, breathing fire into Simon's already disorientated world.

'*You will always have me. Sometimes people are just meant to meet and be together.*'

Razor teeth, famished predators, easy prey. Simon fell head first into the tank of ferociously hungry piranha fish. The water spumed savagely, instantly bespattered with a plume of red blood. The creatures of destruction weren't borne of procrastination as they hurriedly sliced and tore through Simon's mistrustful, green-eyed skin & bones. Serrated remnants, floating in the carmine water formed the consumptive words that brought catastrophe splurging into Simon's vulnerable veins.

'*You will always have me. Sometimes people are just meant to meet and be together.*'

Chapter 39
Deprivation

'She dived into my welcoming brain,
Swimming so ferociously against the grain.
Interweaved and mingling through my circulation
Composing the scripts of my dreams
Leaving me thunderstruck with potent elation
Cascading fluidly through my bloody streams.
Injecting desired goodness with no abrasion.
I smile and I gush and palpitate with a rush
As her wake ripples and contorts my swelling crush.
A delusion so bewitching, forcefully twitching
All my nerves, my hearts swerves, vibrant creation
A daunting future, starved of passion,
Damning deprivation.
Bursting at the seams, squelching dissolution,
Mangled into submission, decaying fruition.
I am deprived of the stimulus, it deadens my beating
The love of my life, my heart it's cheating.*

'What's that you've got there?'
Intuition emphatically barked at Simon, pre-warning him like a guard dog trained to pounce. He already knew before he unexpectedly snatched the white sheet of paper from Ash's hands, that it was categorically going to annoy him.

'Oh, it's just something I've been writing. Just my silly words into a poem. Err, of course you can read it. It's just something silly.'

Simon was engrossed by the words, each penetrating his brain, long before Ash gave him the permission to read it. It seemed like hours before Simon raised his head from the white sheet of scrawling. Ash's words were scrambling around the circuit in his head, each word in a race attempting to overtake the other......'VROOM!' as they passed each other to take pole-position before being awarded the prestige of being the first word to shoot from Simon's mouth. There could only be one winner. A word that was born to win and succeed faster and more ambitiously than any other word in the competition.

'Deprivation!' Screamed out at full throttle, leaving all the other words trembling in its whirlwind speed, wondering if they could ever match the marvel of such a stunning performance.

'Deprivation!' It did a customary lap of honour, whilst the other words were only preparing to fire out.

Second and third place were also touted as born winners, albeit no match for the talent of 'Deprivation'!

'Twitching! Swelling!'

'Simon. They're just silly words. They really don't mean anything. Just silly, stupid words!'

Ash was also overcome by the winning words, forcing him to hunch his shoulders and cower in submission, as the victors wallowed in the glory.

'Deprivation! Twitching! Swelling!' They held hands for one last, joint lap of honour.

'You nasty little man! You dirty little pervert! You're talking about my girlfriend, aren't you? You're talking about Teresa. I can't believe this!'

'Yes. I mean no. I mean, it's about her and it isn't about her. It's just silly words, I told you. No harm, just silly words.'

'Silly words! No harm! No fucking harm! You're twitching and swelling about my girlfriend! Deprived of her and you're telling me they're just silly words!'

'I didn't mean it like that. You've taken it all wrong. I'm not even like that. It's not meant to be perverted, you're just reading it wrong. I'm so sorry but you are reading it wrong.'

'Admit it, you fucking pervert. You want to fuck my girlfriend. Admit it! Admit it! Admit it! You want to fuck her, don't you?! You do, don't you! You do! I know you do! Fucking admit it, you filthy little cripple!'

'No, no, no, no, I don't. You've got it all wrong. I just like her and these are just harmless words!'

'Ash. It's here in black and white. You want to fuck her. I know you do. You've always wanted to fuck her admit it, you disgusting cripple. Fucking admit it! It's here in black and white and you fucking wrote it with your own hands. 'I smile and I gush and palpitate with a rush, as her wake ripples and contorts my swelling crush. A delusion so bewitching, forcefully twitching.' Your writing. These are your fucking words! You want my woman! You selfish bastard, after all we've done for you, you want to steal my woman and destroy my life! Don't you? You do! Don't you? I know you do! And I want you to admit it right now! Or you'll be sorry you ever set eyes upon my Teresa and you'll be sorry, you fucking gush and palpitate! You will wish you'd killed yourself at the same time you killed your girlfriend when I've finished with you!'

The angered torridness from Simon's mouth, thundered a heated mist over Ash's face. An abandoned, debilitated pet, caught in the incinerating blaze of headlights, blinded, panic-stricken with no way to turn, nowhere to run, except to humbly accept the damning hand of fate that was imminent, the double-thud of tyres crushing his weary bones into the tarmac, with only one dying wish, that it's an uncomplicated death and not the agonising brutalised slow departure of bleeding torture, prolonged with regrets silently waiting for their performance before the shift into darkness.

'I know. I know. I know. I'm sorry they've offended you, I don't know what else to say, it's my poetry, it's my writing, it's the way I express myself, I know what you're thinking but I'm not a pervert, I adore Teresa because she's literally saved my life and of course she is an amazing and attractive woman but I would never disrespect you or her, not now, not ever.'

'C'mon, cripple, tell me you want her, tell me you want her. Tell me you love her, you gushing bastard! I will fucking hurt you, if you don't admit it! Tell me you fucking want her! I'm not going to ask you again! This is your final fucking chance! I will fucking kill you if you don't tell me! Tell me! Tell me! Tell me! Tell me! Tell me right now!'

Spitting blighting words into his face, Simon demonically shook the wheelchair as his blood gorged eyeballs burnt their enraged stare deep into Ash's vulnerable spirit, further breaching the gaping cracks. Goodbye spiteful world. Ash could smell the familiar aroma of death lingering in the vitriolic air, with the zig-zagged rubber about to leave its fated pattern over his defenceless body and in those micro-seconds before his impending demise, his flimsy heart surrendered a hopeful white-flag confessional.

'I want her! I want her! I want her! Are you happy now?! I've always wanted her. I love her! I love her! I want to fuck her! I love her! I love her! I want her!'

A seismic reaction in the pit of the earth, grinding plates of earthy annihilation resembled the coalition of acerbic acids consolidating their potency deep inside Simon's jaundiced belly. The assimilation of botheration, enviousness and uncertainty of his relationship with Teresa, struck the deafening gongs of doom, as the bubbling volcano surfaced in the guise of his temper and jarred emotions.

'Fuck! Fuck! Fuck! Fuck! Fuck! Fuck! I knew it!'

Assuredly, there was calm as the dizziness from Simon's head-but between Ash's dripping eyes left expletives ringing in his ears, with a lightening of the burden unduly lifted. This uncustomary confession didn't end with priestly forgiveness but with a searing pain in his skull as the priest pushed Ash's wheelchair back against the wall and swiftly staggered into another room, with a barrage of demented words, laughter and sobbing all collaborating into a senseless chant, intermingled with the distinct sound of rattling through drawers and cupboards.

Chapter 40
Goodbye

Dearest Teresa,

This is the most difficult letter I've ever had to write but I had to write, so you can see my thoughts in black and white. Before I begin please understand this is my final decision and I'm hoping you will respect it and not attempt to change my mind. It really is what I want to do and I know you will want me to follow my feelings. The kindness you've showed me through my rehabilitation is much more than I could have ever asked of any human being, I didn't even know people like you existed in the world, with such humanity that you'd rescue me from despair and even give up your own space and home for me. Your kindness has been, without any doubt, nothing short of miraculous. After two weeks of your unadulterated attention and amazing cordiality. I've decided to move back to Hillrush House. I had a long chat with the authorities today and they can accommodate me again from tomorrow.

There are many reasons for my decision but for now, suffice to say, even though I know I'm not a burden upon your life, I want you to get on with your existence and I'm certain mine will sort itself out. Of course, my renewed positive outlook wouldn't have been possible without your huge kindness and support, therefore I will forever be in your debt and grateful for the angel you are. Thank you for everything and I hope your life with Simon continues to go from strength to strength, you two have a bright and beautiful future together.

Ash.

'Wow, I wasn't expecting that. What on earth happened? What did he say when he gave you the letter?'

'Nothing at all, darling, except will you please give this to Teresa and then he buggered off to bed saying he wanted an early night because he had a headache. Why? What does it say in the letter?'

'And that's it? That's all he said? He wants to go back to the institute and he's going tomorrow. I'm just gobsmacked he wants to return to Hillrush after what happened there. I thought he was happy here.'

'That's all he said, darling. He did seem really happy, we were even joking around just before he handed me the envelope.'

'Well, if that's what he wants, it's what he wants and he's welcome to leave. I just hope he knows what he's doing. He's been through a lot.'

'I understand that, Teresa, but if he's made his mind up, then we should be happy that he's happy doing what he wants. That's a shame really. I will miss him. I got used to him being here. I know I initially moaned at your decision but ultimately it felt right to have him here.'

'Maybe he's just feeling he's become a burden and feels uncomfortable. I guess everyone has a sense of dignity, I might speak with him in the morning and see if I can change his mind. Hillrush House is really not the place for him, that hell-hole will just destroy him. He's got to understand he's not a burden.'

'I know what you're saying, Teresa, but sometimes you need to listen. Listen to what people are saying. He's a grown man, he can make grown up decisions, so you can't patronise him and treat him like a child that doesn't know what he's doing.'

'I'm not patronising him, Simon. I just care, it's in my nature to care and because I care, I worry. I worry that he's been through huge trauma and he's feeling helpless and on top of that I know he will feel he's a burden on us, therefore he's possibly making a rash decision. I just can't let that happen.'

'I understand, Teresa. It's the nurse within you. It's the nurse that cares so much. Well just ask him how he feels. I guess you'll soon know whether it's a real decision or a knee-jerk one. It's been a long day, shall we go to bed?'

'Yes, I'm tired too. I'll be with you in a minute.'

The words from Ash's letter danced in Teresa's eyes as her stare peered through the black ink and crisp ivory paper, they were almost attempting to decipher themselves as they weaved a patchwork of listless colours, rearranging themselves into something resembling a uniform pattern but still their systematic randomness shone through. This was not their intended message.

'What's wrong, Ash? Why are you torturing yourself like this?'

Teresa's mumble simultaneously choreographed an agonised tear that dripped onto the letter, smudging Simon's name and rippling down the paper as it struck its salty destruction through the word 'future' directly below 'Simon'.

Chapter 41
Hillrush House

'I'm sorry I had to call you here but as you're his only next-of-kin, you are the only one we can call at times of emergency or concern.'

'That's fine. I've been so busy I haven't really had a chance to visit since Ash came back here. What's wrong? What's the emergency? Is it Gloria again?'

'It's not really an immediate emergency but we thought you should know. No, it's not Gloria. For his first week back we've given him his own room and to be fair we think he's settled back in quite easily, of course it's early days yet but at least the first six days seem good. Oh and by the way, talking of Gloria, she's gone to a secure facility, after her attack on you and her repeated attacks on Ash, she was simply too much of a danger not be in a secure area. You really did have a lucky escape from her didn't you, it was all caught on our cameras so she really didn't have any grounds to protest at being relocated.'

'What is it then? What's wrong? What's wrong with Ash?'

'I'm afraid he's been self-harming. There are cuts and wounds all over his body and he admitted he did them himself and signed a statement that no one else was involved. To satisfy the law, much to Ash's disapproval we had to take pictures, here take a look at these before you go and see him.'

Six separate photographs, six separate sets of wounds. Without warning, the mutilations were proudly spread on the reception desk and in pessimistic unison bleated like six little lambs gasping for their final breaths as the hungry, rabid wolf tore through their woolly coat and squeezed shut his sharp incisors into their warm, young bloody flesh.

'How? How? How? How? How did he do this? Tell me how did he do this? How? How!?'

Teresa was shaking as she pointed to one of the photos, she gasped and sighed out the only words she could muster as her entire

178

body prepared for a grief-stricken deluge to condemn the afflictions rudely staring her in the face.

'It's not nice, is it? He must have squeezed and twisted it hard and kept squeezing it and twisting it until it was swollen and then even more till it bled, that's the only explanation. He did it to both of them. We didn't want to ask him the gory details once he confirmed it was all his own work.'

'But, but, but I've never seen a chest that sore, not through all my years, never ever!'

'I'm afraid so, love. He did it to himself. You can ask him about it, he might tell you how he did it but approach the subject cautiously, he will be quite embarrassed, as anyone would be. These other cuts are more traditional lacerations that a self-harmer often does. It's just not nice. God only knows what goes through their heads to want to feel such a horrible pain. I don't really understand it myself. The thought of it just makes me shudder.'

Standing to attention were the cuts on both arms, paper-cut thin but razor blade deep. Horizontal ones, parading with the vertical and the diagonal. Disjointed slithers of self-branding, achingly seared into the skin.

'Surely this is negligence on behalf of Hillrush House. How on earth did he get hold of the blades to do this? How could you be so slapdash to let a patient do this to themselves? Why didn't anyone notice this was going on?'

'We couldn't notice, love. There was nothing we could do.'

'I don't understand. This is gross negligence. Of course there was something you could have done. This should have been prevented!'

'I'm sorry to tell you, love. Ash's statement clearly states these wounds happened before he was readmitted to the hospital. I'm afraid he already had them before he came through these doors. These photographs were taken on his first day here.'

'No, no, no, no please God no! This just can't be true!'

Teresa's face shrivelled with disbelief and anger as tears dribbled down her cheeks with the dreaded realisation Ash's self-harming was done at her home. The bloody lesions jumped from the photos and clapped in alliance, at last they had been understood, finally the truth was unearthed. The visualisation of pain suddenly attached itself to Teresa's nervous system as every carving of the blade, every spurt of blood from Ash's chest, every wince he had suffered, catapulted itself ferociously through her trembling body.

Dragging her feet through the corridors of misery, Teresa's thoughts fired a dedicated volley of shots perforating the limited shield she had left against the perpetual bombardment of embittered happenings in her life.

Bam! Bam! Bam! Bam! Bam! Bam!

'How much more can I take? What did I do so wrong to deserve this?'

'Under my nose. He did this under my nose. In my home. Under my nose. He must have been so sad. Why was he so sad at my home? What did I do so wrong?'

Abruptly, a ceasefire. Teresa's biting apprehensions scrunched themselves into a crumpled sheet of paper to be unscrambled later, as Ash's sedated face destroyed the final remnants of protective resolve Teresa had left. Victoriously her stinging deductions simmered down. Everything this man had become was portrayed in one cumbersome artistic piece of work from his forlorn facial expressions to the slightness of his withering legs barely making an impression under the rough beige quilt cover. A deserted, lamentable endurance swathed in charitable bedlinen, embellished with the acute scars of an unintended reality in which the physical pains subserviently bowed to the monstrous mental butchering inside his sleeping head. Teresa's own life nervously giggled and side-stepped, embarrassed at the vastness of this troubled soul, helplessly sleeping away the hours and days to the cessation and ultimate happiness of a dismembered life.

'What does he live for? What keeps him alive?'

Ash's arms were both above the cover, both garnished with slits of dried blood, a pattern of lines with little significance except reckless heartache, underneath his left hand, his father's literary jewel.

'Crumbling into defeat, my cherished thoughts incomplete, my godforsaken future still gleaming ahead but the road, crazy, twisted and crooked in spirit and intention. Scream heart, scream loud, it's you that persists in pumping my life afloat. I listen to you and I ignore you in equal measures and as long as you insist on thrusting life through my veins, I will keep walking my misshapen pilgrimage, through this hellish world, knowing that I endure hell to be mesmerised by my heaven.'

The visible words from the chapter Ash was reading, recited themselves to Teresa in his dulcet words, astonishingly answering her turbulent questions about his devastating non-existence.

Two dots of blood had seeped from the two wounds on Ash's chest, almost crying for attention, as they stood proud, staining his wispy hospital issue shirt and once again pre-empting the straightforward question 'Why?'.

Teresa's frown as she walked away from her slumbering inmate towards reception, registered further confusion, triggered by the streaked green and white cushioned flooring furbishing the hospital wards. Her memory jumped at the incidental reminder of being attacked by Gloria and feeling her head against the spongy floor.

'Ash was asleep, so I'll come back tomorrow.'

'Sorry, I forgot to mention, he's sedated to help him sleep. I'll tell him you visited, I'm sure he'll be delighted.'

'Oh by the way. You said I had a lucky escape from Gloria. What do you mean 'lucky escape'? How was it such a lucky escape?'

'Well, my dear, your friend saved you!'

'You mean Ash. Yes, he shouted my name just in time, otherwise Gloria would have caught me unaware.'

'My love, he didn't just shout your name, he probably saved your life!'

'I don't understand. What do you mean?'

'Don't you know? Ash stopped her from strangling you. We assume she was going to kill you!'

'How did he persuade her to do that? How did he stop her?'

'He didn't persuade her love. He pulled her off you!'

'Who did? Ash can't. He can't walk. Who stopped Gloria?'

'Oh yes he can. Don't ask me how, my love, but I'm telling you, Ash, the person asleep in bed forty two, physically stopped you getting strangled. Maybe, he can sometimes walk, he certainly didn't hesitate that day as he leapt from his bed and pulled the scrawny cow off you and then kept her down until security arrived. It's all on video if you want to take a look.'

'No. No, it's fine. I believe you. I'll take a look next time. Actually, I'd like to take a look now. I'm so bloody confused.'

There was no sane balance in Teresa's head. Rationality thwarted and splattered into distorted fragments. Disturbing and perplexing, her belligerent mind was scattered in a heap of turmoil as dazed thoughts came dressed as conspiracies and agitation.

'Here you go, my dear, there's no sound but at least you can see what's happening.'

Sound was not necessary, as the visuals projected a million descriptive words, far greater than any dialogue could possibly manage.

'Goodbye, love. See you tomorrow.'

The video was still playing as Teresa, bemused and disorientated walked out of Hillrush House, without any parting pleasantries. The entirety of her communication organs and brainpower were dumbstruck and fixated with the final video image as she turned towards the exit and left the building. Ash restraining Gloria in a twisted lock, involving his arms and legs, after thrusting aside his bed linen and promptly galloping from his disabled bed, with a brazen, nonsensical disregard for the historic shambles that plagued his days.

Reception at Hillrush House was always subdued, people didn't visit humanity's deranged, fallen creatures. Jilted by a manufactured ordinariness, a society whose standards have been concocted to the utopian ideal of what is commonplace, rejecting people by what the mass populous consider as normal. Hillrush House, one of the hundreds of such disposal organisations, incarcerating the repudiated, camouflaging them into unimportance and, by twisted default, securing them into the impervious world, in their own isolated non-existence, wasn't a haven for concerned visitors and relatives. For the duty nurse it was back to the limited communication of Hillrush's residents, as her only rational person, petulantly departed the building.

'You missed your pretty visitor, my love. Hopefully she will be back tomorrow. She looked really worried today but I had to tell her, it's my job to tell her.'

The nurse mumbled to herself, whilst attempting to straighten Ash's dishevelled bed sheets.

'There you go, all done. What are you dreaming about today? Who is in that mind of yours? Who are you talking to? What are they doing to you? Sleep well, my love, sleep well. See you later.'

Ash gripped his father's book as his body twitched and his mind explored the depths of its ability to conjure from the spellbound to the theatrically disturbed. A solid tempered steel hand tool, possibly developed from tongs used to handle hot metal in the Bronze Age, particularly useful for bending and compressing a wide range of materials. Short clutching, serrated jaws, allowing the force of the rubber hand grip to be amplified and focused on an object with heavy, commanding precision.

Grimacing with an intense shooting pain, Ash squeezed the pliers, shutting the angry, crocodile action upon one of the two protruding points on his naked chest. Braced, into his wheelchair by the force of his other hand on the armrest, Ash enforced the self-mutilation until a squirt of blood syringed itself from the mangled swelling. Contorted relief as he achieved his goal, blood squirming from the wound, weeping and meandering its way down his trembling torso. His elation and accomplishment, short-lived, the other nipple needed the same crushing treatment as he swapped bridling arms and snatched the pliers into his other hand and once again gritted his teeth with the same ferocity as the squashing jowls of the blue handled pliers.

'C'mon, you can do this! C'mon, you can do it! We need to see blood! We need another squirt. If you don't make it squirt, then I will and you damn well know, if I do it, I will pull it right off and leave a gaping hole! You really don't want me to do that, do you?! You really don't want me to leave a huge ugly gaping, bleeding hole. So, c'mon Ash, you can do this, you can squeeze this one just as tight. C'mon! C'mon! C'mon! C'mon! That's it, squeeze! Harder! Harder! Harder! That's my man! Well done! Well done! Just one more little squeeze, so we get the same squirt as the other one, c'mon you can do this!'

Blood lactated from the wound and the determined cheerleader faded having encouraged Ash's goals.

'Where were you when I needed you, Dad? Why did you desert me? Why did you let me go? Where were you?'

Ash's tears diluted the red stream flowing down his blistering chest, the saltwater soothing the plier's handy-work. Even in dreams pain can be relieved, particularly by familiarity.

'My dear Ash. This is your wrongful life, an evil rigmarole you don't deserve. I know you didn't ask for it but know this, I am by your side and I will always be by your side and at those times when you need me the most, I will lift you. I will lift you high. I will lift you from this pain that rains on you every day. I won't let you down, I won't leave you. I will never leave you until your days are happy again, I will stay by your side until your world is complete. I will stay until you need me, until you can smile and live the life you deserve. I won't let you down, Ash. I won't and I never ever will. Your world will be complete.'

Dad's voice boomed its mindful peace and Ash's dreams of self-destruction immediately converted to floating blissfulness, amidst the searing pain of reality that brushed through into his imagination as his squirming agitated his actual injuries under the coarse bed linen.

Chapter 42
Devouring

Creeping, sliming around my bones.
You were always there, isolated and confined.
Released from your cage, anger that clones.
Internally they know you will applaud my moans,
As you dissect and disease, pillage and plunder
On the outside, they will look and wonder.
Why was I born with the chemical blunder?
Devouring, lunching, crunching my goodness
Striking famine and fever in your destructive wake
God's holy body you dismantle and break
Relentless and ruthless until the last breath I take.

'Thank you, Simon. Not the most romantic poem I've ever read but I suspect the condition you carry hardly evokes romance. Are you not feeling good today?'

'Sorry, Teresa. It's just how I'm feeling at the moment. They're just not very encouraging at hospital and once again today, they made me feel like my life will end soon, as this scourge continues to devour me. It's just getting me down, that's all.'

'I'm sorry, Simon, that's awful. I wish I could do more. It's just not been a good day today. I went to see Ash. He was asleep but it so happens, he'd been self-harming while he was here living with us and your poem just puts everything into perspective. I'm just sorry I haven't really been much support for you. I really am sorry.'

'Hey, that's okay, honey. You've got a lot on your plate. I totally understand but that can't be right, there's no way Ash could have self-harmed himself, we would have known. Did he tell you that himself?'

'No, as I said he was asleep but he confessed to Hillrush House that he did it himself and they showed me the horrific photos. I really wanted to ask him why. I feel like I've been a massive failure. What on earth made him do that? How could he do that to me, after all I did for him? I really want to know what he was thinking and what made him do it. I'm so confused at the moment?'

'I wouldn't bother, darling. Who knows what was going on in his mind? I don't think he will ever make any sense. Maybe, I'll go and visit him and cheer him up. I don't suppose he gets many visitors.'

'You're right, Simon. Yes, I'm sure he would appreciate a visit. He might even tell you what was going on in his mind. Sometimes, it's easier to do that to someone that isn't medically connected.'

'Yes, you never know what he might confess. I might go there tomorrow, it'll take my mind off myself for a while.'

'You will be better soon, I know you will be. We were meant to be together. I just know we'll get through this.'

'I feel it eating me away, Teresa. Slowly devouring through my flesh, cannibalising my body. Sometimes, I just want to slice out the tumour myself and be done with it.'

'I remember Dawn randomly saying she would support me through this, I wish she was still here, I hardly knew her but for some reason she just wanted to help me, help us through the ordeal. There was such a comfort about her. She once said 'Teresa, there is always a way. There is always another door just waiting to be opened. You can't always see it but it is there. I can help you find the door. I can help you open the door and I will be waiting on the other side to welcome you into your renewed world.' I now wonder what she meant by that. There are no doors to open.'

'I'm sure she could have helped but I'm not sure what door there is for me, surely there is no door when I could be dead soon from this thing growing inside me. I know you're upset about Dawn, so I won't say anything. I think it's suffice to say we'll just never know, will we?'

Chapter 43
Legacy

'Well, well, well, a second visitor in as many days. Some people never get a visitor and lucky Ash has had two in two days. Yesterday it was a pretty woman and today it's you, at least Ash is awake today, he was really upset to miss his visitor yesterday.'

'Yes, that pretty woman is my girlfriend, thank you very much. Now, which way is the lucky patient. I can't wait to see him. I'm sure I will make it up to him for missing her yesterday. He'll be delighted to see me.'

A smile replaced the scowl on his face as Simon walked away from reception into the direction the nurse pointed.

'I will be careful. I know. I understand. I know you're always there.'

Simon heard the familiar voice of Ash as he approached his isolated ward.

'Ha, ha, ha, got visitors, have we? Talking to the dead again are we? Hello fruitcake, I thought I'd pay my old friend a visit.'

'I knew you were coming, Dad told me you were on your way.'

'Oh for God's sake, man! Your dad is dead. Fucking gone! No more! Doesn't exist. Of course, had you ever made the funeral you'd actually know that for sure but you were too busy killing your fucking girlfriend, weren't you?'

There were no more tears. Ash was all cried out but that didn't cease the almighty crash of his already shattered heart, as his anxiety levels were attempting to burst from his brain.

'What do you want Simon? Why are you here? Are you just here to hurt me?'

'Hurt you, Ash? Hurt you, Ash? Never. I never want to hurt you. I'm just here to make sure you've kept your promise because if you haven't kept it or you don't keep it, then yes, I will hurt you. I will hurt you so hard that the death of your father and the murder of your girlfriend will be like a lovely walk in the park on a sunny afternoon. Oh yes, I will hurt you hard.'

'I haven't done anything wrong. I have kept our promise and I will always keep our promise.'

'I'm glad to hear it, Ash, because you know exactly what will happen if you ever break our promise. Remember this, Ash? I thought I would bring it as a lovely little reminder of what can happen.'

With a delicate clunk, Simon placed an object on Ash's bedside table. The tears that had so far escaped from showing their frustration, duly mustered up their pent up angst and congregated in Ash's eyes, a place they were accustomed to and no longer felt strangers to materialise in, showing their combined empathy.

'Oh you do remember. You remember them well. Lovely, aren't they? Oh I do love a set of pliers. They are so useful around the house, they can do so much but at times they can be so angry and you know what they can do when they're angry, don't you Ash? Ah yes, I can see, your chest still remembers what they can do. Do you want me to remind you what they're capable of?'

No words formulated. This very moment was the most helpless Ash had ever felt, he shook his head and tightened his hold over the only consolation he had left in his miserable life, his dad's book. Lifting the intimidating blue handled tool, Simon snapped it next to Ash's nose, causing him to jolt his head and a solitary tear to feverishly trickle down his contorted face.

'And don't think that heap of shit will help you. If I'd written that I would have killed myself too.'

'My dad didn't kill himself.'

'Maybe not your dad but your mum did, didn't she? Probably because she read that awful book and we all know why she killed herself, don't we, we all know why she took her own life. Don't we? You're from an entire family of freaks, aren't you? All of you depraved, all of you fucking bonkers.'

A grievous collision was imminent, merely seconds of collaborative memories, hurtling towards an interweaved constellation of misery. Holding onto mum's desperately suspended torso, cricks in her neck crunching obstreperously louder than a hungry bunch of feeding crickets. Dreaded noises, sulking grief, the aroma of mum's slightly perfumed legs as they were pressed into Ash's face, the broken landscape of dad's facial expressions, ageing a year as every fateful second slipped by, the Eiffel Tower screaming its fear of the conclusion that had already crossed its watchful looming frame. The consolidated orchestra of death replayed the farce through Ash's senses, weighing thickly upon his head, which he bowed in impending defeat and sobbed.

'C'mon, my good man, there's no need for that is there, you don't need to cry, it's not as if your crying is going to bring them all back is it. They're gone. I understand you could have done more to keep hold of them but hey you can't go back now, can you? All dead. All gone. Just little Ash and his stupid book left.'

Ash rained tears as his ears deciphered Simon's comments, hearing the smirk on his face as his cutting words tore and lacerated the ounce of resolve and dignity he had left to hold his head an inch higher than the wretched depth it had sunk to.

'Well, I might as well tell you why your mum killed herself. Do you want to know? I think you should know and I think I'm the one that should tell you because as you know I'll do it with real feeling. Do you want to know, Ash? Well, I'm going to tell you anyway.'

Scared frigid, stillness, tensing every fibre that can be forcibly controlled, with the sight of the growling, fearsome mass of sharp teeth, glossy tan coat and bulging muscle of an anger fuelled Rottweiler about to be unleashed by its sadistic owner, with only one intention. Blood and carnage. Ash closed his eyes and just waited for the heavy, pneumatic jaws to sink into his flesh, grasping his trembling bones underneath, as the dog-owner released the frothing, antagonised beast, with a single expression 'Go on, get him, boy!' that translated into dog language as 'attack and bite the scared, cowering man, to make my owner happy!'

'She was a fucking murderer. Your mother killed someone. Your mother, the evil bitch actually murdered someone. There you have it my good man. That is why she took her life because she couldn't live with the fact that she took another life. There you have it indeed, like mother like son, no wonder you turned into a murderer too. It runs in the fucking family!'

The Rottweiler ferociously shook his head as Ash's brittle bone grated against its sharpened incisors. The pain as skin, bloody tissue and serrated muscle adorned the unyielding jaw, had reached an unbearable crescendo, there was no more agony possible, all of Ash's pain receptors were overloaded, smoking feverishly, at the fullest capacity available, they weren't constructed for this industrial level of affliction.

'Typical of you to be so selfish. Not even a thank you for telling you the truth, not even an acknowledgement of my kindness in being so honest with you. You just sit there feeling sorry for yourself, I've got things to do. In fact, I may as well tell you because I know you want to know, I know you enjoy the twitch it gives you. I'm going home to take out my disappointment at your selfishness, on Teresa's body, yes I will give her a good ramming, I will make it hurt and yet she will enjoy it so much. You? Well you can just sit there in your wallowing pity and think about that and the fact that your mother was a murderer. Goodbye fruitcake and do not forget our little promise.'

Ash recoiled with Simon's parting gesture, a swift pinch of skin on his cheek with the pliers, leaving a red mark and a spot of blood encouraging a blister. It had no effect. A deep numbness blanketed Ash's body, he had been switched off. Life was at its darkest depth. The faintest flicker of hope shining in the distance was finally extinguished into tormented nothingness.

'That was awful. I saw that. I will make sure that man never comes to see you here ever again. You're a good man and you don't deserve such an evil person in your life. Let me see your cheek where he touched you with that horrible thing he was threatening you with.'

Velvety words trickled over Ash, leaving a residue of sweetness, washing away the hostility of Simon's unwelcome visit, the woman's fingertip on Ash's face injected warmth and friendliness, as he strained to make eye contact with his kind visitor.

'Thank you. It's my life now. It's all I have left. People like him, this bed and no hope for anything to ever be any different. I asked for it. I asked for all of it and here I am getting everything I have ever deserved. This is my life.'

The woman's eye's smiled before her mouth made any movement. She wasn't wearing hospital clothes, she must be someone else's visitor, a normal, amiable visitor, not there to threaten, harm or scar but visiting through human caring, the kind that would visit a friend or close relative.

190

'You know life can change at any given moment, things happen, directions alter, in the same way badness comes about so can goodness. You must never give up on hope. Make hope the last man standing and hope alone will fight, fight and fight again and hope will never, ever give up, not until you give up on hope.'

'I don't think I have any hope left, it's all been stolen and dragged through the mud. I think hope has actually given up on me.'

Ash squeezed his book as the words fumbled through his mouth, with a trail of bleakness, an opaque bitterness, leaving a residential taste of discouragement on his lips. Even the magnetism of clasping 'Make my World Complete' had evaporated, its usual alchemy proven to be a fallacy, discredited, defamed from the pedestal it once commanded from.

'Hope will never let you down. Hope will stand by your side. Without hope your heart will truly die. Even if you only have the smallest, tiniest smidgen of hope, that will do but never, ever let go of it because it will never let go of you, it will never give up on you. While you have hope you will have light.'

Redness blushed Ash's hands as his grip on 'Make my World Complete', tightened, attempting to wring out ounces of hope and optimism that it normally shrouded Ash's dreaded days with. Gritting his teeth, searching for the magic to pour from its pages and deluge him, his frustration built a defence against the welcoming onslaught from this prized possession.

'What's your book?'

'It's the last book my father wrote. It's the only thing I have left in the whole world. It's probably the only hope that gets me through my days.'

'If that's the case, why don't you read me something from it? I'd really like that, then maybe as it's an emblem of your hope, it might shine for you. That will make my day if you'll do that.'

Unwavering bricks from Ash's defensive wall of frustration and woe tumbled as his visitor's voice soothed his soured thoughts and spruced up the crumpled pages in his persecuted mind and the compulsion, catalysed by an aroused gush of fortitude from the throttled book, to read, effortlessly nudged aside the anguish that was dominating him. Ash un-grappled his book as its pages flicked open on a chapter titled 'One' and a smile that was inconceivable only moments ago creased over his heckled face.

'Truth or falsehood; is there one synchronised to align with you or is this a game of coincidence with no agenda and no pattern?'

Ash looked up at his visitor, her eyes glimmered in a sky of abject darkness, exuding a brightness Ash had only ever seen in Teresa's eyes. He continued to read from his dad's book, the words danced a harmonised order as they leapt from the page, wallowing in the pleasure they were bringing, remembering the elicit emotions the author poured into them.

'I pondered that very question for the multitude of days I lived a half-life, oblivious to the other half wandering aimlessly through life in an identical bubble of unknowing rapture. I concur the universe embarked on a masterplan, in which every living person is a unique thread entwined into the gargantuan blanket of humanity, destined to a life manufactured along its cumbersome journey. Anomalous to each other, unaware that the thread you are is incomplete until tied to the closest parallel. One can never know until 'the one' arrives, creating the most compatible knot, and the universe smiles as his witless frolic completes.

There is one. There could be one of many that were severed but we serve our master, oblivion. What we don't know, what we don't witness, what we don't see, what we don't sense, bears no part in the narrow, shallow life we tread. There is not an adventure, an escapade waiting us to discover the one, you cannot travel to nirvana. You cannot embark on an expedition in search of the one. The universe plays his behemoth game of correlation, engaging two of his pawns to meet by pure fluke. I wrote about love. I pondered about romance. The universe watched, listened and learnt and without warning, fiendishly grabbed my aloofly floating raft on an endless sea of mediocrity and plunged my soul and sanity into the deep end, washing a tsunami of completeness over me. She was the one. My unconsummated half. An astray thread had discovered the immaculate twine, bonding, braiding and entangling to conceive perfection.

She was my world. She remains my world and my world knows no boundaries, no restriction and no rules. There is no force strong enough to break the unbreakable bond, union and connection of a world that is complete. Death itself cowers, his morbid smirk reduced to an unconventional grimace, his power over life weakened, debilitated, his tables turned, twisting his legacy into a zest that even his scythe of blackness cannot disjoin and darken. Life is love, love overwhelms death. Synchronisation or coincidence? Were my musings on love leading me to the one? Did I contrive the coincidence, synchronising it into my beliefs and thoughts? There is no bona fide explanation for encountering the love that I lived for, the love that gave me life, the life that I dreamt into existence and there she was in the flesh, bones and glorious technicolour, awaiting my frayed thread to fuse with hers, as our DNA danced an infinitive waltz, chemically amalgamating, cementing an eternal collaboration. Boundless fulfilment, ceaseless enchantment, we were destined to be as one. Were we lucky to have found each other or did our vibrations through the universe magnetise our energies together, drawing and pulling us to the same location and desire that we dreamt of through every waking moment? I will never know the answer, albeit she was the answer. The answer to my prayers, making my world complete.'

Ash closed the book. The warmth of words blossomed through his disjointed thoughts and flowered his irreverence towards life, linking his disconnect with a flowery chain of aromatic flowers.

'Make my World Complete', the fiery torch that shone through the deathly quagmire, there was an insane alchemy lurking within its battered pages, a sorcery that metamorphosed its black and white musings to accommodate any emotion the reader was embroiled with.

Ash's agitation had mutated into sparkles of hope, temporarily forgetting he had the pleasure of an audience.

'Did you enjoy that?'

The woman's gaze was glued to the words still fluttering as butterfly kaleidoscopes, mesmerising her with their hypnotic charm; 'Make my World Complete', had brazenly taken another consenting hostage. No ransom required, willingly captured within its magical bewitchery.

'I don't know what to say, except I just never knew, I really didn't know.'

'Know what?'

'That words could mean so much. That just a few lines could have me so taken by them. That I could be so lost with just a few simple words.'

'My dad had a way with words, especially when talking about my mum. I hope they are still together now. He made his love sound so eternal!'

'They will be. They will be. Words like those are beyond this life and are inscribed into hearts, not just books. I have to go now. I will come again and you can read me more words. For now, you and your dad have made my day complete. Thank you so much, Ash, forget that horrible man that was here before, he doesn't know a thing about you and your family and above all never, ever give up on hope. There is always hope and I can tell it will always shine its glorious light upon you. I just know it will. Goodbye, Ash, don't you dare give up on hope.'

'Thank you. I won't. I won't give up. Goodbye, yes, please come again.'

An ethereal touch upon Ash's hand and synchronicity, coincidence and destiny fought for the highest podium of recognition as Ash reprimanded himself for rudely not asking his visitor's name. Insults, pain and dwindled self-esteem following Simon's unwelcome visit, entirely washed away by a torrid stream gushing by his bedside. Ash's sum total of redeeming light over darkness people now equalled two, one who resided in the fibre of his body, Teresa, and one whose name he didn't ask, but her brief presence swishing through his life left an indelible mark with an exclamation sign shouting the mystery woman was meant to feature within the landscape of his tumultuous life.

'Thank you, Dad. I know you are always there and I know no matter what happens, you watch over me. I know you sent the woman to my bedside and I know you will always look after me. I miss you every day.'

Chapter 44
This Charming Man

Bristling with ruffled charisma,
Character, buoyant and brilliant
This charming man, conjured from blood and bones,
Once resilient
Your womanly touch, the unknown factor,
Crazy, unfounded breach
Putting pointed signals from cupid
Within my manly reach.
Slashing, scratching,
Pulverising the unreachable roughness
Smoothing, planning, sanding,
Sharp edges cut and rounded
Releasing the coarseness, flowing
With seasons unfounded.
The sun, the moon, the stars, the galaxies,
Infinity founded.
You exploded my mind, opened my heart
And out it poured.
Emotions, personality, connectivity blazing it soared.
This charming man, changed, modelled and moored.

'I love it, Simon. What inspired the words?'

'Obviously you did, my love. Ever since I've known you're into reading again and ever since we got back together, I've been inspired to write and this little piece is nothing, it just shows how you've changed me.'

'That's lovely. But you're not kidding me, Mr Driscoll, you've always been charming. In fact it was your killer charm that had me hooked in the first place!'

Teresa smirked as she read the passionate collection of words again.

'You've certainly got a knack with words, Simon, but you always had that, you've always had a certain way about you that just melted

195

me and actually made me weak at the knees. I love this. Keep it up and you might have your own version of 'Make my World Complete' soon, talking of which how is our estranged patient?'

Filtering through the still air between them, Teresa's words connected with Simon, a literary string of grenades exploding into 'This Charming Man's head 'Boom! Boom! Boom! Boom!' Four concussive detonations, ruffling his charisma and character into submission, rousing the slumbering antagonism beneath. Four pealing blasts, one attributed to each word 'Make!....My!.....World!.....Complete!'

'Why do you need to bring that book into everything, I can do so much better. I wish you would just forget the mad man, his father and that dreadful book. I am so sick to death of Ash. He has gone and he will never ever be back, so can we please forget him and his stupid world!'

'Simon. You need to calm down. That was a compliment. Make my World Complete is one of the most amazing books ever written. Why does the mention of Ash and his world make you so angry? What's the real matter? What's underneath it all? Is there something I just don't know? You really need to tell me. I was only complimenting your wonderful words.'

'Teresa! There is nothing wrong. Don't you dare try your psycho bullshit on me! I'm not your patient and by the way, just in case you've forgotten you're not a nurse anymore and furthermore, no it isn't a good book, it's nothing more than a loser talking about the love he can't have because he's an idiot, like his son. What the fuck is so good about such a pointless story!?'

'I don't want to argue with you. There is no need for this argument. If the book winds you up so much, I won't mention it again, albeit I just don't understand why you're so angry about it all. It's a book and Ash was a patient. Simon, your anger is not justified at all. What is wrong with you?'

'I am not angry! I am not fucking angry! There is nothing wrong with me, nothing at all fucking wrong with me! I just don't get why you're so hooked on that invalid, what's his hold over you? Why are you so naïve, he clearly twisted you around his finger. The man is a lunatic and yet he has you totally addicted to his bullshit, to the point it's coming between us and wrecking our home! Why can't you see what he's done to us? Just explain to me how he's done this to you. Explain! I want an explanation! I deserve an explanation! And you are going to give it to me! C'mon, Teresa, explain! Explain! Explain! Fucking explain! Now!'

Red Alert! Red Alert! Red Alert!

Teresa's latent memory instantly smashed the emergency glass and punched her sleeping, subconscious thoughts into the buzzing reality of ringside, the front row of her brain.

Round one. A flowing gush of adrenalin burst through her veins as the pummel shook her head and jolted the hormonal tsunami into creation.

Round two. Asphyxiation as all other open thought avenues drowned into immediate submission. This was sheer dominance.

Round three. Recognition, as her dormant memory prepared to throw in the towel, knowing it was doomed to fail. This was no match for the ordinary.

Round four. It's a knock-out. It's over. Teresa was floored as her subconscious, with a swift blow, was battered into her conscious. Simon's familiar idiosyncratic jolt as his right hand erratically scratched his head, just above his right ear, sparked a thousand sleeping memories and Teresa fully understood the potential of the escalating conversation.

An agitated characteristic that had heralded the most debased outcomes between them. Simon's already weak control mechanism had been overwhelmed, his right hand action was precisely the same one before, he stuffed the poem into her mouth and physically assaulted her, the very same movement before the vilest dialogue spouted from his enraged mouth. Every degradation, crippled conversation and debauched aftermath had been preceded by his arbitrary itch. Fretting, Teresa's words stumbled from her mouth, as the surging adrenalin prepared her for a ghastly outcome.

'Can we just please forget it? I'm sorry I mentioned it. I promise never to mention it again. Please, Simon, let's just forget it.'

'I'm sorry, Teresa, but I really need to know and you're going to tell me and I know, that you know the answer. So, just spit it out and we can move on. Just tell me! Tell me why you have such an obsession with that freak. What has he done to you? What is it? C'mon, just tell me. I need to know and you are going to tell me!'

'Simon, there is nothing to tell. There is nothing to say. Honestly there is nothing. Can we please drop the whole subject?'

'I already know. So just say it. Just say it and we can move on. Just tell me. Tell me, Teresa. Just tell me before this gets any worst!'

'Why should it get any worst, when I'm telling you there's nothing to say? You're being crazy now, you're scaring me. This is ridiculous, Simon. Just stop! You need to stop right now!'

Scratching his head like a flea bitten mutt, Simon stood up and barked out his ferocious rabid words. 'Or what? What the fuck will you do, if I don't stop? I will stop once you tell me the truth. This is all your fault, fucking tell me! Tell me right now! Or you'll be sorry! You'll be sorry you ever met that freak or ever opened that stupid fucking book!'

'Tell you what, you stupid man. Tell you what! I don't know what you're talking about. Sit down, Simon, just sit down. You need to sit down and calm down. Sit down now! You're really scaring me! Just sit down!'

'Don't tell me what to do. How fucking dare you tell me what to do. Fuck you, Teresa, fuck you and your crippled lover boy. Fuck you both! You fucking deserve each other. You're no different to that bitch Dawn. You cannot tell me what to do. No one tells me what to do. No one. No one!'

'What do you mean I'm no different to that bitch Dawn? What the hell has this got to do with Dawn? Simon, tell me now what you mean. I need to know what you mean! Why have you brought Dawn's name into this!? Simon, what the fuck is going on? Tell me now! Oh my fucking God, why the hell did you mention Dawn? I need to know! Simon!'

Spluttering her words, the air remained motionless. The picture stopped, grinding to a halt as if the projector had jarred, only letting the reel progress one slovenly frame at a time, conversation slurred, the colours of the scene blurring at the edges, brushing them into a smudged haze. One subject within the segmented movie moved at its regular pace, focused on the kitchen door, he marched with a mission and disappeared from the confusion of the room. The film scene was frozen. The stillness of time as multiple thoughts, ideas and potential outcomes meandered together, slushing into a gruelling mixture with the remains of her adrenalin wave. Amplified by the cluttering racket from the kitchen, conjuring images of metallic objects, that on any other occasion would be ignored or simply unregistered as the noise of normality but today, this particular moment, mingled with Simon's mumblings of 'I'll fucking show you!' 'I'll show you! 'I'll show you right now!' 'I'll fucking show you!' the rattling thunder-bolted up Teresa's spine, juddering into her already inundated head, as his name trickled from her palpitating lips,

'Simon, Simon, Simon, Simon, Simon, Simon, Simon!'

Chapter 45
Beginnings and Endings

'Now, young man, you must be Simon. I've heard so much about you.'

'Yes, it is Simon. Who is this?'

'Oh I'm Dawn. I was just calling to talk to Teresa. She's told me so much about you.'

'Oh yeah. All good stuff, I'm assuming?'

'Of course, young man. Your lovely lady dotes on you and is very worried about you too.'

'Worried. What's she worried about? Why's Teresa worried?'

'She's worried about your illness but she is a nurse and at least she knows how to cope.'

'My illness! Teresa told you about my illness. I didn't realise you knew each other so well.'

'We've met a few times but I was a nurse at your hospital so it was a natural conversation to have. How are you feeling nowadays? And what treatments have they put you on. I know the staff quite well, so I know they will look after you and get you through this. Who's your doctor? I'm certain I will know him.'

'I'm sorry, Dawn, but I'm really shocked Teresa has told you about my illness. I'm not sure I appreciate being discussed like some specimen. As for my treatment and my doctor, frankly I don't think it's any of your business!'

'Hey, hey I was only comforting Teresa because she was so upset and she felt much better sharing her burden. I know it's none of my business but Teresa is a very special woman and offering her a shoulder to lean on was the least I could do. I understand you're upset and I understand you're going through so much with your illness too. I'm sorry if I've said the wrong thing. I was only trying to help.'

'Okay. Maybe I overreacted. I just haven't been feeling myself since this scourge took over my body and the treatment isn't helping much, it just makes me tired and grouchy all the time and I don't even know if they're giving me the right treatment for my needs. I wish there was an easier way. I wish there was some way I could support Teresa in return. This is a very difficult time for me and for us.'

'I know, young man. You're going through the trauma of being unwell and unsure. That will have put strains on your relationship without a doubt. I know the head doctor of Oncology at Walton Hospital and I will ask him about you and your treatment and nudge him to prioritise you, it's the least I can do, after all it's not about what you know, it's about who you know, isn't it, and he will do as he's told, we go back a long, long time. He will already know you, he's a kind caring doctor that knows all of his patients personally.'

'Dawn! I know you want to help and I know you care but I will only say this once and I want you to listen very carefully. Keep your nose out of my fucking business or you will regret ever meeting Teresa!'

'Now, now, young man. Why are you getting so angry when I'm trying to help you? Dr Weston-Mayers is a good friend and he can help you. That will help you and the lovely Teresa. Why wouldn't you want my unique offer of help and by the way you should never threaten a woman, especially if all she's doing is trying to help you'

'Fuck off, Dawn! I don't need your help. We don't need you! Do not ever contact Teresa again, otherwise you will suffer, that is a promise. If I ever find out you've spoken with Teresa again, I will hurt you. I will really hurt you!'

'Well young man. You don't scare me. I've been to prison you know and I've dealt with real thugs, not just cowards that hurt women. You don't scare me, you could never scare me! I will speak with Teresa and we will grow our friendship and it will last forever, unlike you young man, you will be outed for the lying, cheating animal you really are!'

'You've done it now. Those badly chosen words only mean one thing. Tonight, I will physically and mentally show Teresa what an animal I really am and when she screams in agony, when she cries out for help, I hope you'll be proud of yourself because it will be your fault she will suffer so much, I'm so looking forward to it. If you're lucky enough, maybe I'll do the same to you one day. Now fuck off before I come round there and sort you out right now!'

'You can't hurt me, Simon, you can never hurt me and for the record, I've already spoken to my good friend Dr Weston-Mayers, he's never heard of you. Walton Hospital has no record of you or your illness. You are a cheating liar and I will tell Teresa what you're doing. Now fuck off yourself, you vile little creature!'

Chapter 46
Hold my Hand

'Well I can only say you've surprised me beyond belief and you have no idea how much it has restored my faith in human nature and the belief that honesty is always the best policy. Well done, young man, well done!'

'Thank you, Dawn. I'm just sorry I turned up at your home unannounced but I didn't know what else to do after you rightly put the phone down on me for being the vile little creature that I am. By the way it wasn't difficult to sweet-talk your address out of Walton hospital, you may want to warn them of that in the future.'

'Well, young man, that's your lovely charm. No wonder Teresa is besotted by you and believe me, she will totally understand why you made the story up. Hey, I don't know what lengths I would go to, to get the love of my life back into my life. I'm so glad you're going to tell her the truth tonight and I'm so glad it's been inspired by little old me.'

'Oh you inspired me so much. You made me believe it was the only path left for me to solve my challenge once and for all. Thank you for helping clear my clouded thinking. After today we can all move on and be truly happy, once again I'm so sorry and thank you for the lovely cup of tea, it's just what I needed.'

'No more apologies, young man. Save them for your good lady. Not only will she appreciate your decent turnaround but she will be proud that you fought for her the way that you have. Now on your way, make haste. You have a wonderful woman waiting for you and waiting for the rest of her life to unravel.'

The sound of an old oak door, heavy and a burden on the rusted hinges that have held it up for so many years, Dawn's eyes creaked open. Shards of light syringe injected themselves into her aching pupils, as a jaded deluge of gratitude washed over her, in the opening micro seconds of her weary awakening following a blissful deep sleep, it had been an uninterrupted night, decidedly rare and disproportional to the aging process.

'Oh you've decided to wake, have you?! I've literally been waiting for hours!'

Dawn's feeble wisp of gratefulness was scythed from her throbbing head, immediately usurped with quaking panic, as her scattered mind attempted to backtrack its memories and make some sense of the gleeful voice shouting across the room.

'What? What's going on? Oh my God! What's happened? Why am I on the floor? Someone please help me! What's going on! What's happening? What's going on? Please, please, please help me! This is all a mistake, please help me! Please. I can't move. What's going on? Please help me. Please help me. I can't move. I can't move! Oh my God, I need help!'

'Help? Help? You don't need help. Why would you need help with me here? Help from what? That's what I'm here for, to help you!'

Dawn craned her neck as every cellular fibre intrinsic to holding her together antagonistically worked in the opposite direction, springing her movements back, her body was an over stretched elastic band, rubberised, unable to operate and pinging back to the original position, with the added disincentive of searing needling stabs of pain ripping through her awkwardly stretched skin.

'Oh, of course. You can't move, can you? Whoops, silly silly me, I apologise, I forgot to mention, I'm afraid your tea had a couple of these little babies in it. People call them date-rape drugs. Personally, I prefer to call them, 'how to shut up an old loud-mouthed bitch who is intent on ruining other people's lives' pills. Normally one does the trick but for you, as you're so special, I gave you two. Which is thankfully, why you can barely move. Great, aren't they? In fact, they're fucking genius! I mean, I was doing all sorts of wonderful things to you and you didn't even budge once. You just lay there loving every second of attention I gave your body. Your mouth was a tad still but it was still warm and I guess the whole idea was to shut it in the first place but thank you, it was all good for me. I've never been that intimate with a woman your age before. I highly recommend it.'

Dawn didn't need to see a face, the voice alone made her plead with her brain, that this was a hilarious dream, concocted by an over active mind that loved to play with emotions and senses. He rattled the tablets in her face brushing her nose with the glass bottle, echoing through her ears as kettle-drums banging out their Caribbean symphony, with a rhythmic reminder of when she must have left her tea unattended for mere seconds as she had fumbled around her kitchen cabinets, to find some biscuits for her unexpected guest.

'Simon.' Dawn's trembling words slurred from her pained throat. 'This is all a mistake. Don't do this. Please don't do this. I won't say a word. I will never repeat this to anyone. Please, Simon. Please, Simon. Please. Just make it stop. Just let me go. Please let me go. Please.'

'Oh I know you won't say a word. You've no need to convince me of that. I already know you will be silent. I already know you won't tell a soul. You won't tell anyone because you can't tell anyone but that didn't stop you threatening it before, did it?'

Dawn inherently knew to shut her eyes as Simon walked closer and raised his gloved fist, just giving her the briefest glimpse of her assailant, with whom she had waved goodbye to at her doorstep. The smell of glove leather sifted through the darkness of her memories and transported Dawn back to her mother, as her olfactory senses painted a picture of cold winter mornings, safely walking to school holding hands. Today the recognisable safety was crushed as a new memory of leather was registered with a frenzied punch to her face, sending the crunching resonance of breaking cartilage in her nose deep into her bruised skull.

'Nice hit! Your face is so good at taking all kinds of hits, isn't it? I don't suppose you enjoyed that as much as the pleasure I gave your face earlier! Well don't worry, where there's pleasure there's always pain and I guess, where there's pain, there's always pleasure. So, now I must give you some more pleasure to balance it all out. You're really making me work hard, aren't you!?'

There were no tears. Dawn was motionless, barely twitching as Simon tore and wrenched her skirt from her frozen torso and ungraciously pushed her legs apart.

'This is what you need. This is all you needed, you should have just said so. Rough and hard, just like you are. Take it and be grateful. I don't suppose you get much at your age!'

'Love you, Mum. See you later!'

Dawn's memories took control and diverted her from harsh reality to the rare moments of bliss that had enraptured her life once upon a time.

'Love you too, Dee. Be a good girl today and later you can have your favourite sweets. Strawberry lollipops.'

Dawn's world was complete as she waved watching as mum walked away, girlishly giggling that she was guaranteed her favourite strawberry lollipop tonight. Unclutching Mum's hand was always racked with the potential of a nasty, cumbersome world, just waiting for the protective parent shield of magic to be removed, before unleashing its wrath.

Turmoil, destruction and anger had chased Dawn for the entirety of her life, Mum lost her battle to cancer, whilst she was still at school, Dad had never been present, a minor hoodlum, violent, unsociable and frequently in and out of jail, Mum was all that Dawn had in her tiny existence. At the age of sixteen, alone and parentless in a scheming world, that was ready and poised to tarnish the fine lines between right and wrong, Dawn, at each defining corner of her journey, took the wrong turn, directly taking the path least socially desirable, always the route with the maximum anti-social exposure and abandonment. Bitterly discontent, crime after crime led to incarceration, duly protecting the world from her acrimony and revenge. It was whilst in jail, locked away from a disharmonious existence, that Dawn learnt her most valuable lessons in appreciating life and helping others do the same. Twisted in its regime, the free world only brought her miserable miscreants that held her hand and drove her into hell and then in imprisonment, her salvation, a single person that saved her and through warmth and kindness, rebuilt her lost faith in humankind and the power of having her hand held again, leading her to the greatest version of herself. Two individuals secured and contoured her life. Two unconnected people without who she would have passed life without seeing the beauty that is omnipresent but has to be bitterly fought for. Mum was her protection. Shielding Dawn from the drunken blows of her father and the acerbic approach of a misguided and affronted world full of people that took revenge for their misgivings, rather than challenging life and squeezing out the goodness that is available to those brave enough to battle and brawl for it.

'Fight for your right, fight and you will see the light
There is darkness in the shadows, waiting to pounce.
Fight little Dee, fight for the light with every ounce.

Your prize is happiness, the sadness to flounce.
Inside you is greatness and awe.
Hold my hand and I will show you the door.
Hustle and bustle for goodness and you will see.
The world awaits you and will set you free.
This universe is created for your living spree.
Go, little girl. Go live and be
The world is yours. It's all yours, Dee.'

Night after night, Mum would read the 'Poem for Dee'. Instilling hope and belief to conquer the world and stay happy, avoiding the dark corners, prevalent on every doorstep, within very soul.

'Whenever there is darkness, Dee, stretch out your hand and I will hold it. I will always guide you to the light. That's my role, that's my only role, to always show my little Dee the light and keep her from harm.'

Rebecca was her salvation. A fortuitous partnering whilst in prison, Rebecca delivered Dawn from total destruction, once she had already become hostage to a degenerated life of infamy, from which the depraved individuals she felt sisterhood with had repealed her. Violently rejecting her from the only impregnability in numbers she had in her world. Dawn had plummeted to the lowest, grandest level of renunciation, she had been cast-aside by people that were already cast-aside by society. There was no further level of revulsion any individual could descend to. Their coincidental union gave Dawn the essential hope she desperately needed for her new dawn and carved a life of caring and kindness for people.

'Hope will guide you and hope will keep you alive. Deep, deep inside your heart you have to believe you will be okay again. Even if you only have one tiny ounce of hope left that one day you will heal, then you need to hang onto that because that one ounce of hope will get you through, that single ounce will give you a reason to live. Sometimes, all you need is hope!'

Rebecca's mantra on hope, instilled within Dawn that an ounce of hope would keep the heart alive, a miniscule ounce was all that was needed to cling onto life and see the light at the end of any tunnel, no matter how long or how dark it was. Hope was the light twinkling in the distance, a beacon leading and showing a path through the eclipse and keeping the inner belief breathing. Come what may, hope kept human spirit ablaze with certainty.

'Mum. Where are you? Mum, please hold my hand. Rebecca, where are you? Please hold my hand. Please come to me. Please hold my hand. I need you. Please hold my hand. Please hold my hand. Please come and hold my hand. I need you. I need you both. Please come to me. Please come!'

'No one is coming to get you. No one is going to hold your hand. You only deserve pain and luckily for you I'm the best person in the world to give it to you.'

Simon, lifted himself from Dawn's twitching body, whilst pressing down hard with his large strong hands, exerting the entirety of his weight onto her pelvic bone, expending his last ounce of physical angst, until the crunching sound from her pelvis excitedly announced it had taken the brunt of the pressure and consequently eased his desire to inflict a grievous parting gesture upon her defiled frame. Staring upwards for a glimpse of heavenly solace, Dawn's ears picked up a distant clattering sound emanating from her kitchen. Sounds of metal. She closed her eyes and filled her hammered mind with strawberry lollipops.

'Mum. Rebecca. I need you. I need you. I'm alone. I'm dying. I need you here. I need you close. I need you to hold my hand. I need you to take me with you. I need you to show me the way. Please come. Please come and save me. Please, Mum. Please, Rebecca. Please!'

Simon returned from the kitchen.

'Look! I found something very useful, something to help me shut your mouth for good!'

Straddling her shattered body, Simon sat down on Dawn's recoiling stomach and gleefully wafted the kitchen knife past her barely open eyes. Dawn mustered the last ounce of strength and raised each hand two inches from the floor as the flaming light of hope was extinguished and two women appeared, kneeling beside her to hold her hands.

'Come with us.' Their hallowed whisper drowned Simon's spluttering hatred.

'Come with us. It's time to leave this world.'

Chapter 47
Control

'All I've ever wanted is an ounce of loyalty. Just one person for once that can show me some fucking loyalty. Is it really that much to ask? Is it me? Do I just want too much? Am I being unreasonable? Surely, just one little iota of loyalty wouldn't go amiss. Surely, I deserve that?'

Mumbling incoherently, Simon's conversation with himself, halted as he stepped out of Dawn's house, closing the door behind him with a parting glance.

'Tut, tut, what a mess. You are so messy. Don't lie there all day, will you. My dad would have whipped my arse if I'd left a mess like that.'

'Simon, you're a worthless piece of shit. You will never be anyone or anything. I can't believe my son is such a failure! People will always walk over you. You're a weak walkover. A doormat! I can't believe you carry the Driscoll name and yet you are not a Driscoll, you can't be, you're just not good enough to have my name. You're too weak to have my name. I think I'll change it to Simon Dipshit. That's much better. From this day on, I rename my weakling son, Simon Dipshit. Now get out of my sight, Dipshit, I've got work to do!'

Dad's words vibrated through Simon's head, cleverly attaching themselves to any remorse that dared to enter his body, sweeping it away long before it was even in the same postcode as he was in.

'Now who's a fucking Dipshit Dad? I'm in control. I control the world. The world is all mine. Mine. All mine. I hope you're watching. I hope you're happy now. I'm not weak. No doormat here, Dad. Can't see anyone walking over me. Can you, you fucker? Can you see anyone walking over me? No Dad, you can't can you. Who's fucking weak now, heh? Not me! Not Simon Driscoll. No doormat here. I am in control!'

'So, let's look at Dipshit's track record this week. You've excelled yourself. You're at a new level of useless. Oh what a shining star my boy is turning into. You've let yourself get bullied and to top things off nicely, your school report is shit. Well done son! Well done! You must be really proud of yourself. Well I am. I'm really proud that you're a bigger loser, a bigger Dipshit than we ever imagined. Bravo King of Dipshits. Bravo! Well done, Dipshit! Well done, loser!'

The comedic applause from Dad's huge hands, bombastically echoed around the living room. Mum, demurely peered down at the carpet, counterfeiting a smile and tried not to catch Dad's, looking for approval stare, Simon's siblings roared with laughter, almost choking as they gasped for air to laugh even louder, as Dad clapped for a full minute. At thirteen, the oldest of three children, Simon bore the brunt of Dad's caustic nature, stinging his confidence, which subsequently weakened his resistance to the wide open world of dominant characters throughout his life.

'I hope you're clapping now, you prick. I hope you can see how much control I now have. You taught me everything I know, Dad. Well done, you prick. I've got more control than you ever had. I've got more control than you could ever have imagined!'

'Why can't you just be like your brother and sister? They're younger than you and so much better than you will ever be. No control, no future, no idea, no son of mine! You will have to learn the hard way, Dipshit! You will have to learn that life is not about being a doormat. Life is about wiping your feet on doormats, about being in control but you, I think sadly, you will always be a doormat. You will always be walked over, always trod on like dog-shit. There's another name to describe you, Mr Dog-shit. Get out of my sight, Dog-shit, go and find someone to walk over you!'

Mum consistently attempted to appease Simon's crumbling self-esteem by quietly defending Dad's destructive commentary, whilst battling her own dwindling morale, after fifteen long years of marriage.

'You know what he's like Simon. He doesn't mean it. It's just his humour. He does love you, like he loves all of us. He just doesn't know how to show it properly. I know you're not weak, I know you're not a loser. I know you'll go far. I know how good you are and so does your dad.'

'Hey Mum! Are you watching too? See how far I've come. You were always right. You always knew. You always knew I wasn't a loser. I hope you're up there telling that prick that you told him so! Go on, tell him. Tell him now. Tell him how far Simon Dipshit has gone. Tell him how I now control my world. Go on, tell him!'

'Could you really be any worse than you are? You're sixteen now. You've failed all your exams, you've left school, now fucking what? What are you going to do now, Mr Dipshit? What now in the grand scheme? What plans does a Dipshit have? You started off as a failure, I knew you would be from the moment you were born and boy was I right. A failure then, a failure now, you son, Mr Dipshit, you will die a failure. You will never be anything worthwhile. You will always be a useless, fucking Dipshit! Worth nothing! Not to the world, not to yourself and certainly not to me. What a fucking loser!'

'I'm not a loser, Dad. I'm not useless. I'm not a Dipshit. I'm not going to be, a doormat. You've never loved me. You've never cared. You've always hated me. You've always tried to destroy me because you are nothing yourself. You're an old man and you still have nothing and now you don't even have any time left to get anything. You're a bitter and twisted, evil old bastard. You're the loser, not me. I will be a success and you will just die soon. I hate you, Dad! I hate you, you nasty bastard! Everyone in this house hates you. Even Mum hates you because you've already destroyed her life, you've already made her miserable. We all fucking hate you. We all despise you. We all wish you were dead!'

'Get out of my fucking house, you fucking Dipshit! You ungrateful little bastard. Get out and never, ever return. Just get out of my fucking sight. I should have killed you at birth. Get out of my fucking house. Leave now. Go! Get out. Get out! Get out of my fucking house right now! I never want to see you again!'

'Fuck you, Dad! I still hate you. I still hope you suffer every day. Did you like what I've just done? Did that make you happy? I hope Dawn comes to find you and jumps on your fucking balls, you deserve it old man! You deserve it all. Well that was in your honour. Thank you for giving me the green light to control my world. I have more control than you could have ever had. I not only control my world, I control all of the people within it. Thank you, you fucker!'

With every step the contented glow emanating from Simon's face complemented the stretching of his huge smile. Lighting him with a sense of personal achievement. A sense of order, controlling the loose ends of his embittered life. Closure with Dawn was already landmarked history as Simon's thoughts turned to the cornerstone of his personal achievements and his signature smile magnetised all that crossed his path as he waltzed his victorious walk.

'It's your smile. I love your smile. If I don't stop looking at you, you'll have me hypnotised and then I will have no control and you'll be able to do anything you want. Stop smiling at me, I just cannot handle it. It's a weapon of mass destruction. You have no idea do you?'

'Oh really. Well that's a lovely thing to say. You're making me blush. I never knew my smile was anything like that. Thank you. That's got to be the nicest thing anyone has ever said to me!'

'Oh, you have no idea. I saw your face lighting up the room as soon as you walked in. Heh, some people light up a room when they walk out. You, well you certainly lit this room up when you walked in. It was like someone switched a floodlight on!'

'Wow! Thank you! That's just so lovely. I can't believe I'm hearing this. It's the best thing I've ever heard. Have you been drinking? Is this alcohol talking?'

'Of course I've had a drink. I wouldn't have the courage to say what I've just said to a complete stranger otherwise. So alcohol isn't talking but it's certainly supporting me, that's for sure. Supporting me to say what I wouldn't otherwise be brave enough to say. I did get encouraged by my friends too, they really pushed me to come over to you.'

'Well, I'm glad you did. You've made my day. Nope you've made my year. Nope, better still, you've made my life. I've never had such lovely compliments from a complete stranger. By the way, my name is Simon, and thank you.'

'No, thank you, Simon, for being so pleasant in return. Are you sure no one has ever complimented your smile, I find that so hard to believe. Well anyway, you're welcome and you needed to be told. My name is Teresa and it's lovely to meet you.'

Two independent worlds collided as the unequivocal moment took control of the unexpected accidental encounter. Simon's pace gathered momentum, thoughts of the fortuitous liaison still pounded his heart with glee, shrouding any comprehension of the barefaced calamity that became the embodiment of the Simon and Teresa story.

'We've been together for a month now and I can honestly say, it's been the greatest month of my life. This is a difficult thing for me to say but I'm going to say it anyway, so I hope you don't mind but I've written it all down for you to read, sometimes the words don't easily come to me, so it's best that I put it into writing. Please read it when I've gone and let me know what you think. I don't know how else to express myself. This whole experience has been so new to me and I totally understand if it's not what you want to hear.'

'Thank you, Simon. I've had an incredible month. I'm sure it's what I want to hear. You've been a dream. I will read your letter and I will let you know. Oh, I'm so intrigued now, I can't wait to read it. I will call you later this evening after work.'

Dearest Teresa,

I'm not brilliant with words, so please forgive me. This was the only way I could think of getting what's in my heart and in my mind across to your heart and mind, in the tiniest hope that you feel even half of what I'm about to tell you. Teresa, you must promise to tell me if this is not what you wanted to hear. I need to know what you think and I promise I won't be insulted or upset at anything you tell me.

Here goes. I can honestly tell you from the very second you walked over to me at Le Petit Rouge my world changed, I thought I was dreaming. I thought it was another cruel joke played out by God to tease and trouble me with all the beauty I wished for but was never granted. Even now I say to myself every waking morning, it's all a dream and yet every waking morning I'm born again the second I realise you are for real and that magical moment, exactly four weeks ago, really did happen. I never, in my wildest dreams, imagined I would find a woman like you, one that walked over the way you did, the way you captured me in your first sentence. I never imagined that my feelings could explode the way they did within seconds of meeting someone. I live my days mesmerised by the whole happening. As I write this letter that's twenty seven days, eight hours, fifteen minutes and twenty six seconds of wondering how I became so lucky. Teresa, it frightens me that you have become so much to me in such a short period of time, that in four weeks you have literally become all I think about, all I wonder about, all I need and all I could have ever wanted. This might frighten you but that's not my intention. The intention of this letter is simply to put down in words how wonderful life is with you in my world. In fact you have become my entire world. What I'm really trying to say, is the three words that make me feel so vulnerable, three words that zap my strength from me but give me a new strength, one I never knew existed for people like me. Three words that mean more than any other words in the universe. I guess what I'm attempting to say is, Teresa, I LOVE YOU!

I never believed I would tell any woman those three words because I didn't believe any woman would make me feel the way you do. It's a magic that was reserved for the cinema and not for creeps like me who were always destined to be with someone for the sake of being with someone, not the real deal, not the magic, not the fairy-tale, just mediocrity and falseness like the rest of the world. You have made me believe in magic again. You have completed my faith in love, romance and beauty. You, Teresa, are more than I could have ever wished for. You are so incredible that I fear losing you more than I fear the loss of my own life. My days are suffocated with the dreaded thought that I could lose you and go back to being the loser I was born to be, just a nobody in a world of nobodies. That's why I felt compelled to put my feelings in words, so that you know how cherished you are and what you have done to my little world. How you came, you conquered and you changed my life from just living, to life itself and all the beauty it has within it. You have made me believe in me again. I never believed that was possible. I never believed that would happen to someone like me. You have made me whole and given me a sense to live.

I know it's only four weeks and this is a lot to take in but I read somewhere once that one must take the opportunity as it arises, otherwise it may never come again. So, here I am, after only four weeks, vulnerable, weakened and completely besotted, walking on air, living the dream and loving life and it's all because of you and only you. Please put me out of my misery and just tell me to go away if this has shocked you, or it's just too much to handle. I promise I will understand. The last thing I want to do is suffocate you with my hankering love. I await your reply. I couldn't not tell you how I feel. This is real love, Teresa, for me at least that's what it is. I LOVE YOU!

Yours Forever
Simon.

Chapter 48
Possession

'What do you think? Does it make me look fat?'
Reluctantly inching her way from the bedroom, knowing Simon didn't appreciate evenings when Teresa wasn't home, she cagily pondered the age old question that haunts most women wearing something new when they're not entirely sure about how it fits around their curves, especially if their self-esteem is not as enduring as it once was.

'Wow! You look amazing. That's a very sexy black dress and it suits you.'

Instantly a forceful injection of confidence syringed its way through Teresa's bloodstream, fluorescently sparkling red corpuscles into accelerated vibrancy, whilst projecting an electrifying shiver along her spine into the back of her brain, signalling floaters of low self-esteem to be bludgeoned into oblivion. The surprise answer showed itself etched upon Teresa's face, almost expecting a negative grumpy remark. She lit up.

'Damn, I knew I should have bought the shorter and sexier version!'

Teresa's confidence barked at her with a notion of regret.

'Really? You really think that. You really think it suits me. I'm so please you do. Thank you, Simon. That's made my day.'

'Of course it does. It's a little young for your age and probably a little too tight around your tummy and arse but that's expected if you're going to squeeze into a dress that's too small for you. Hey, you still look sexy. You always do. I love it!'

'Ha! Ha! Ha! Ha! Gotcha! Teresa's banished and beaten stalwarts of dwindling self-esteem barged their way back to stand proud and undefeated, as her posture drooped into a lacklustre stance.

'Oh Simon! I thought you were going to be positive for once. I thought you'd like this dress. It's my right size and the woman in the shop said it looked stunning on me. Why can't you say things like that, just for once?'

215

'What?! You want me to lie to you. Of course the woman in the shop said that, she wanted a sale. She was hardly going to say, it's for a girl in her early twenties who hasn't got a flabby belly and a fat arse was she? If you don't like my answers, you shouldn't ask me questions. I'm probably the only person that will tell you the truth. The dress is just too tight for a woman of your age and lived-in shape. You just look like you've tried too hard. You don't look terrible. You just look like a lot of weighty women that try and hide their lumps and bulges. Like an overfilled sack of spuds but hey, I love spuds, so it kind of works for me!'

'Cry! Cry! Cry! Cry! Cry!' Teresa's waning confidence demanded a reaction, one that directly matched her broken spirit.

An ocean of tears surged forward, welling and pushing out a trickle over her freshly applied mascara, meandering a stream of blackness mixed in with her porcelain beige foundation down her cheek. Teresa stood nailed to her seventh step forward, lingering for a chasm to majestically appear beneath her, plummeting her into another abyss, away from the embarrassment of a child waiting to confess their incontinence. Holes and words were scarce, in their notable absence the tears compensated in a choreographed torrent yielding the force of Niagara, drenching her delicately brushed, powdered, daubed face onto the elegantly embroidered neckline, creating an oatmeal coloured decoration, leaving behind the blushing pinkness of her raw skin.

'What are you crying for you, silly woman? I told you I like spuds. You're gorgeous, Teresa. Who cares if you look a little bloaty, most importantly you know I love you and you know how it turns me on when you cry like that. Not that you've got anything to cry about, you look stunning even with all those lumps and bumps. You need to get going or you'll be late, carry on like that we'll be going straight to bed and I will physically show you how amazing you look.'

There was no eighth step. Teresa created her own roadblock as Simon's verbal assault whacked her full frontal in her disrobed face, whooshed past her ears and with a double-back surge, gathered a commanding momentum, bashing into the back of her trembling knees. Teresa collapsed, trudging the eighth step and solemnly bowed in defeat.

'Well, that's not going to get you there, is it, not only that you've just ripped your dress. I told you it was too tight. You may as well call it a night, don't bother with the party, you don't like your boss anyway, stay here and I will make sure you have a fantastic evening and I will prove to you again what an adorable sexy woman you are and how you always turn me on so much, like you are now. After almost a year together, you know what it does to me when you're on your knees like that, don't you?'

Words were uncooperative, jumbled and erratic cemented in her throat, impotently anticipating an instruction to speak out or disintegrate into formulations for another day. Enlightenment barged in as the lucid sound of a zipper descending, the brusque tilting upwards of Teresa's drooping chin, swiftly followed by an unpalatable taste, deviated the words into a gagging mumble.

'This is what you wanted! This is it! C'mon, baby, it's all yours! You don't need a party, you don't need other people! All you need is this. You turn me on so much, even when you look like a sack of spuds. Come on, do this! I love you so much. Oh Teresa, you're just the greatest!'

Glued shut. Teresa's eyes persisted on staying closed, not even the spouting waterfalls billowed from within them, circumnavigating around the unwelcome guest vigorously invading her face.

'Oh shit! The party. I'm late! What's the time? What's going on? Where am I?'

Confused questions machine-gunned themselves as Teresa demurely opened her eyes, abstractly shooting holes in her reluctance to recall the debacle of the evening before. The protagonist dress, crudely torn, dead, having suffered a volley of verbal and physically sadistic abuse, lay crumpled bereft of resolve or design, on the floor next to her. 3am in the morning, the party already concluded, along with the rumours of Teresa not being in attendance, arousing suspicions, following the well chatted debacle of her fading confidence in buying a new dress, coaxed by her feisty colleagues to just do it in a carelessness approach and still no Teresa.

'He probably stopped her coming.'

'It's him. You know how much she wanted to be here.'

'He's jealous of her. Probably didn't let her out.'

'We've all told her to leave him. Look at the way he has changed her. He's possessive. He's just taken over her life because he doesn't have one. It's time for her to get rid of him and go back to the lovely Teresa she always was, not the reclusive wreck he has turned her into.'

Voices rattled through Teresa's head. Potential conversations. Gossip, assumptions and home-truths wrapped themselves around her aching limbs still adorning the eighth step she never took. The dress that heralded her break from damaged esteem and the cataclysmic decline in her self-worth, zapped and eroded during the demanding nine months of her relationship with Simon, shouted an abundance of confidence, with greater boldness and certitude than when it adorned her body. A scrunched mess of black material, caked in spoilt make-up and a sub-consciousness of bullying and demeaning sex, acutely spelt the barefaced truth. It was time to close the door on Simon Driscoll.

Chapter 49
Relentless

'Where is your fight? You were blessed with the mighty, the fearless, the unrelenting. The almighty power to defeat, conquer and resolve. There is no challenge, there is no confrontation. There is no battle that can overwhelm your congenital blessing, ingrained deep within every pulsating molecule of your human form. The Universe, subservient to your omnipotence, relentlessly forged a union with the sun, moon and stars to compose the sovereignty you behold. Eons of architecture assembled your warrior capabilities, for they all understood the degrees of botheration that were biding their time to engage you in combat. Your enemies patiently acknowledging their time to advance already penned, just waiting, suited up in their brawniest armour. Bodacious soldiers of desperation, hopelessness, dejection, agony, discomfort, depression, anxiety, desolation, bleakness stomping their feet in contemplation of the fear and fury they will unleash upon you. Little do the marching hordes know, little do they understand your relentless might in overpowering the onslaught, of crushing their bold objectives, of crippling their actions. Incumbent within your mind, soul and body a nucleus of ultimate fire, searing dynamism, designed to defend against the mandatory aggression destined for human-beings.

This is war. There will be pain, there will be casualties. You will be maimed, tortured and crucified. Your bones will be ground to a fine chalky dust, peppered with the scarlet hue of your evaporated blood, homeless and abandoned from its pumping motivator, your once flowing heart. Yes, your once four-valve beast compressing and dilating to drive the red liquid of life around your body, wrenched and torn with emotions and disruptions, now an empty mush, crinkled, cracked and void of pulse and swell, barren, defeated and annihilated. Stand up soldier! Stand up! Stand up now! Believe in your ingenuity and mastery. Wake up your slumbering behemoth, breathe fiery anger upon your adversaries, hold them in the palm of your hand and splutter them into extermination and, as those crumbs of resistance flutter to the ground, jump! Jump high and with your concentrated force pulverise them into the earth. Oh they will return, for they too are invincible but with each defiant comeback, you are reborn, evolved and prepared to resist the confrontation. You are enough. You have enough. You are all you need. Stand up and fight!'

'Ah I love this chapter. It was always one of my favourite ones. Always ready to fight. Relentless. I love it. It means so much. So true.'

Ash's face glowed. It was his mystery visitor, her raven hair wispy and curled over her face, raised by her escalated cheekbones, lifted by her broad smile which illuminated the gloomy ward.

'Oh sorry. I didn't see you there. Wow! Hello. It's wonderful to see you again. I was wondering when you might come back. I didn't even get your name last time. How long have you been here?'

'I've just arrived. How have you been? Are you any more hopeful since we last met?'

'I've remembered what you said about hope last time you were here. I've remembered it well. I do have hope. I do believe but I still feel down sometimes. I can't help it. My life is crushed. I can't even walk.'

'Hey. Hope is so magical. Hope is all we sometimes have. Hope is all you sometimes need. You will get through this. You will make it and you will look back and realise everything happens for a reason and takes you where you need to be. There is a pathway destined for you and you can't avoid it. You just have to keep travelling and keep fighting your way through and believing you will!'

'But if it's destined, then why bother fighting? What will be will be and it's going to happen regardless of any fighting I do or don't do.'

'Yes but you can also steer your destiny, it can take a number of routes, it can do a number of things. Imagine for a second if you hadn't got angry at Jolene. Imagine for a second if you had driven slower on that fatal day.'

'How do you know about Jolene?! How do you know I was angry?! How do you know about the crash?! I need to fucking know! You need to tell me right now! Is this a set-up?! Who the hell are you?! And what do you mean you love this chapter and it's one of your favourite ones. You didn't even know about this book that last time

220

you were here. Something isn't right. Who are you? Who the fuck are you?! Tell me now! Who are you?!'

'Don't fret, Ash. I'm not a set-up. I'm not your enemy. I'm on your side and always by your side. I'm only here to help you and get you through.'

The visitor placed her hand upon Ash's trembling fingers. A shroud of calmness after the tornado brought silence and comprehension. Words assembled and travelled towards Ash's mouth but stayed still and silent upon his lips.

'Your father sent me. I'm your mother.'

Chapter 50
Time

'Who are you talking to today?'

Oblivious to the unoiled, clanking wheels of the tea trolley approaching, Ash's ward nurse appeared with his afternoon beverage of insipid tea and soft digestive biscuit.

'You're always talking to someone aren't you? So who was it this time?'

A cyclone of emotions whooshed around Ash's head, spinning, ricocheting around his suppressed thoughts, striving to piece together words.

'Mum. I was talking to my mum. It was my mother!'

The sentence mischievously splurged from Ash's mouth, knowing it would be met with criticism and unwelcome scorn.

'Were you really, young man? Your mother, was it? You were speaking to your mother. That's lovely, and how is she today? How is your dear mum?'

'I didn't know it was my mum. I had no idea. I thought it was just a random visitor last time she was here. She said Dad sent her. She told me Dad sent her to me.'

The words knowingly dashed out, teasingly enticing cynicism from the nurse, while she nibbled a biscuit meant for the patients. Spluttering crumbs from the remnants of her stolen snack the nurse moved closer to Ash's bedside.

'I believe you. I know your mum died when you were just a boy but I believe you when you say you met her. I believe in life after death and I also believe people never really die. They stay with us forever. I don't think you're a fruitcake like everyone else here does. I honestly believe you. I also think you're very special, I just don't think you realise that yet. Anyway, here's your tea. Enjoy. It's fish and chips for dinner tonight, see you later.'

'No, wait. Please don't go. You really believe me. People think I'm mad but you believe me. Why am I special? Why do you think that?'

'Yes, I believe you and I just know you're special, I've seen it with my own eyes. I also know your time will come and when it does, the world better watch out. Now, I really must go, otherwise the rest will kill me if their tea goes cold. See you at dinner.'

'Thank you, nurse. Please just one more thing before you go. Just one more thing. What is it that you saw with your own eyes?'

Ash reached down and squeezed his legs. Nothing. No sensation, no reaction. Visually his limbs were intact, coldly staring at him, bluntly adding their silent weight to his hips, glued in to the sockets but severed of any wiring. Ash's legs were a flimsy pair of trousers. Physically present, hanging in the right place but alien to the wiring of his torso. Disconnected and void of any sensation. Unscathed and on exhibition, emotionally exposed but physically redundant. They were bashfully making a mockery of the nurse's answer to 'What is it that you saw with your own eyes?'

'I saw you jump out of bed and save your friend from being strangled. Your legs are supposed to be severely damaged and yet you jumped like a horse and sprang into action. You're special, my lad, don't you ever forget that. You are special indeed!'

The cyclonic rush confronting Ash had the debris of a fallen town hurtling around it. Awash with remnants of homes, objects and possessions from a thousand people and hundreds of houses, collectively unidentifiable, lost in an uncontrollable hurricane. A swirling mess of so much that once made immaculate sense but now a disengaged hodgepodge of blurred agitation. Handcuffed into meekness, Ash reached for the only countermeasure available in his bereft state. 'Make my World Complete'.

'I find myself wandering without purpose. Why am I here? What is the point? What is life all about? Pay bills and die! Is that all I have? Pay bills and die! Is that the unique, bewitched circle of life I was destined for? Is that it? Is that my full spectrum of existence? Will my death really matter? Will I be remembered by anyone? Will my legacy be worth any more than the bills I paid? Here I am sat still and pondering my very reasons for being alive, for being pushed out of my mother, straight into a world that has done nothing but bombard me with reasons not to be here. My oxymoronic life mocks the definition of the word 'life' and nudges me into death. Please give me purpose, give me ambition. Give me the inspiration to be here, on this listless, grey planet. I'm not here to just pay bills and die. I want more. I want to know why I was born. I want to know why I am here. I need to understand the absurdity of what I'm living for. I don't want to live my life in vain. There has to be something more than this!'

A fertile patch on the horizon.
An escalating thirst drying my weary bones
A distant drumming, beating a crimson rhythm
Flummoxed, bewildered, drowning in solitude
Mother, you bullied me into life and pushed me away
You watered me with your loving spray,
I have no education for this worldly fray,
For the desperate battles I fight every day.

An astounding revelation, wrapped in a solitary moment, without caution, you vividly grasp why you were born. Your purpose for being alive sledgehammers into your days and smashes through the walls of uncertainty that shrouded your life so unremarkably. No label, no indication, its arrival halts you in your tracks and consigns your questions to oblivion. Obliterating the years of inquest, the laborious examinations of 'Why'. Bereft of warning, there it is! Shining its distinct light and highlighting the only question you have left in your cynical repertoire 'where have you been all of my life?'

'I wrote that for this lovely woman here. The purpose and love of my life.'

A Pre-Raphaelite's version of the world. The backdrop filtered into hues of anaemic blue, a conspicuous ambience. Fatigued hospital furniture, exemplary props converging upon the focal point. Emotionally crippled patients frowning into their tepid white mugs of tea. Sunlight pouring through the Victorian framework of a chalky window, beaming through the dust weighted air upon the protagonists of the piece, equidistance from the blanched walls of the institute. Warmth erupting from a couple clasping hands, where colour and atmosphere explode into benevolence. They are kindness, glowing goodness, sunlight cruising through despair, devotedly lighting the facial expressions of their bedridden company. Ash was home. Pain dashed through his skin, immediately vacuumed from the air with the presence of his cherished guests.

'Mum, Dad, you're here. Stay with me.'

'We can't stay, son. We don't belong in this world. We're only here to see you. One day we will share the same world but now is not the time. Your days in this world are not complete.'

'I don't have anything to live for. There is nothing left in this world for me. I want to go now. I want you to take me with you. I can't live in this world. I have nothing. Nothing. Just nothing without you. Please take me!'

'Your life has been tragic but it's not over. You still breathe and while you still breathe, you have hope and while you still have hope you have life and while you have life you have a purpose to fulfil. This is not your time, Ash.'

'I'm already dead. I have no hope, no life and no purpose. I am dead. I have nothing, nobody, no reason. I want to go now. This world has no place for me. I want to go, Dad, I need to go. I'm not staying here any longer.'

'Son. You have to listen. I can only say this one last time. You need to listen. Please listen. If you go now, you will kill all of our hopes and dreams. We've come so far and yet it will have been for nothing. We know you didn't come this far to only come this far. Our story is not over, your story has barely begun. Our time on earth might be over but we still live to see you live, this is not your time to leave. There will come a day when we come for you and we will all be reunited but you still have years of memories, years of happiness, years to make us smile, knowing you are happy. Yes, you've lost it all. Jolene is gone forever but, and this is what you must know, having lost your life was the opening of another door, the door that was meant for you, you may not see that yet but you will and it will all make perfect sense. See these legs? They are yours, you control them. They are fixed to you and can be fixed by you. Yes, they can walk, yes they can stride and yes they can run but until you tell yourself that you are not dead and that you have a life to live they will remain useless. Son, this is our final chance. Feel the rays. You are strong, you are everything you think you're not. Be big, believe in yourself and believe in what I'm telling you. Your story is alive. Your story needs you. Your world will be complete, it awaits for you to open the door and welcome it in with open arms. This is it. This is your moment. This is what you have lived, hurt and died for. It's time to stand up and take what is yours. It's time to make your world complete!'

The sun circumnavigated its life giving spray, energising Ash's face with glowing warmth, it seemed hotter than it should be but the heat was blindingly welcome in this morose yet uplifting, crossroads moment. Somehow it filtered its florid beam through the dust laden air with laser accuracy, syringing itself through his pores, vibrating his skin as it poured its burning yellow goodness into his pallid skin. Natural vitamin D never felt so addictive, filling Ash's flesh and bones with vitality and heated gusto. A limp empty glove, filling with a forceful hand, fingertips expanding the material, as its flaccid demeanour stiffens and eradicates the spiritless lethargy into a fist of confrontational aggression.

Chapter 51
Don't Give Up

'The stars are shining so bright for you but they're not waiting for you. Your time is far from complete, so don't you dare give up. This is not the end. This is merely a beginning, a rebirth, a cruel maze you have to find the courage to escape from. On the other side there is sunshine, brightness and all the love you've always wanted. Don't give up! Don't you dare give up! This is not your time. This is far from your time!'

'Who said that? Where are you? Is that you? Where are you? Where are you? I can't see anything! Please don't go. Please don't leave me. Please help me! I can't see you!'

'Who are you talking to? Of course you can't see anything, you stupid woman, I've wrapped a bandage around your stupid head. Great thing about being in a nurse's house, oh sorry I mean ex-nurse, that there's always a bandage nearby.'

Simon slid two fingers into the bloody mouthpiece enveloping Teresa's cocooned head as far as they would go, pressing firmly down into her jaw. The rasp as they brushed along her dried tongue shuddered through her head. There was nothing in her stomach to be sick with as her throat dryly spluttered on the forced intrusion.

'I have to say, this has been my greatest idea to date. Wrapping your fat head up in bandages and cutting a slit for your mouth, shame you didn't sit still and the scissors slipped, nevertheless you seemed to enjoy what I put into this hole last night and being as lucky as you are there's plenty more of that and it feels so much nicer when I can't see your face. Your mouth seems very dry my dear. Don't worry you'll get something to lubricate it soon. It's about the only thing your mouth has been good for. Now, I told you I was getting some sleep, so why have you woke me with your mumbling so early? You're not gagging for it already are you? Anyway, tough! You'll have to wait. I need a shower. I fucking stink of you. Don't go anywhere will you! I'll go and clean up before I give your mouth something to chew on.'

Teresa's mummified head absorbed another rush of tears from her blinded eyes, innocently soaking the wetness as part of their inherent role to absorb.

'Don't cry, my dear. Please don't cry. Yes, it's me. I too am a casualty of Simon's evil but you will get through this. I just know you will.'

'Dawn. Dawn, is that you?' The words scraped through Teresa's arid throat, as her drained tongue glued itself to the top of her mouth, the distant sound of showering drowning her attempts.

'It is me. I am here. I want you to survive this. I want you to live when I couldn't. I know you will. I know you can!'

Teresa's face ached as her frowns of cheer and distress blended with the clenching springiness of the stained wrapping tightly binding her head, Simon's words still bouncing around her head from the last time she saw light.

'Oh you bruise so easily. Your eyes look uglier than usual. Oh dear your nose is bleeding too. Unbelievable how you can't take what you've literally asked for, isn't it. Well, I found this lovely bandage in the kitchen, so I will do some nursing, show you how it's done and bandage up your grotesque face!'

'Please don't leave me, Dawn. Please don't go. Please stay.'

Mumbling her pleas between dusty coughs, Teresa's senses collaborated into pin-pricks of confused pain. From the bind of her wrists to the twist of her arms behind her back, the ache of stillness had amalgamated with the pang of cuts on her forearms. Every molecule of her frame was injured. Her absent coordination unable to diagnose the source of her agonies, bunched them together into a mass of teasing misery, as her mind endeavoured to burst memorised joy into the grisly ring.

'Now, now, little Tessa. Why are you crying? What on earth has happened? I didn't bring you into this world to cry over the little things in life. If you do that, how on earth my dear, will you cope with the bigger things?'

'I know, Mummy, but a boy pushed me over and look my knees are scraped. It hurts, Mummy. It hurts.'

'Let me look at that. It's nothing, Tessa. We can clean that up in no time. Now stop sulking and listen to me.'

'Yes, Mummy, I'm listening.'

'Boys will always push you because they don't know how to behave but you must always stay strong, you must never, ever give up. You'll never become a nurse if you give up will you?'

'No, I won't, Mummy.'

'Good girl, Tessa. One day you will understand that the world is full of bullies but there are some people that can completely change your world and will make it beautiful forever, until that day don't you dare give up, don't you ever give up.'

'I won't, Mummy. I will never give up.'

The warmth of Mum's hand brushing over Tessa's brow, over her head and gently stroking her was all the comfort she ever needed all through her life. Through all the twisted turns of her years mum's words always brought relief from the disappointments and let-downs.

'I won't give up. I won't give up. I won't give up!'

'What's that? You won't give up. Good! I'm glad to hear it. I'm all fresh now and you know what I need don't you. Such a shame your hands are out of action. Looks like you'll just have to get on your knees again. Oh well, It's about the only thing you're good at. You sound like your throat needs something to soothe it. Come here, bitch!'

Chapter 52
Goodbye

'Don't you dare give up, don't give up! Don't give up! Remember what Mum used to say. Don't ever give up. You can't give up. You just can't!'

Embryonically curled from the parting gesture of Simon's barefoot kick to her abdomen, Teresa stirred and choked. Her words were strained and impossible to be forced from her swollen mouth. Formulating them in her mind was the last form of communication open to her deteriorating body. She couldn't recall what had happened, everything was silent after hearing the words 'Come here, bitch!' and the rough clasp of her shoulder as Simon pulled her from the sofa onto the floor. There was no recollection. She could hear a distant rumble, guessing he was still nearby and she could taste a metal saltiness in her ulcer gorged mouth, a claggy batter of blood and oral molestation.

'I'm done. Goodbye. I need to die now. I need to be gone. I know I'm dying. I know I'm going. Goodbye.'

'No, Teresa. Your time is not up. Your time is not now. You will get through this. You will survive!'

'Dawn. This is it. I've reached my final hurdle and even I can't jump over it. I've fallen. I'm broken. I'm bleeding. I'm dying.'

'I know it all hurts. I know you are close but you're not going to die. I need you to hold on. I need you to stay alive. Hold on Teresa. Hold on my darling. Hold on. I will hold your hand. Just don't let go of life just yet. This is not your time, Teresa!'

Dawn vibrated through Teresa's head. She could feel the burning warmth of seeping blood, pouring internally from her punched and kicked organs, all of them battered into defeat, relinquishing their life breathing abilities to sitting still and taking their last breaths whilst being drained of their pumping red fuel.

'No, Teresa, no! You're not saying goodbye. This is not your goodbye. This is not your day to leave. Come back! Come back and be brave. Come back. Your world is not yet complete. Today is not your day!'

'I can't feel anything. Everything is numb. Everything is gone. I'm cold so cold. I'm feeling so cold. Goodbye, Dawn. I'm coming to be with you. I'm coming to where you are. I'm coming to where I belong. Goodbye, world. Goodbye, world. Goodbye. I don't want to be here any longer!'

Teresa's blood was at a crossroads, torn between the lacerations on her breasts, arms and thighs to the beaten liver, kidneys and stomach as her body trembled into shock syndrome and began its melancholy road to ceasing operation and shifting into oblivion.

'Goodbye. Goodbye. Goodbye. Goodbye. Goodbye'

'You're not still mumbling, are you? For fuck's sake, what do I need to put in your mouth to stop you mumbling?! I am not taking the blame for this shit! You asked for it, bitch. You asked for all of this. Looks like I'm going to have to finish the job and be done with you. I think it's time to say goodbye my love. The world hates you and doesn't need you anyway.'

With a gentle stroke of her twitching cheek, Simon moved Teresa onto her back and gripped her around the neck with both his hands.

'I am so fucking angry with you, bitch! You have wasted my time and wasted my fucking life! How dare you! How fucking dare you!'

Spluttering upon her contorted face, Simon's fury belched as he shook Teresa's limp, bleary head causing her eyes to rattle within their weary sockets and irretrievably roll to the back of her twitching mind.

'Hello Teresa, welcome to the story of your life. I'm it. I am your life and here's a preview I've prepared. Please sit still and watch the world of Teresa Ann xxxxxx'

Teresa was home. Serenity in her childhood cinema where mum brought her every Saturday morning to the Kids' Club. The red velvet seat engulfed her frame as she slumped into its doughy softness. The cushioning was deeper, with greater comfort than she could remember from decades ago and the arm rests had clearly been reupholstered, they were always gnawed down to their bare metal barely gripping onto the torn material and foamy cladding. Mum was absent. Always so close, holding Teresa's hand but not today. Teresa acknowledged she wasn't there but today it didn't seem to matter, today Teresa didn't feel lonely, lost or uncomfortable, there was an invisible blanket of calmness shrouding her. There was safety and companionship, even though she was alone. Yes, this was home. The cinematic extravaganza lit up her face as her eyes bore the weight of life gradually dripping away and her lids felt heavier and heavier. Her smile ached in her cheek bones as the images flickered at lightning speed, a carousel of happy moments, gambolling through all her living years.

Straining to watch the movie to the end, the relentless images that pieced together this woman's life ceased with their parting gesture, her last recorded days of contentment, the poignant yet blissful memory of sitting with Ash at his bedside talking about 'Make my World Complete', with his prolonged smile burning its blithe symbolism into the screen. The film was over, transformed into a blinding, yet soothing whiteness. Teresa's eyes clasped shut.

Chapter 53
Make My World Complete

'She was my breath, my depth, my being
God, I apologise. You weren't alive. I didn't believe
But only you had the prowess to conjure this miracle
Only you had the power to implore untold glory
To besiege my days with the greatest story.
Born in heaven, celestial from above,
Man's ultimate victory wrapped in love.
I now live my days with my conquering crown
In the distance my worries burdened with a frown.
For if utopia is this woman, then there must be a hell
A bottomless well, into which I will drown
My world will be incomplete without her
My sun will set and my heart will cry
All my wishes will crumble and I will die.'

Broken, deserted, lonely, searching for the only drop of water that can quench this thirst. My throat is parched, a sandstorm gusted into my face, blown into my mouth, granules of sand grating on my vocal chords. Exasperated words scratching to be spoken broken into unrecognisable bloodless tedium. Surrogate libations are widespread and I drown myself guzzling them in copious volumes but still this arid life, born to connect with her, pines for the only celebration that can intoxicate my mind, raise my spirits and attempt to taste this food on my tongue. Sweet, salty and sour commingled into bland, tasteless mush, pushed into an unwelcoming stomach that churns and churns edging to send it back, unwilling to process it for purposeless nutrition, the energy of survival that has little ambition to fulfil its goals. Inspiration to open my eyes to the beautiful world to which I am blind to see, I visualise its grandeur but images do not formulate until we gaze out together, brushing the earthly hues into our very own picture, painted upon a canvas created for our eyes to colour a world that is pallid and blanched into submission.

Sounds collaborate their symphony as they trundle to be heard; gambolling into my ears, they clatter into nonsensical noises, clattering that cannot be redeemed until I wake and hear the twittering of birds, singing me their dulcet anecdotes, without her ears my feathered friends goad me to become an enemy, to lash out at their pointless harmonies. Be gone! Be gone! And take your aggravating chirping to the window sill of someone who cares, not one that will shoot you dead for daring to serenade my sadness.

Dismembered fingertips, eroded to numbness. What is there left to physically touch, to send the electronic signals to my apathetic brain, belligerently failing to recognise sensations. My senses are disconnected, void of their duties, lacking in the discipline they need to satisfy their job descriptions. Redundant roles, bereft of direction and necessity. My world is disrupted, fallen. Sight, sound, touch, taste and smell have turned their back on me, paying allegiance to the leaders that kept them animated, who fought in the trenches but now my heart and mind, dying, war embittered and injured. The irreparable damage has been done, slowly bleeding to death. I remain abandoned and empty, a life incomplete.

Trickles of sunlight poured through the chalky window blooming radiance into the bleak, paint crumbled walls of the long-term ward. In the background the cluttering morning noises and waking groans worked in unison filling the disinfected air with the daily melody of hospital rigmarole.

Adorning the bedside table, next to the only greeting card and plastic jug of stale overnight water, the virtuoso of love and hope 'Make my World Complete', absorbing the filtered sunshine, re-energising itself, bolstering its meaningful words with the life engorging rays.

'Where am I? Where am I? Where am I?'

Echoing around the empty room, the croaky voice turned to a spluttering cough, phlegm sheening the cotton-mouthed throat allowing enough lubrication for a shrilling scream.

'Aha, you're awake are you? It's about time you woke up.'

'Where am I? What's going on?'

'You've woken in a daze. You've been out for a while'

'Where am I? Where am I? What, what are you doing here? Dr Sommers! What the fuck are you doing here?'

'That's a fine way to talk to your old boss, isn't it? You had to come back one way or another didn't you?'

'How? What has happened? Why am I here?'

'Teresa, dear, you've been out cold for twelve days now. Welcome back, we've all been rooting for you but you still need to rest, you're a long way from recovery yet.'

'How did I get here? Simon. Where's Simon? What happened?'

'Calm down, dear. Calm down, you'll hurt your throat, he damaged that too. In fact he left you in quite a disgraceful mess.'

Clouds gathered, Teresa's crumpled thoughts positioned themselves into an explanation. The whiteness. It was all over. She was dead. Doomed to repent in the only profession she worked for throughout her entire life, now in death she had returned as a patient. The ultimate misery, eternal purgatory in a hospital bed, with the one person that halted her dream career and changed the course of her life. Dr Sommers. The buzz of questions frantically hurtling through her head was deafening.

'Why am I here? I'm dead! Why here? Of all places. Here? With you! Why? Why? I need to know. I need to know!'

'You're not dead, you silly woman! You're alive. Barely alive, I might add. Severely battered and bruised, bed ridden but most definitely alive.'

'How? What happened? How was I saved? I was dead. I died. I remember dying!'

'You really don't know, do you? I did wonder. You must have lost consciousness, judging by the crush in your windpipe. You must have faded out just before you were saved.'

'Saved? Saved how?' Teresa croaked out her words, each one grating the letters as they barely formed in her gravelly throat.

'Tell me. Tell me! How was I saved? How?'

'Ash. That's how. Ash saved you. He burst into your home and stopped Simon from killing you. He's a hero. Ash is your hero.'

Teresa could hear and yet the words were jumbled. Whizzing around a race track, attempting to overtake each other, scrambling for pole-position. The speed whirred into blurriness and blurted out into a nonsensical sentence.

'Don't be cruel. Dead. Dead. I'm gone. Dead. I'm no more. Go away, Sommers. My life, no more. Ash, Ash, Ash! I can't take this. Just let me be, just let me go. I've lost everything, at least let me have peace!'

'He's been here every day. Every day reading from this book. Every single day, sometimes for hours on end. Just reading and reading. Over and over again. Every single day.'

'No, no, no, no I don't believe you. I don't believe you. No!'

'Yes. It's hard to believe. He walked up your stairs and forced the door open and grappled Simon to the floor and held him down until he was taken away by the police and you were brought here by the paramedics. You were fighting for your life. It took all our might to bring you back into the world of the living. Yes, it's all down to Ash. Ash is your saviour!'

Teresa closed her eyes, building a soft dam as the river of befuddled tears welled behind them pushing out a trickle that rolled down her face and plummeted from her chin upon the crinkling, crisp white linen of her bed.

'I'll be back later. You need a lot of rest, Teresa. Your body will take time to recover from the damage it endured. Goodbye, and welcome back!'

Clenching her eyes tighter, ignoring Dr Sommers squeaking shoe departure, Teresa felt droplets cascading down her face accelerating their departure as the damn constricted.

'I'm not going to open my eyes. I'm not going to open my eyes. I'm not going to open my eyes.'

Intuitively from learned experiences of dreams, Teresa knew the unlikely situation would change if she simply kept her eyes closed, cold-shouldering her bizarre surroundings into oblivion.

'Whatever happened to the happy ending I was supposed to have, why did I tumble and trip at every obstacle? Why did I let Simon back into my life? He broke me, he broke my world. No, it's my fault, I let him break my world and I let him take my life away. I let him do everything. It's all my fault, I caused this. Therefore I deserve this. I don't deserve heaven, I don't deserve my happy ever after. I deserve hell. Hell in a hospital. Bedridden hell. This is my hell. This is what I deserve!'

The line of separation was faint. Separating the conscious and subconscious as Teresa flitted between the two states of being.

'I gazed upon her. I gazed my love. I gazed my future. She was the purpose of living, the missing letters that made my equation complete. Algebraic tangles were ironed into loving simplicity. Me minus her, was zero. Me minus her, was incomplete. Me minus her, was no point. Me plus her, was happiness. Me plus her, was life. Me plus her, was destiny. Me plus her, was my every breath. Me plus her, was love. Me plus her, was my world. She made my world complete.'

'Is that you, Ash? Is that you?'

'I'm here right by your side.'

Teresa opened her tear-drenched eyes and there he was, standing tall, clutching his father's book, wide-eyed and glaring at her childlike, a child simply cherishing a guarded treasure, knowing that little else mattered in the universe. Just this moment, right now.

Leaning forward, still holding the book, Ash cocooned his arms around Teresa, brushing the wetness from her eyes across his warm cheek.

Whoosh! An immense surge blossomed through Teresa's bruised body, a whirling hurricane swiftly spinning through her, escalating upwards to her head as the eye of the storm stirred her heart and wrenched it apart with a thunderous beat. Remnants of a cracked, broken and flawed history crammed closely together, cowering and crumpled in a sheet of tightly screwed up paper, unwanted, tossed away by the force of the cyclonic rush. Elated, as the twister straightened her convolutions and brushed them aside, Teresa was weightless, relentlessly floating in anti-gravity. It had been scooped from below her feet, leaving her feather-light with nothing pinning her down. Their heat exchanged frequencies, boiling their commingled blood in unison, synchronising their pelting heartbeats into one vociferous boom. Meandering rivers of salted tears blended into a waterfall of bridled emotion.

There were no words. An elementary twenty-six letter alphabet had yet to evolve past mankind's attempt to understand the philosophy of enchantment. Vocal expression wondrously commandeered in an unequivocal moment as two entities collided and contrived a singular complete world.

Lightning Source UK Ltd.
Milton Keynes UK
UKHW021831091221
395377UK00009B/594